I0542412

A S H E S

RAYNARD GADSON

Published by
Poseidon's Ink Publishing
New York, NY 10037

This book is a work of fiction. Names, characters, places, and incidents are the product of the author's imagination. Any resemblance to actual events or locales, or persons living or dead is purely coincidental.

Copyright © 2013 Raynard Gadson. All rights reserved.

No part of this book may be reproduced or transmitted without the written permission of the author.

ISBN-10: 0615831125
ISBN-13: 978-0615831121

For the ones who read "Home Again."
Not only did you bring the Douglases to life,
you brought me to life.

CONTENTS

PROLOGUE
GREENVILLE, NORTH CAROLINA – 1986

It was the last time my mother and I saw each other alive. She was resting at the foot of the stairs, her body twisted in several unnatural positions. Her face in similar, painful contortions; her eyes staring straight at me and growing darker and darker until with one final blink, they were closed forever. I always told myself she was aware that I was standing there in the darkness. That she'd seen me watching her die in front of me, and did so believing I knew that my father was the one who killed her.

The plague of that night wasn't the trauma a seven-year-old boy would endure after watching his mother die in such a manner. It was the nagging question of whether or not her decision to succumb quietly to death was for selfish reasons. Was it more important for her to be relieved of the situation instead of overpowering the desire to let go and somehow harness her last breath in order to cry out to her child?

I stood there, watching the blood trickle from lips that just two hours earlier had kissed me goodnight and for the last time told me "I love you." She was dead, and I was left alone in the dark, paralyzed by my own resounding heartbeat. I felt my father's stillness on the stair landing above. He had started a descent, but stalled on the first step. I pressed myself against the wall, hoping to merge into it and disappear into the space underneath the staircase.

My eyes were stinging, and it would only be a matter of time before my sobs became uncontrollable. Fifteen minutes ago it wouldn't have mattered because they would have been swallowed up by the sounds of argument emanating from my parents' bedroom upstairs. Now, however, one teardrop hitting the hardwood floors would break this silence like a sonic boom, and he would know I was there.

The stairs began to creak, a foreboding alert that he was descending. I squeezed my eyes shut, imagining him turning the corner and finding me there, a disappointed look on his face preceding a threatening "Why are you out of bed?"

What would I say? The screaming match they'd been having was loud enough to wake me, but the truth was I'd never gone to sleep. I'd waited up for him, hoping tonight would be the night he'd make good on his promise to be the one to tuck me in. There's a lot to be said of a son's belief in his father. It's unrelenting. The promises came and went like ghosts, leaving only the painful memories of what once had life. But trust in what he told his son had me gripped by the throat. I had to count on him to breathe, or he'd take it away and all I knew about hope would be left in a tangled slump at the bottom of the stairs.

The stairs stopped announcing his arrival, and for a fleeting moment, the fear subsided. In that moment, I saw myself in bed surrounded by all the expensive toys Mom had given me in consolation for having to share Daddy with his work as a resident at St. Joseph's Hospital. And he was there, standing over my bed, making another promise that one day soon he'd be a doctor, instead of leaving Mom to explain that all of his absences were so that I could have a better life later on.

I opened my eyes again to the darkness of her ill-fated 'later on,' and the muffled sounds of Daddy's staggering effort back up the stairs. I looked over to the base of the stairs where Mom's eyes had said goodbye to me, and allowed my pupils to dart from left to right hoping the darkness would at least permit my peripherals to establish her figure there. She was not. The realization struck like lightning. Her body was being dragged up the stairs behind me by her murderer.

Until this point, my experience with death was limited to

several goldfish and a dog. I'd gone through enough to ask all the requisite questions about God and Heaven, and knew that digging a grave for an animal's carcass is what normally happens after it dies. I knew a funeral was a ritual ceremony that helped people find closure. I also knew Daddy wasn't taking Mom's body to the backyard.

My first instinct was to follow. To peel myself away from the wall and look up to see if I could spot him over the railing. Something inside of me needed to know if maybe Mom wasn't dead. Perhaps being the doctor-in-training that he was, Daddy noticed something about her that indicated she still had life.

I inched closer to the foot of the stairs and waited, finding a pool of her blood spilling off of the landing and onto the beige welcome mat on the inside threshold of the front door. I leaned over it and peered up the staircase, expecting to find my father peering down at me from the top, a disapproving glare that could cut through the darkness and lure me towards his wrath like a beacon. He hated it when Mom would let me stay up past my bedtime, even when it was in wait for him to come home. That detail always infiltrated their arguments. This time was no different.

Daddy came home tonight later than expected, as usual. Mom had just put me to bed after my numerous attempts to convince her to let me stay up. It was past eleven o'clock, and as much as she didn't want me to go to bed having been let down by Daddy again, she had to have known his reaction to me still being awake at this hour would be a bigger problem.

I heard his car pull into the driveway right at midnight, and I hopped out of bed. My room was on the first floor, and the driveway was right outside my window. Catching a glimpse of him at all during the week was like catching sight of Santa Claus. He came in after I was sleep, and was gone before I woke. Our family was the mistress to his shifts at the hospital.

He walked through the front door and I heard him drop his keys on the floor. He must have missed the desk where he usually puts them. I ran over to my bedroom door and opened it just enough so that one eye could look out into the hallway that ran parallel to the stairs. He was lingering at the front door, just at the end of this hall. Even in the dark, I could see that he was having trouble pulling off his jacket.

Bare footsteps sounded on the stairs. He paused, forcing his eyes to adjust on the figure descending the stairs toward him.

"What are you doing up?" he asked Mom. She had stopped midway down the stairs.

"If you're gonna come in late every night, the least you could do is come in a bit more quietly, don't you think? Daniel's got school tomorrow," she replied.

He grunted.

"If you'd put that boy in the bed earlier then we wouldn't have a problem."

"If you'd come home before midnight once or twice a week... he's waiting up for you."

"And you *let* him?! That's responsible." He stepped over into the living room, out of my line of vision. I saw her shadow cross the hall from the stairs, following him. "You know, you could try putting a book in his hand every now and then instead of the remote control, Cath. There's your reason why he's so slow at 'grasping concepts'."

"You are unbelievable." I could still hear her arguing. "You barge in here after midnight every night of the week, reeking of liquor - and you're calling *me* a bad parent?!"

"That boy's got you wrapped around his finger. Everything he wants you go get it for him. Now, I forget, where is it that you work again?"

She didn't respond.

"Thought so," he spat. He tried to leave her in the living room, but she followed him across the hall and up the stairs. Their voices got louder despite the fact that they were a floor above me.

"There's only so much I can tell him to get him to understand that you don't hate him," I heard her say. "The water guns were your Christmas gift to him. That bike was for the A he made in math."

"*One* A."

There was a brief break in the argument, and I could hear the closet being yanked open and something heavy hitting the floor.

"You're... you're not going anywhere," Mom was saying. "You

are not gonna leave me to do this by myself."

"You're both sucking me dry and I'm tired of it," he yelled. "You expect me to manage all the bills around here on one paycheck – if you want to call it that. You're giving that boy everything he points at, and for what? C's and D's! And you're up here climbing down my throat every time I want to grab a beer or two after a 12-hour shift?"

"And then drive home wasted," she retorted. "Way to handle things."

"Baby, if I didn't do *something* to knock this edge off, none of us would be able to handle it."

I could hear his heavy footsteps starting towards the stairs, and her bare feet sounded like they were dancing around him.

"So what is leaving gonna do? It's not gonna make anything better. Unless you want Daniel to end up in some foster home."

"You know what, save the guilt trip. Maybe when you have to scrape just to barely make this rent, you'll find out how necessary that bike and those water guns are."

I knew they were at the landing of the stairs when she yelled that I was his responsibility too.

"Let go of my arm, Catherine!" Daddy said with a force I'd never heard before.

In the endless second following his order, I heard Mom's body come tumbling down the stairs, landing at the bottom. I stepped out of my room and into the darkness. My eyes adjusted just in time to watch hers close.

And now she was no longer there.

A light went on at the far end of the upstairs hallway. The dark splattering of blood trailing up the stairs helped my curiosity win its fight with fear. I slowly started up, clinging onto the railing, and only pausing for a moment when I noticed Daddy's shadow briefly eclipse the light coming from the bathroom at the other end of the hall. Their bedroom was adjacent to the bathroom, and the two doors opened against each other. It was a construction mistake Daddy had been meaning to fix, having accidentally gotten stuck in either room several times because one of us forgot to close the other door.

I reached the top of the stairs and spotted Daddy kneeling

beside the tub on the far wall in the bathroom. His body was obstructing my view of whatever was inside the tub, but my suspicions were soon confirmed when I saw Mom's leg draped over one side of the porcelain rim. Was he washing the body? Was she alive?

My pace started to quicken as I made my way towards the bathroom with hopes that Mom was still alive. I stopped when I noticed the cabinet beneath the sink was wide open, and various cleaning agents were strewn across the floor. When Daddy had finally finished fidgeting with trying to fit Mom perfectly into the tub, he reached for a full bottle of Pine Sol and poured it over her body.

My eyes watched wide and glazed as he lifted a book of matches in his right hand, and fumbled with bringing one of them to flame. After another moment of hesitation, he dropped the match into the tub and fire engulfed my mother. I watched as he stared at his wife for a few moments, and wondered what his face would reveal when he turned around and saw me standing between him and the stairs.

He stood up, still with his back to me, and I darted behind the door to their bedroom. I couldn't leave him alone. I couldn't *be* alone. I needed to see that he was crying, so that I would know it was okay to cry too. I only knew to trust his reaction.

He turned to the sink and vomited, perhaps not noticing the flames crawling up the shower curtain. Perhaps not caring. He caught his reflection in the mirror above the sink and stared at it for a while as the flames grew. Then, I saw him lift his trembling right hand, curl it into a fist, and smash it into the mirror, shattering the image. The sound startled me and I jumped against the bedroom door, which slammed against the bathroom door, pinning it shut.

"Daniel?!" I heard my father scream in the same tone he used as he told my mother to let him go.

At the sound of him saying my name, the tears became rivers I couldn't control.

"What did you do?!" I cried, stepping out into the hall and standing in front of the bathroom door.

"Daniel, open the damned door!"

I continued to cry as he banged against the door, trying without success either to force me to open it or break it down.

He stopped for a moment, I assume to try to douse the fire that by now had grown almost as out of control as anything else in this house tonight. Smoke was seeping from underneath the door, and I could hear the faucet running. He came back a few times to bang on the door but I just stood there, again paralyzed, but not so much this time by what he'd done, but by what I'd done. My father's son.

"Daniel, you gotta open this door. Please." His plea became desperate, as if he knew what was about to happen.

I started backing away from the door, afraid that I would have to follow through with this, or live with his consequences.

Before I made it halfway to the stairs, a loud explosion finally broke the door free of its hinges and spread the fire to the surrounding rooms. The ejected door came hurling towards me, and spun vertically allowing me a glimpse of my dad's burning flesh pinned against it just before slamming into me.

The last image I saw that night was fire.

O N E

WESTMORE COLLEGE – APRIL 2011

Some scars don't heal. At least not on their own. The remedy then becomes using a mask of some kind to cover them up. Learning how to conceal old wounds turns into a trade, and lies will weld themselves to flesh like metal.

Professor Carter Owens stood looking across the small, stuffy classroom, waiting for a hand to be raised among any of the twenty students.

"Come on guys, your GPA isn't hanging on one wrong answer," he said. "Ethan, yours actually couldn't get any worse. Give it a shot."

Ethan Foster looked up from his social sciences textbook and tried to ignore the sneers from his classmates.

"I don't know. Thrill?"

"You're telling me that you think a person is predominately motivated by thrill to continue doing something over and over again?"

"Well a serial killer isn't going to keep offing people if it makes him feel sick. He's getting some kind of pleasure from it. Right?"

Professor Owens walked to the large black board behind him and scribbled "thrill" beneath the word "MOTIVE."

He was least engrossed in this part of the course, and normally waited until near the end of the semester to delve into the criminal mind. It never seemed to matter, however. Most of the students opted to take his social sciences class because of the lure of the subject, and criminal behavior attracted college kids like moths to a flame.

"So that was your real reason for having to take my sociology class three times? It was thrilling?"

More sneers. Ethan was tired of it, and having been on this court with Professor Owens before, he knew a comeback was necessary.

"Maybe it was just thrilling for you to have a lacrosse star in your classroom three semesters in a row."

"Former lacrosse star," Professor Owens corrected.

It was where the mutual disrespect between the two of them had been born. Ethan's first class with Professor Owens was general sociology two years ago. Admittedly, Ethan was more concerned with his jock status than with the assignments Owens was all too strict about. His lackluster involvement with his schoolwork led Owens to believe Ethan had ridden his sports scholarship to Westmore College, and had every intention of using his significance on the team as a horse-drawn chariot towards graduation.

Ethan's free ride came to an abrupt halt when his grades in Owens' class got him ejected from the team. His nagging suspicions that Owens' subjective grading was a little more personal in his case were confirmed while he was taking the same course the second time. There was nothing he could do other than whatever was necessary to even stay in school at that point – and give Owens a real motive to hate him: succeeding anyway.

For Carter Owens, working to prove your worth was branded into him at a young age. His parents were slaves to the 60s. The Woodstock era had arrested and sodomized them, and their son paid the price for it. Back then, he was known as Owen Carter, the bright young boy who knew that doing the best he could in school was his only sure way of outrunning the statistics. Any child with a similar home-life – with parents who spent every dime they saw on mushrooms, pot, and sex parties – would have lost themselves in the battle for attention. But little Owen knew the best way to not end up a reflection of his parents was to drive himself to being the exact opposite. He worked hard in school and took two or three jobs during the summer to get himself through medical school.

Some days he would catch himself staring out at his students and realize one accident in his past had turned all of his ambition against him. The accident was love, or what he thought was love. During his senior year of high school, he met Catherine Hutchison. The passionate part of their romance was like a firecracker – brief but explosive. When the show was over, the colorful array of bigger-than-life firework confetti was stifled by the suffocating fog of smoke left in its wake. In the four amazing months of passion they shared, a child was conceived. It was the accident that caused one irreparable crack after another in Owen Carter.

He married Catherine out of duty, knowing more than anything that he would not abandon his parental responsibilities the way his parents had. The obligation to his son's future and the determination to find his own success were at constant odds with each other, and by the time he had started his residency at St. Joseph's Hospital, the two goals collided – the cracks connected and the glass shattered completely.

With layers of lies surgically masking the scars from that night twenty-five years ago, Professor Owens turned back to the class just as Genevieve Davis's hand went up.

"Genevieve?"

"People are products of their environment," she said. "It goes back to the whole nature versus nurture argument. Child molesters are often former victims themselves, right?"

"Interesting point," Owens responded. "But what if I asked all of you what you think is the difference between what drives you to complete college and, say, what drove John Gacy to rape and murder dozens of young men? How would you answer that?"

"Gacy was gay," a younger student, Darren Gabriel, contributed from the back of the class, soliciting snickers from several of his classmates.

"Achievement?" piped Kaylen Winston, refusing to give Darren the attention he wanted.

"Okay, what about Jack the Ripper?" Owens retorted. "Could it not be argued that he set out to successfully achieve the riddance of prostitutes in Great Britain? What if I told you that the same thing that drives most of you to succeed drives others to murder?"

He paused, allowing them all to consider.

"Think about it," he continued. "For most of us, making good grades or succeeding at something positive gives us a sense of confidence, which means on some level, we feel inferior. Getting an A on a term paper gives us a sense of superiority. In Gacy's case, perhaps the only way he felt he could reach that same sense was to emasculate someone."

"But wasn't it still ultimately for the thrill?" asked another student, Jackson Young. "Otherwise why repeat it?"

"Thank you," Ethan murmured.

"A person who has always made straight A's on everything all through school – don't you think at some point it might get mundane? And yet they still make A's," Professor Owens offered.

"So you're saying it's habitual?" Kaylen asked.

"I'm just trying to get you all to think about this," Owens said. "Motive is a complicated concept. It's very rare that just one of these factors contributes. You can't base a serial killer's motive on psyche or environment alone. You can't just say that the Unabomber was insane, or that David Berkowitz was possessed by the Devil. Most people just say that because it's the easiest explanation. You can say: 'John Gacy was mentally ill' and be done with the conversation, and nobody would argue. But it's hardly ever that simple. It goes deeper than that."

"I still say childhood experiences are ninety-nine percent involved with the motive of a serial killer," asserted Genevieve. "I mean, it's our childhood experiences that compel us to succeed in academics."

"And what differentiates your childhood from Gacy's?" Professor Owens asked.

"Hopefully a lot of things," she responded.

"Exactly," Owens said. "Gacy, Manson, Luis Garavito, Ted Bundy... you can't just call them all crazy. You can't just say they must've had bad childhoods. To really understand what drove them to murder, you need to factor in a lot of different things: their pasts, what was going on in and around them at the time, and often even their perceptions of their futures as well. Sometimes it even has nothing to do with their childhood. Sometimes it's triggered by a recent event. Sometimes it's personal, sometimes it's scientific or religious, sometimes it's political, sometimes it's emotional."

"Sometimes its sexual," came another voice from the back of the room. Many students turned in their desks expecting to find a proud smirk on Darren Gabriel's face, but even he was staring in Lucas Dutch's direction.

"Come on," Lucas continued. "We've all seen dozens of movies where the killer's always chasing after the chick with the shortest skirt. Half of those are based on true stories."

"He's right. To a certain extent," Professor Owens said. "While many of the killers in movies are based on real people, their motives get watered down, or as Lucas pointed out, sexed up."

"There is nothing sexy about torture," Genevieve chimed in.

"They just ain't doing it right," Darren responded, tossing Genevieve a wink.

"Before this goes NC-17," Professor Owens interrupted. "How about we steer all of this passion to your final assignments."

Ethan couldn't help but acknowledge the sudden strike of dread overcoming him. He slouched even further in his chair, hoping to ease the discomfort. Owens' entire course was comprised of two grades: the midterm, on which he'd received a D, and the final. He knew Owens loved having him over this barrel, his life a dangling marionette show.

He listened as Professor Owens declared this final project to be something he'd never assigned before. The class would be split into groups of five, with each group presenting a thoroughly researched, fifteen-page case study of a serial killer.

For Ethan, there was little relief in knowing four other students would be responsible for his grade. There was always a chance Owens would group him with four A-students, knowing Ethan would get comfortable and not realize a D on this final project would bring him back to Westmore for a fifth year while the other students' A-averages only dropped to a B.

When it came to Owens, Ethan was just a mouse in a maze of paranoia. The struggle to escape had become impossible ever since Ethan fell in love with the professor's 17-year-old daughter, Havana.

T W O

The difference between secrets and lies – lies are woven together like a fuse. Ignited, the flame races towards the TNT of secrets, which explodes with often fatal results.

Owen Carter arrived in Miami twenty-five years ago, floating on a raft of dynamite. He had just memorialized his young wife Catherine and their seven-year-old son Daniel in Greenville, North Carolina, and wanted to be as far away as possible from the memories of the tragic night that ended their lives and left his a charred canvas of secrets.

The night of the fire remained his ghostly passenger until he met a young Cuban nurse named Lucinda. Lucinda assisted the plastic surgeons that performed the final reconstructive operations on Owen's fire-tinged body, and then fell madly in love with the evasive patient despite his refusal to discuss the events of the night of the fire.

Over many months, she visited him, bathed him, fed him, and eventually brought him to her house for post-op care. For many nights, his tears spoke more than he ever did, seeping through the walls into her bedroom, where she fought back tears of her own. After two years, she mustered up the courage to confront him about his lamentations. His answer surprised her.

"I spent most of my life pouring myself into school and work, promising myself to be more than what my parents were," he told her. "This is failure."

"You haven't failed," she said. "You can go back to school and become a doctor. You can finish what you started."

"It's too late. I'm twenty-nine years old now, and every dime I had saved up to pay for school went into my family's memorial and all these surgeries. I look in the mirror now, and I don't even see the guy who wanted to be a doctor."

"What *do* you see?" she asked.

He hesitated.

"A monster."

"The scars will heal." She tried to comfort him. "A year from now, you'll be as beautiful on the outside as you are on the inside."

He allowed her to think he meant the outside scars, and gave in to the need to be held by a woman who thought he was beautiful.

"To go through what you've been through, losing your wife and son..." she let the atmosphere swallow the thought, and embraced him.

It was the first time he felt emotion break through the numbness he'd held onto ever since the night of the fire.

She agreed to help him deal with the stress of the vague explanation he gave her as to how his family died. Her support came with the insistence that he attend weekly sessions with a psychologist that she would pay for in hopes that talking to *someone* about the details of what happened would afford him restitution. He conceded, but made a conscious effort not to retrace the steps of what happened that fateful night, and whenever pressed for his memories, he would tell Lucinda that the psychologist was making no progress, leaving her with the task of finding another one.

Despite the secrets he tried to keep under lock and key, day by day he started showing signs of strength. He legally changed his name to its reverse as one of the steps to shedding the old life, and soon he had enrolled at a local college as a grad student in the field of sociology, aiming to earn a master's degree and a certificate to teach. He had been told by one of the revolving psychologists that doing so would quench his life-long thirst to complete college, and choosing a path outside of medicine would prevent him from reliving painful memories associated with his previous experience as a resident.

His relationship with Lucinda turned into something he hadn't expected. Several months into their courtship, he realized that his vow not to be distracted by love again had waned. Either that, or he had reached the maturity level where he could handle it. He proposed to her on his 31st birthday, and a year later they were married with a baby on the way.

Havana Danielle Owens was born in 1993 and was named after the birthplace of her mother. Shortly after Havana's second birthday, Carter stunned Lucinda by suggesting they move their family to North Carolina – the state it'd taken him more than five years to mention to her by name. He told her that having Havana triggered something inside of him that made him want to attempt to finally get over the tragedy in his past. He felt facing the fear and the pain he had been running from was the only way to finally move on.

The seemingly overnight decision to move back to North Carolina was one that Carter didn't want to give himself time to talk himself out of doing. He convinced Lucinda that this was the healthiest thing he could do for himself and his family.

And it seemed to be just that. Their first year was understandably tumultuous for Carter, even though they decided to settle in a town that was over an hour away from Greenville. He was behaviorally erratic for months, and often spent days or even weeks either emotionally or physically absent. At his request, Lucinda and Havana gave him the space he needed to heal by these means. In time Carter Owens had fought himself through the demons of his former life in order to provide his new wife and daughter with the husband and father he felt they deserved. Things were falling into place by the fall of 1999 when Carter accepted a position as adjunct professor of sociology at Westmore College.

The acclimation was much easier for Lucinda and Havana. Lucinda quickly found work at the local hospital, and Havana started school and made friends without missing a beat.

During the winter of Havana's junior year of high school, one of her after-school activities crossed paths with a collegiate initiative, and Havana met Ethan Foster, a junior at Westmore College. The two of them were assigned to chaperone a group of elementary school students on a field trip to Westmore. Havana was involved via Campbell High School's "EleMentor" program, where high school students spent several hours a week mentoring kids from local elementary schools. For Ethan, volunteering was more of a necessity. Failing Professor Owens' general sociology class brought his GPA down, and cost him his sports scholarship. Paying for school became the full-time job that further took a toll on his grades. Westmore had a special program that helped students in similar situations get additional course credit through volunteerism, so that maintaining their scholarship funding didn't take their focus away from education.

Ethan signed up for Westmore's "Students Achieving Together" program, which allowed grade-school students to interact with college students and learn the importance of staying in school. The idea was that grade-school students are inspired by seeing the effects of achievement on their peers.

Havana took an immediate notice of Ethan. She got his phone number off of the contact list they handed out at the beginning of the campus tour, and a week later, called him under the pretense of wanting to schedule a second tour with a few middle-schoolers who had missed the first one. He wasn't too interested in doing so, and tried to brush her off a couple of times. A month went by, and when it looked like she wasn't going to give up, he agreed to meet her for a cup of coffee and discuss a time for the tour to take place.

An hour into their meeting, the tour had taken a backseat to his rant about a certain professor of his who had chewed him out in front of the entire class. When she realized who his most hated professor was, she tried to abort her mission to schedule a second date – sure that once he found out Professor Owens was her father, he would want nothing to do with her.

Figuring it would be easier to rip the band-aid off in one quick motion, she admitted it to him, and was surprised when his interest settled on how she managed to survive in a house with this man for all these years. She told him that her dad had spent most of his thirties in a kind of pain that he kept bottled up, and she and her mom just learned how to skate around it. Hearing this brought Ethan to the threshold of sympathy, but he refused to enter, explaining that no amount of pain justified his tendency to embarrass students at his leisure.

Havana agreed, and shared with him particular childhood memories of waking up in the middle of the night only to find her dad in a cold sweat, lying on top of the covers next to her, cradling her protectively. She never assumed, and never asked what it meant.

"It wasn't weird to you?" Ethan asked her.

"Not at first. I was only six or seven years old at the time," she responded. "After a few years he stopped, and suddenly he was just overbearing and judgmental. Maybe I've just gotten used to it."

"If he's anything like he is in class, you shouldn't be," Ethan said. "Nothing is ever good enough."

"He's definitely the type of person who thinks you need to prove yourself," she told him. "You don't earn something you never worked hard for."

"But who is he to assume I didn't work hard for my scholarship?" he asked, glad to have someone he could talk to who didn't judge his paranoia.

"Athletic performance and academic performance are two totally different things. There are some really dumb jocks getting drafted into pro-sports these days, and you know it."

It was Havana who convinced Ethan to adopt the "succeed anyway" mentality where her father was concerned, and he found being able to talk to her was like easing the pressure of a blood clot. Before either of them knew it, they were meeting frequently to commiserate, and feelings were conceived.

Their first kiss was an accident. They met at the county fair for the July 4th fireworks show. She had sneaked out of the house and was very nervous that her father would show up on a last minute decision to take advantage of the Westmore students and faculty Free Admission Night. She hadn't told him yet that she even had a clue as to who Ethan Foster was, and knew it scored points for her with Ethan.

They spread out a blanket on the lawn in front of the Ferris Wheel, among dozens of other couples and families, to watch the fireworks. Their spot was near the fair entrance, and Havana sat on the opposite side of Ethan so that she could have a clear view of the gate to look out for her father.

It was a moment right out of a 1990's romance movie. Havana leaned over away from Ethan to retrieve a digital camera from the purse that lay on the blanket to her left (she had been tasked to get a couple of pictures for a yearbook spread). The fireworks show started with a thunderous Roman candle. Unprepared, the boom spun her around with a jolt. She hadn't expected Ethan to be facing her, and her lips landed an inch in front of his. Their eyes found each other's, and their moment there paused as three or four more fireworks went off around them, brightening the sky with various shades of blue, purple, orange, and red.

Ethan was the first to move, bringing his finger to her chin and gently gliding it forward, setting her lips in motion toward his. The kiss lasted for only a few seconds, but of all the fireworks they saw that night, nothing was more memorable.

Their romance remained a secret until that November. The Friday before Thanksgiving, Professor Owens made a sarcastic remark after overhearing Ethan telling a friend that he had a date to go see some horror flick at the local movie theater. When he got home, Carter learned that Havana had a date planned for the same movie. He pieced two and two together and set out to confirm his suspicion. He arrived at the theater just as the movie was letting out, and spotted Havana and Ethan laughing near the entrance. He got out of his car and rushed over to them, enraged at her for going out with a guy nearly five years her senior.

She met his accusation with a very inventive cover. She told him that the date she came with tried to get fresh, and Ethan had come to her aide. Carter didn't know whether or not to believe her, aware that if it was a lie, they both had enough time to concoct it. Regardless, the story did nothing more than bring their individual actions under heavier scrutiny.

By the end of Ethan's second turn in Owens' general sociology class, the only thing standing in the way of him passing was the final. With Carter's suspicions growing, the three weeks between Thanksgiving and Winter break found Ethan and Havana at a necessary distance. Havana knew they had to continue to sell the lie to her father, and Ethan knew his grade depended on it.

When he passed the course with a C average, he thanked Havana for her encouragement and support by stepping in front of the proverbial bullet. More than anything, Ethan knew how difficult it was for Havana to keep up the lies under her father's roof. The best way to ease that burden was to break the news to Carter that he and Havana had become friends.

"You must think I'm stupid," Owens told him.

"I already know you don't like me," Ethan explained. "What sense would it make for me to get sexually involved with your daughter?"

Carter raised an eyebrow of surprise.

"What I mean is, I understand that boundaries exist here," he corrected. "Your daughter and I are just friends."

"With hormones," Owens added. "*Teenage* hormones."

"I'm twenty-two."

"Exactly. What twenty-two year-old guy is ever 'just friends' with a seventeen-year-old girl?"

"This one," Ethan told him. "What kind of idiot would I be to stand here and tell you that I'm sleeping with your daughter?"

"I don't overestimate your critical thinking skills, Mr. Foster," Owens replied. "You probably feel safe that you won't have me again during your final semester at Westmore."

Of course, Ethan's foresight failed him, and social sciences ended up on his class registry for the following semester. Dropping the class after their conversation about Havana would have been the smoking gun to what Owens' already suspected about Ethan's involvement with her, so he had to endure the five months of psychological torture in order to save face.

Havana adored what Ethan tried to do for her, but hated the cost of it. Upon learning that he would have Owens again in the spring, Ethan told her that their relationship had to be sex-less until he graduated in June. It made frustrating sense. They could face Owens if they ever had to about their friendship and he wouldn't be able to smell the lie on either of them.

She feared, however, that this pause in their intimacy would pull Ethan away from her, and losing him was not an option.

✝ ℍℛ𝔼𝔼

Professor Owens dismissed his class after naming them off alphabetically in groups of five. With just a few weeks to complete the project, many of the students were locating their group members as they exited. Ethan found his team near the front of the room.

Genevieve Davis was a straight-A student. She grew up in a 1950's sitcom. Her dad was a successful realtor and her mom was a homemaker. They raised their only child, Genevieve, in a cul-de-sac outside of Charlotte, and enrolled her in a private school until 7th grade. When Genevieve was 16, she told her parents that she wanted them to send her to Europe with some of her girlfriends the summer following her high school graduation. The trip changed her life. She returned to the states on a mission to learn as much about European culture as she possibly could, and then move to England or Greece.

She majored in World History, and intended to teach it in an institute abroad. The only unforeseen hitch in her plan was Ethan.

Genevieve met Ethan during freshman year. He was the all-American jock, with the rare mix of cocky and southern gentleman that her parents had sheltered her from. Newly released from their orbit, Genevieve was immediately drawn to the forbidden fruit. She was still, however, the duck waiting to become a swan. She was a late bloomer, and had become accustomed to wearing drab outfits considering it pointless to even try to fit into the league of buxom post-puberty bombshells. She figured she was nothing Ethan would notice, and her crush became something she would learn to live with, which was no small feat since the two of them had had more than a few classes together, and whenever groups were assigned alphabetically, nine times out of ten her "Davis" was grouped with his "Foster."

And Lucas Dutch would always be in the midst as well. Lucas had known Ethan practically since they were in diapers. They were always the two on the playground fighting over who played which Power Ranger. Their friendship had been born out of convenience, but over the years turned into the most reliable friendship either of them had ever had – even though neither would admit it. Competition dominated between them, and continued until high school when Lucas opted out of sports to focus more on earning academic scholarships for college. His parents were far from broke, but Lucas had a keen interest in forensic science, and the degrees he wanted would require more than what his parents had put towards his college fund.

All things considered, he decided to sacrifice some of the perks of his high school years in favor of helping his dad and uncle repair and resell old cars. With the three of them working together, the business turned a heftier profit than they had expected, and Lucas was on his way to Westmore to get his Bachelor's in criminal justice before heading to a bigger school for his Doctorate in forensics.

It was his ambition that attracted Reagan Edgefield to Lucas. At first, the distraction scared her, and she adamantly resisted it for the better part of their junior year. They had both been taking Psychology 315 with Dr. Kershaw, who was easily the most difficult professor at Westmore, known for his full-class, all-essay exams and monotonous lectures. Following the first exam, Lucas found Reagan sitting outside Dr. Kershaw's office in tears. He sat down next to her without saying a word, and pulled out his exam paper, revealing the "F" he had just received.

"Can't be much worse than that," he said.

She didn't respond. He shoved the paper back into his notebook and sat back.

They stayed there for about half an hour before she started to get herself together, avoiding his gaze.

"Let's do this again sometime," he called after her. She stopped, turned back to him, and smothered a smile before continuing on her way.

Following the second exam, she found him sitting on a bench in the cafeteria. She took a seat next to him without saying a word, and pulled out her exam, revealing the big red "B."

He took the paper from her and gave her a proud smile.

"Thank you," she said.

"For what?"

"Making me realize that I never want to look that pitiful again."

From then on, he tried without success to get her across from him over a cup of coffee, but her excuses went from having a boyfriend to not being emotionally available. She was a Psyche major, and pulled out every manipulative trick she knew to prevent herself from being sidetracked by his persistence and charm.

Near the end of that semester, he approached her with one final proposition. The final exam was coming up, and both of them were looking at a C average in the class.

"What do you say we study for this beast together?" he asked. "It's *not* a date. We can even go to the library, where other people are not on dates, too."

She lowered her eyes, sending him the signal that she didn't want to hurt his feelings yet again.

"How about this..." he continued. "You and I study for this together. If both of our final grade is still a C, you'll never hear from me again."

"And if we both make B's?"

"One dinner to celebrate," he said. "...and you'll never hear from me again."

She chuckled.

"It's a win-win for you," he told her.

Following a heavy hesitation, she agreed, and their final grades ended up being B's. To fulfill their agreement, she met him at a local diner where they feasted on two large ice cream sundaes. He told her that his ambition came from watching the way his dad's face lit up whenever he restored an old car to pristine condition. It was the manifestation of knowing that you'd gotten yourself into the position of doing what you know you were made to do. Being a part of someone else's ambition makes your own that much more desirable.

In turn, Reagan told him that her mother used to be a well-respected nurse before she abruptly took off when Reagan was a baby, leaving her father to raise her. Amid her dozens of unanswered questions grew abandonment issues that followed Reagan into her teen years, and created the shelled-up introvert Lucas would find struggle in cracking.

The idea of becoming a psychologist was suggested to her during high school. She had taken one of those online tests that assessed her social likes and dislikes to determine what career options would be most suitable for her. According to that particular quiz, psychologists were more or less required to keep emotional distance from their patients, and could usually give out better advice than they themselves have put into practice. That seemed to suit her perfectly.

At the end of their date, she thanked Lucas again for all his help, and told him that the "never hear from me again" part of his proposition wasn't necessary.

He turned to her with a sly smile.

"That's great, but the agreement was that we'd have dinner," he told her. "What we just had was dessert."

"I know," she tossed at him as she climbed into her car. "Next week, we'll do lunch."

Needless to say, their "dinner" never happened. Instead, they would go out for a lot of late lunches and very early breakfasts.

Darren Gabriel was the youngest of the group. He was one of only two sophomores in the class, and decided he had to be very vocal in order to prove he could hold his own against the upperclassmen. His juvenile sense of humor repeatedly gave him away.

Darren grew up in Chicago, where he was the product of a broken home. His dad left him, his mom, and his younger brother and sisters when Darren was ten, forcing Darren to become the man of the house prematurely. The area where they lived was at the intersection of several gang territories, and one of his young sisters had become a casualty of the ever-engaged turf war. Darren's mother never recovered, and spent her days without much hope that any of her children would make it out alive. Several years after his sister's death, Darren asked his mom if he could go live with his older cousin James and his family in Raleigh. She had clearly lost even the will to care by that point.

Once his aunt and uncle heard about the situation, they arranged for Darren's mom to participate in an intense post-traumatic stress recovery group therapy program, and accepted Darren and his two remaining siblings into their home. The accommodations were tight, but they felt a lot safer.

Darren worked his way to Westmore, receiving some help from federal aid. His mother had finished with the program in time to attend Darren's high school graduation, then she and the other children moved back to Chicago, leaving their old apartment for one closer to the suburbs. Darren wanted to stay in North Carolina to attend Westmore and study sociology so that he could come back to the old neighborhood and try to start programs for inner-city youth that would help prevent what happened to his sister. His mother took a second job to help him pay for it.

Last year, his 15-year-old sister got pregnant and the money his mom had been sending for his tuition decreased substantially. He ended up selling the car his aunt and uncle had given him as a high school graduation gift, and was forced to accept a monetary donation from them and several local churches that desperately needed to see a young African-American man aiming to do something positive with his life and for his old community.

Darren squeezed between Lucas and Reagan, forcing Lucas's arm from around her shoulder.

"Alright, check it out. We absolutely have to do something crazy with this project. I'm thinking re-enactments if possible."

"Re-enact silence," Genevieve replied.

"Vieve, I was thinking you could be one of the victims. You already have the look," Darren said. "I mean, dead can't look much worse than that, right?"

Lucas chuckled in spite of being elbowed by Reagan.

"Can we all just get focused here," he covered, with a sudden shift in demeanor. "It's already gonna be hard enough as it is to make a decent grade with Foster in this group."

Ethan took offense.

"Good to know you've got faith in me, bro."

"It's not you, it's Owens," Genevieve added.

"Seriously," Reagan agreed. "What kind of morbid human being assigns his college class to research serial killers?"

"I think it's gonna be fun," Darren said.

"You would," Genevieve shot at him. "You get off on this kind of stuff, don't you? Going through one mutilated body after another like you belong in one of those *Saw* movies. Creeps me out."

"It's just a case study," Lucas said, coming to Darren's defense. "Nobody here can say we're not intrigued by things our minds aren't naturally wired to comprehend."

"Well I'm not intrigued," Genevieve said.

"Come on, Vieve." Ethan threw an arm around her. "My future is pretty much riding on this grade. You already know Owens is ready to give this group an F just because of me, and that's only going to bring your GPA down, too. We all need to give one hundred percent on this. I need to know I can count on you."

She looked up into his eyes and found support. Before her affirmation could be vocalized, a light rapping on the door drew all of their attentions.

Havana Owens stood in the doorway.

"What am I interrupting?" she asked the group, though her eyes were locked square on Ethan's.

"What are you doing here?" he asked, making his way over to her. "School's not out for another couple of hours."

"Seniors can take off whenever they want to."

"Since when?" he asked her.

"Are you glad to see me or not?" She kissed him, consciously putting on a show for the others whom she knew were watching.

"I'll give one hundred percent to this project if you will," Genevieve threw at Ethan.

He pulled out of his kiss and glanced over at his group members.

"Give us a sec," he said.

"I'm hungry anyway," Darren told the others as they gathered their books and started for the door. "Come on, Vieve. I'll buy you lunch. Make you look important in the cafeteria."

The four of them left Ethan and Havana in the doorway, Ethan widening the space between them by taking a step back into the classroom.

"I know what you're doing," she said, following him in. "I told you I don't care."

"What are you talking about?" He was genuinely confused.

"It's so hot when you're protective of us."

"Let's get you back to school."

She closed the door, sealing them together in the classroom. He grabbed his books off the corner of the front desk and looked up in time to catch her lips with his. Her kiss was ravenous.

For a moment, he gave in and enjoyed her form against his. When the kiss had broken he pulled away, tracing her bottom lip with his finger, and smiled.

"You're a very bad girl."

She lifted her almond eyes to his.

"I could do a lot worse," she said.

"Well breaking out of school to come *here* to be with me needs to be it," he told her, ushering her to the door. "We are just over a month away."

"A month is too long," she said. "It's really bad when I'm walking around jealous of Lucas and Reagan. To think that they're doing more than we are is something I can't live with."

He chuckled. She reached for the knob and opened the door, coming face-to-face with Ethan's biggest concern.

"I was coming back for my glasses, but it's quite clear Mr. Foster has found something else of mine," Professor Owens said.

"Daddy!" Havana said, caught. "I came by here... looking for you. Ethan told me you were—"

"Class was over," Ethan chimed in. "So I told her you might be in your office."

"I was hoping we could go to lunch," she said to her father. "Like we used to."

"Like we used to when you were out of school for the summer," he said. "It's the middle of April unless I missed something."

"No, no... it is," she said, flushed.

"So what made you think this was a good idea?"

"I don't know. Maybe it was stupid."

"Then let this be another reason why you shouldn't cut classes," he said. "Go back to school and then go straight home. You're grounded."

"But Daddy…"

"Havana." His tone made it clear to her that he wasn't going to hear anymore from her.

She left the classroom, giving a final apologetic glance at Ethan.

"Professor Owens, I know what you're probably thinking."

"I'm wondering why this is the fourth time I've caught my daughter on this campus in the past year."

"Well the first two times she was doing a tour, Sir."

"With you."

"Havana and I are just friends," Ethan told him. His perspiration was a welcomed odor that he hoped would mask the floral calling card Havana had left in his clothes.

"I do hope this friendship doesn't distract you from this project. One more F in my class and you and your friend may find yourselves at Westmore together *next* semester."

"Are you threatening to fail me?" Ethan asked as Owens retrieved the glasses off his desk.

"Of course not," Owens said, starting out of the classroom. "I don't have to. Your work is almost as questionable as the perfume you're wearing."

FOUR

If fear was the fuel that drove determination, Ethan had a full tank, and ahead of him lay the Interstate of getting through this project. Professor Owens was only as intimidating as he was because of who he was, and the more Havana risked them being caught together, the less her ability to soften her father for the truth became.

Ethan's parents were a much calmer storm, but a threat nonetheless. In his prime, his dad had been the town's most revered fire chief, and for months back in 2005 had achieved local celebrity status after literally dragging a pregnant woman in the middle of labor out of a burning house. Medics delivered the woman's son right there on the sidewalk in front of every news station around, and the mother credited Ethan's father, Frank, for saving both their lives.

From that moment, the pressure to conform to the type of family everyone else expected they were turned Frank into a Jekyll and Hyde kind of personality. The Hyde at home demanded with growing aggression that Ethan and his mother assume the roles projected upon them. It was easier to be a family before it was of dire necessity that they look like one. Having to over-think or predetermine every public action began to smother that natural familial instinct, and the outward appearance of their family became a mask, hiding the truth that each of them were longing for the days before Frank saved those two lives. Every now and then the thought of how normal their lives would be had Frank not saved them at all that day would venture from the darkness, but wither in the seconds before being acknowledged.

Ethan and his mom knew how important it was for Frank to present his family as what the people perceived. The house fire had been the most covered fire-related news story in the nine years since the Levenson Asylum fire that had ended much more tragically, claiming the lives of more than a hundred people. Frank's station was one of six dispatched in response to the blaze at Levenson in 1996, and two of his friends lost their lives. That fire turned the entire state of North Carolina on its head, with many people believing the lack of proper firefighter response had led to the escape and eventual murders of a dozen mental patients.

With this house fire, Frank feared another tragic scenario would further tarnish the already-scarred trust civilians had in his particular station, so he operated on behalf of his men. Upon first glance, the woman trapped in the house was not moving. Smoke and heat had obscured all but the large round lump protruding from her waist. He realized she was pregnant, and knew that even if the mother had already suffocated, there was a chance to save the baby.

He fought the flames and prayed as he reached for her. She lay in the triangle created by the floor, the wall, and a big wooden beam from the ceiling. Fire chased itself around the beam and met the wall as soon as Frank got a grip on the woman's arms and began to pull her away. The crack and crash of the engulfed beam brought the woman to consciousness. Her instinctive screams told her she was in danger, but the pain of a contraction erased any concern for her own safety.

"My baby! My baby's coming!" she began crying. "Stop! Wait! My baby's coming!" She was screaming as if her legs were pinned underneath that burning beam, but Frank had a grip and was dragging her out of the building in spite of her repeated attempts to free one hand or the other to caress her unborn child.

"I've gotta get you out of here," he was shouting back at her.

As soon as he'd pulled her out of the house and onto the sidewalk, her piercing scream signaled other medics on site to rush over. Seconds later, her solo became a duet as her son's wail filled the air.

Frank made the front page of every local newspaper, humbly restoring faith and morale in his fire station. His excitement went from zero to sixty before crashing tragically into notoriety, causing him to sustain life-altering familial injuries.

Behind every success is a scandal, and some residents weren't readily accepting how "Hollywood" Frank's heroics seemed. At the time, Ethan had been a junior in high school and several of his classmates regurgitated their parents' suspicions that Frank's stunt was staged in order to bring attention to a fire department that was on the brink of being absorbed by a neighboring station. Ethan's impulsive decision to defend his father landed him several days of out-of-school suspension, and Frank's reaction was far from appreciative. It was the first time in his life he had ever hit his son.

The pressure of living his life as the town's hero was its own curse. He hadn't learned how to reject the projection of others and thus charged his loved ones the cost of this burden. He had to maintain a certain image in public and refused to talk about the emotional drainage he had undergone during the save. Boiling beneath the surface was a fear that periodically erupted like a geyser, and with every retreat, Ethan's mother would encourage her husband to abandon the demands of being in the public eye by retiring, even so much as suggesting they travel. She desperately wanted the family she once knew, ignorant of the fact that time was driving and would soon be dropping Ethan off at college – the on-ramp to a life of his own.

Frank's refusal to retire came along with the justification that Ethan's college tuition needed to be paid for, and while they had some of it squared away, it was hardly enough. The sports scholarship was a much-welcomed relief, but losing it during his junior year of college left Ethan fifteen thousand dollars short. His mom would have to postpone their traveling plans indefinitely, and with the public embers still smoking from the 2005 fire, Frank's heroism was waging war against his health. Retirement would be his only reprieve.

With his parents' anguish in mind, their resolute stand against him dropping out of college, and his newfound support from girlfriend Havana, Ethan went into his senior year with the intentions of earning his Bachelor's degree in political science, and avoiding accruing fifth-year tuition debts. That meant he had to get through Professor Owens, and this project was the only thing standing between him and his being responsible for the stabilization of his parents' financial health and his relationship with Havana.

*

Ethan walked out of the campus cafeteria and into the noisy quad. He strained his eyes against the pupil-splicing sun, glancing around until he spotted Lucas, Reagan, Genevieve, and Darren at a nearby table finishing lunch. He approached, catching the end of their conversation.

"You're like Screech on crack right now," Genevieve was telling Darren. "Why don't you go find somebody desperate enough to give you a second glance?"

"I thought I had," he replied. "You're lucky I have a sense of humor."

"I think *you're* the one who's lucky. That I have any tolerance left," she spat.

"What is this?" Ethan asked, joining them. "I thought we were gonna be discussing the project."

"We got side-tracked by the never-ending saga of Darren Trying to Get Some," Lucas answered.

"Hey Lucas, did you forget this?" Darren asked, lifting his middle finger.

Ethan sat down across from Lucas and Reagan, who was about two-thirds of the way through *Mockingjay*.

"What about her?" he asked, motioning towards Reagan. "She don't look too involved."

Reagan looked up at Ethan from her book.

"Some of us have been waiting for the past half hour for the fifth member of our group to finish dry-humping his girlfriend," she said, stuffing her book into her backpack.

Ethan flinched from her verbal slap in the face. "Look, I didn't mean for that to come out like that," he said. "Havana and I ran into Professor Owens on our way out."

"Making it that much harder for us to actually pass! Thanks, Foster," Lucas said with mock gratitude.

"Anyway," Ethan continued. "If I'm on edge right now, that's why. We really need to come up with a killer... killer," he said, trying to avoid the joke. "We have to knock this one out of the park so I can prove to this guy that I know what I'm doing."

"Can you prove that to *us* first?" Darren asked, seriously. His fragile inflection solicited a chuckle from Genevieve, which he immediately noticed. He turned to her, only to have the hopeful gleam in his eyes met with a shake of her head. He returned to sulk.

"I'm in this one-hundred percent, I already told you," Ethan confirmed.

"Then do you have any suggestions?" Lucas asked him. "We decided the best way to go is to steer clear of the big ones like Bundy and Berkowitz."

"Who?" Ethan asked, confused.

Reagan rolled her eyes.

"Ted Bundy? David Berkowitz?" Lucas repeated, noting no recognition from Ethan. "The Son of Sam?"

Ethan shook his head, vacantly.

"He's blonde," Darren muttered to Lucas.

"Geez, Foster, wanna give us that 'I know what I'm doing' speech again?" Lucas asked.

"Hey, if we're going to be researching one of the lesser known serial killers, then maybe it'll help if we all had Ethan's... blank canvas approach," Genevieve suggested. "Maybe we'll even be able to give opposing perspectives. Imagine if we turn in a project that might even be exonerative."

"You want to go out there and turn somebody in prison loose?" Darren asked her.

"I didn't say they had to still be alive," Genevieve said. "In fact... do ya'll remember all those stories about Terrance Todd and that asylum fire back in 1996?"

"The asylum across town? You mean Levenson?" asked Lucas.

"Yeah," Genevieve continued. "I've been thinking. Everybody in town has some version of what happened back then, but has anybody actually tried to piece the truth together?"

It was a tall order and a terrifying suggestion. The Levenson fire of 1996 had made national headlines after police discovered that a number of patients had escaped into the night, and were each turning up dead in the subsequent months – preyed upon by a serial killer the cops called The Hunter.

"That entire situation is borderline urban legend by now," Lucas said.

"Which makes it perfect!" Ethan noted. "Vieve is right, it'd be an easy case! Terrance Todd was one of the patients. Once they found out he was The Hunter, they realized he hadn't just murdered those survivors, he'd also killed several people in that loony bin before setting it on fire and escaping himself."

"*Allegedly*," Lucas added.

"Calm down Matlock, you don't have the law degree yet," said Ethan.

"We can't turn in a project on a crime we can't confirm happened," he replied. "I think a nice, normal killing spree will be just fine."

"Me too," Reagan agreed.

"Normal is not going to get us an A on this project, and we all know it," said Ethan. "We have to go above and beyond, and The Hunter was the biggest case this state had ever seen. Nobody else is going anywhere near that asylum across town, I promise you. We were all terrified of that place."

"Remember that part in *Nightmare on Elm Street* where that brunette chick said 'This doesn't sound safe,'" Reagan asked, sarcastically.

"I got you, babe." Lucas wrapped a comforting arm around her.

"You're on board with this all of a sudden?" she asked him.

"Well, he's got a point," he answered. "Normal might be fine for Jackson Young and Kaylen Winston, but we've got Ethan Foster. The guy who's doing the professor's under-aged daughter."

"First of all, I'm not 'doing' her," Ethan responded. "Right now."

"We can probably get police reports and medical records that will be full of details," Lucas continued. "We can get statements from local people who remember what the fear was like with the killer and a dozen other escaped mental patients running around. No other group is going to have eyewitness accounts in their project."

Reagan hesitated.

"And she's not under-aged," Ethan continued, referring to Havana. "She's seventeen."

"Seventeen," Lucas reiterated after a moment. "That's gonna be our grade on this project. Can you focus?"

"We're doing Terrance Todd. I'm with you," Ethan answered. "We can easily just focus on the murders following the fire. Weren't there like a dozen or so survivors? People didn't know whether to be scared that psychos were on the loose or grateful that someone was killing them off."

"I think people were grateful until they realized the full scope of what he'd done," added Genevieve. "He killed over a hundred people in that fire, and basically stalked the ones who got out alive. Who knows what he would have done next if they hadn't caught him."

"Or who they *thought* was him," Reagan said, fear seeping through. "The version I heard was that there were two survivors left by the end of his little murderous psycho-hunt, and the police had nabbed them both to protect whichever one of them wasn't The Hunter. When Terrance hanged himself in his cell upon being detained, they assumed he committed suicide out of guilt, and just sent the other one off to some other asylum. The *real* killer could still be out there."

"We don't need to get into the specifics of when and why he died. We can get official police reports that say Todd was the killer, and all we need to focus on are the fire and the murders that followed," Ethan said.

"Are we all sure about this?" Darren asked. "Because I've already titled this project 'The Hunter: From Massacre to Mayhem'."

Ethan stared at Reagan. "Do we need to vote?"

Reagan knew she'd be out-numbered, but allowed concern to nestle into her normally radiant face.

"I know you're worried," Lucas told her. "But look at it this way, it won't be hard to find a motive for a mental patient, so the work is already half done. Plus, it's close to home. No endless nights in the library."

"What about the twelve sources?" she asked. "Can't exactly reference the Encyclopedia on this one."

"I don't even think they've *made* encyclopedias since 1996," Darren said.

"Lucas had a great idea about getting eyewitness statements," Ethan assured her. "I need you on board, Reagan. This will be the most original project he gets this semester."

She hesitated again.

Lucas leaned closer to her and whispered something in her ear, at which she smiled and blushed. His charm was a trademark. He then looked up at Ethan with a slight nod.

"Great," Ethan said. "Let the fun begin."

"Wait a minute," Darren interjected. "Before we all start *the fun*, I was still in Chicago when all this was going on. Any chance I can go get a look at this place? Vieve, what do you say we go down there and take some pictures?"

"It burned down," Reagan said.

"It burned *out*," Genevieve corrected. "It's still standing."

"Sounds like a 'yes' to me!" Darren said, starting to gather his things.

"It's a 'no'," she shot back. "At least until I find out if they ever moved the medical records from that location."

"Why would they need to if all the patients were dead?" Ethan asked.

"My hopes exactly." She gathered her things and tossed her hand towards them, a half-wave goodbye. "I'll get back to ya'll tonight."

FIVE

Reagan pulled her car to a stop before reaching the curved arch of the horseshoe driveway that began and ended perpendicular to Grand Street. Even from this far back, the scorched mausoleum fifty yards ahead of them towered ominously.

"Why are we so far back?" Darren asked from the passenger seat.

"Just get your pictures and let's go," she replied. "I have a quiz that I still need to study for."

He climbed out of the car, his DX-format Nikon digital camera hanging from a strap around his neck.

"You coming?" he called after noticing she hadn't gotten out of the car.

"Just hurry up, will you?"

It had taken a bit of effort for Darren to convince her to drive him up here, but his argument that photos would be good for the project made sense, and if she hadn't brought him this afternoon, he probably would have found his way up here alone.

She knew it might also be helpful for her to overcome her own apprehension. She needed to take a mind-over-matter stance and prove to herself that neither this building nor this project was anything that could intimidate her. She needed to face the beast and belittle it. Lucas had been right. The entire event was by now almost an urban legend, and whatever stories they'd heard had undoubtedly gone through the machine of rumors and speculation.

She watched Darren walk up the drive towards the burned out remains of the structure. To anyone who didn't know the history, it could have passed as an old school building. But natives all across the state still lived with the terror of what happened here fifteen years ago.

A chill overcame her, and she rolled up the windows. There was a seasonable breeze outside chasing away the remnants of winter, but she suddenly felt as if she had pulled into Levenson Asylum's cold atmosphere. She didn't care to find the irony in wrapping her chilled body tighter in her sweater while practically being able to smell the char in the air.

"This is crazy," she said to herself. She opened the door and climbed out of the car, taking in the enormity of the five-story building and its acreage. Bushes and weeds were reckless in the large D of a yard created by the driveway and Grand Street. Darren was in the center of the yard, crouching in front of one of several scraggly trees whose bare branches extended like 3-D veins in various directions. The silence was disturbed by the faint shutter sounds as he snapped one picture after another.

She contemplated joining him, but the trek across the yard looked like a jungle, and her shoes were open-toed. It was a "Stay Out" sign that she was all too eager to heed.

"Are you done yet?" she called.

He stood up and started back towards her. "Can we drive around so I can get closer?"

"Why don't we wait until the rest of the group decides the route we're going?"

"Oh alright," he said, dodging a tangle of weeds. "It's probably not smart to be lurking around out here with you, scared of *everything*."

"It's a burned out mental institution where this mass murder happened, Darren."

"I'm aware of that," he said as they climbed into her white Toyota Corolla.

"And I'm not scared of this, it's just creepy." She started the car. "Do you want me to take you back to the dorm, or do you have someplace else to go?"

"The dorm."

They drove for a while, listening to the local DJ's mix of classic Michael Jackson hits on the radio. Darren scanned through the pictures he had taken, showing several to Reagan who would momentarily peel her eyes off the road ahead to get a glance.

"This one would be great if we could get it projected on the wall behind us when we're giving the oral portion of the report, right?"

"Let's not overdo it," she said. "You don't want to end up with a mess."

"It's not like I'm suggesting we play 'Thriller' behind it," he said. His eyes lit up. "*Could* we?!"

Reagan furrowed her brows at him in disapproval.

"Fine," he conceded. "We'll let Ethan and Vieve make all the decisions." He glanced over at her, hoping she'd take the bait.

She knew what he was doing, and allowed the corner of her mouth to curl into a slight smirk. "I'm not going to be manipulated like this."

"Come on, Reagan... it's *our* grade too," he said. "If you're not comfortable, you have a right to say something. I'm telling them all about my ideas, who cares if I'm outvoted. That way, if we get a bad grade on the count that our presentation was 'lacking,' I can justifiably say 'I told you so.'"

"Darren, I'm fine with doing the project," she reiterated. "Like I said, I'm not scared. It's just creepy."

She couldn't tell whether or not he believed her, or if the dread she was unable to shake betrayed her. She was sure though that once this project was done, her psychology study would narrow substantially.

*

After dropping Darren off at the dorm and making him promise not to go back out to Levenson tonight, Reagan returned home to find her dad making use of the last few minutes of daylight. He had just finished washing his Honda Civic and was drying the car off with an absorbent cloth.

Jeffrey Edgefield was a shadow of the father Reagan was born to. She had no memory of what he was like before her mother left them. All she knew was that he was particularly protective of his little girl. She often caught him staring at her with a sadness in his eyes that feared if they even blinked, his porcelain daughter would be reduced to dust.

Similarly, Reagan could tell there was fragility in her father. If her mother packed anything the day she left it would have been half of his heart. She was cautious in the few conversations they ever had about her mother, Robyn. The bounds of her inquiries ended at how much she loved her work as a nurse at Mt. Victoria Hospital in Greenville, and that she loved her only daughter.

Once as a kid she asked him if her mother loved her so much why did she leave? Jeffrey's glossy eyes connected with hers and he explained that Mommy got lost, and maybe one day she would find them again. She wasn't too young to pick up on the agony this question had brought her father, and decided she would rather not bring him to this emotional place again. She locked all of her questions into the back of her mind, and just accepted that Mommy was gone and probably never coming back. By the time she reached high school, she simply told people her mother was dead.

"You're home late," he noted as she got out of the car.

"I had to meet with a group member about a class project." She could never lie to him, but withholding the entire truth in certain cases was easier for both of them to handle.

"Lucas called," he said.

She tried to read his inflection to see if he knew something she didn't want him to know.

"Said your group's meeting at the library tomorrow." He looked up, inspecting her reaction.

She wanted to tell him it was a different group, but the lie got arrested in her throat and hauled back down to her gut.

"What's going on?" he asked. "Are you alright?"

"I'm fine," she said. "It's five of us in the group. I was with Darren Gabriel."

His eyes narrowed, and she knew what he was thinking.

"Lucas knows him. We went down to Levenson to get some pictures for the project we're working on. My signal must have been low out there. I didn't get any calls on my cell."

"Levenson? *Asylum*?" her dad asked, his concern suddenly turning desperate.

She nodded, hoping that seeing her calm would calm him down as well.

"Exactly what kind of project is this?"

"Daddy..." She started to plead for him to lighten up, but realized pleading would make her look like the 12-year-old he expected she still was. "It's fine."

"It's *not* fine. Do you have any idea--?" He stopped himself, and threw the cloth from his hand onto the ground next to the front driver's side tire. "What's the project?"

She hesitated, trying to decide how much of the truth to give him. When she realized he knew too much already not to go digging for whatever information she withheld, she blurted out the whole of it. "We're doing a case-study on Terrance Todd."

He let a moment go by, hoping she would retract with a giggle and tell him to lighten up and that it was sarcasm. When she didn't, he brushed a hand through his sweat-soaked graying hair.

"Tell me you're kidding," he said.

"It wasn't my idea."

"But you're doing it anyway."

"I was outvoted," she told him. "Everybody wants to know what really happened up there."

"Why?" he beseeched, his face suddenly attacked by horror.

"Daddy—" Pleading at this point seemed necessary.

But he beat her to it. "Reagan, please... you have to talk them out of that." His eyes pierced into hers with a painstaking fear. She repeated his genetic narrowed-brow expression, trying to make sense of the subtext dripping from his appeal. He slowly averted his gaze, and then bent to retrieve his towel off of the ground. "I just don't want you giving yourself nightmares," he said.

"That's not it," she replied, figuring her offering him the whole truth for free before should cost him reciprocity.

He turned away from her, fighting back tears as she approached him.

"Daddy, we're all aware of what this town went through fifteen years ago when that fire happened. It was devastating. It was scary. We know."

He turned back to her, but didn't respond – only allowing his gaze to linger in the space just beyond her.

"Part of the reason the group wants to profile this case is to get some kind of handle on everything that terrified us as kids."

She paused, waiting for him to secede. His eyes found hers again, and saw in them a *woman* that he had raised. Here was his daughter, behind the wheel of her own thoughts and actions, and heading for the freeway like a newly licensed teenager.

"I'm sure we can handle it," she continued, suddenly aware that she was slowly ripping his little girl from his arms. "Unless there's some other reason why you think I shouldn't be involved with this."

"You think I'm being overprotective," he said in a voice that was more comforting than foreboding. His face was a map of anxiety.

"What's wrong?" she asked him.

"There's a lot you don't know." He paused, preparing them both for the rest. "About your mom."

S I X

A red VW Beetle crept into the dark driveway of the Owens' suburban home and came to a stop outside of the closed two-car garage. Its headlights and engine shut off, and seconds later Havana emerged from the driver's side.

Storm clouds covered the moon like it was a precious pearl that must be hidden from the thievery of night. Havana made her way across the manicured lawn, the darkness an accomplice to her post-curfew arrival. She reached the front door, carefully lifted her key to the lock and slid it in as quietly as possible.

She stepped into the living room and silently closed the door behind her, pausing with her hand on the knob. Something intruded the stillness around her; she could feel it.

"It's late," she spoke, waiting for her eyes to outline grey shadows against the blackness.

"I didn't think you noticed," came the gruff reply.

"I'm more perceptive than you give me credit for," she said.

A lamp flicked on, and as the dark curtain gave way to dim luminance, she found her father sitting in the furthest of the plush twin armchairs that sandwiched the couch.

"I don't think you are, Havana," he said. "I told you to come straight home. Did you think I was kidding?"

"I think you were a little extreme in grounding me for leaving school during my lunch hour. All the seniors do it."

He stood up, but the switch to a more intimidating stance didn't cause her to back down.

"Let's not pretend that your little visit to Westmore today had nothing to do with Ethan Foster," he said. "That's why I grounded you."

"You're reading way too much into that, Daddy," she replied, hoping it sounded convincing. "Ethan and I are—"

"Just friends," he finished. "I've heard."

"You don't believe me?"

"I grounded you, and yet you're sneaking in here at one o'clock in the morning," he illustrated. "What is your definition of trust?"

"I'm sorry," she said. "I honestly didn't stay out this late on purpose. If I did, do you think I would have bothered about being quiet just now?"

"I don't care," he barked. "Next time you decide to come home at one in the morning without bothering to call anybody, the locks will be changed. On purpose."

She wasn't exactly surprised by his reaction, but it was much more intense than what she had expected.

"I will be eighteen in a few months." The words came out before she had a chance to stop them. "None of this will matter."

He approached her, a grim expression covering his face.

"You don't think so?" The serious look in his eyes sent a chill down her spine.

Havana shifted her view past her father and noticed that her mother was awake. Lucinda had emerged at the foot of the stairs.

"Mom," she said. "I didn't mean to wake you."

"Are you just getting home?" She made her way into the living room and stood at her husband's side.

"I lost track of time," Havana replied. She shifted her gaze back to Carter. "Are we done?"

Before he could answer, she started past them and headed towards the stairs.

Until today, she had been pretty good at keeping her anger in check. She knew from an early age that there was a side of her father that she didn't want to provoke. On several occasions, she had seen what an irate Carter Owens looked like, and the spectacle was unsettling.

Nothing she had ever seen before affected her the way his

threat just did. Perhaps he had a reason to exaggerate his point like that, but the seriousness behind the delivery of his words haunted her like a ghost.

She entered her bedroom and closed the door, isolating herself like times before when she only allowed these particular walls to see her cry. She remembered her mom telling her of how Carter used to do the same thing, closing himself off to leak tears from the emotional and psychological wounds of a past that was to remain veiled behind the curtain of darkness.

But shadows were stubborn, and every now and then a storm cloud would descend, and any attempt at a normal conversation with him was met with a downpour of acid rain. His mood would become dark and thunderous, a sudden and unwarranted strike like lightning that seemed impossible to avoid. He would bark orders intolerably, and give up completely on fair treatment. Those moments were few and far between, but even one occurrence was enough for Havana to know it was more than just blowing off steam. She would press for details, only to be told she was too young to understand. Over time, she became conditioned to the evasiveness, and eventually gave up asking why.

From what she could piece together, life had left her dad behind. He had lost his previous wife and son in some kind of tragedy that left him with a parasitic rage. That the world continued to spin in spite of what had happened made it worse. He either refused to or gave up on staying in touch with whatever remaining family members he had, so she and her mother had never met them. Whatever outlet he needed in order to release that inner chaos probably wasn't legal, and bottling it up inside was the only other option. In finding love with Lucinda, he had evidently figured out how to repress enough of it to maintain, allowing for the occasional uncontrollable hiccup.

His attitude towards Ethan from the beginning seemed curious even after they surmised that it was likely Ethan's free ride to college that embittered him. Pursuing a relationship with Ethan after finding out how her father felt about him was never out of spite. She loved her dad, and had high hopes that once she and Ethan were able to outwardly express their love for each other, Carter would be accepting of their relationship. In order for that to happen though, she fully understood that Ethan had to prove himself to him in the classroom. Jealousy hardly seemed like enough of a reason for Carter to make things this hard for Ethan. She assigned the rest of it to Carter's growing suspicion of their secret love, and as much as she hated having to lie about her feelings for him, she knew how badly Ethan needed to finish college on time.

With their relationship just three months shy of a year old, the excitement of arranging accidental meets and stealing only a tender caress in public had worn off. The whole secret nature of their relationship was a third entity, and it was getting in the way. Whatever moments alone they could snag were usually in the vacant parking lot behind the fairgrounds where they had their first kiss, and would only last for half an hour at most so as not to solicit questions from Carter when she got home later than expected. The only thing that prevented his suspicions about their involvement from being confirmed was proof, and he was like a piranha waiting for the tiniest fleshy slip.

Why it mattered so much to destroy Ethan simply because he had an easier time getting into college than Carter did was the one recurring subject of speculation that Ethan and Havana could not entirely wrap their minds around. There had to be more to it, and Havana was itching to dig for answers. For days she tip-toed around the conversation, only holding back for Ethan's sake. If she approached it the wrong way with Carter, he would tie it all together and the results would be catastrophic.

She had started with a simple question: "Was it hard for you to have a job while you were in college?"

"I had to do what had to be done," he replied.

"Do you think I should get one?" she continued. "I just don't want to have too much on my plate."

"The more responsibilities you have, the less likely you are to hang yourself with whatever web you will have managed to create by then," came the confusing response.

"What does that mean?" she asked, mildly offended by the way his statement was delivered. "I don't have any intentions of spinning any kind of web. You really don't have much faith in me, do you?"

"Just stay focused," he said. "Things have a way of really getting ugly in spite of your best intentions."

"Do you feel more entitled since you worked your way through college?" she pressed. "I guess I just don't understand the pay-off. I thought part of the whole idea of college was to experience freedom."

"The *idea* of college is to further your education," he stated with a mocking tone. "You are not going there some spoiled, party-hopping brat. Especially not on *my* dime."

He was a steel door, and she had taken to it with a lead pipe. The reverberations of their conversation hurt her more than it opened him up. Perhaps if she had a better plan of approach, or if she could flat out go to him in Ethan's defense. But she knew if that happened, their relationship would be ripped apart by the force of nature.

And she still wouldn't understand why.

S E V E N

The spacious second floor study room of the campus library was unoccupied when Darren entered. Usually, there would be several groups of students either seated at the rectangular oak conference table in the center of the space, or huddled in any of the four corners of the room. Saturdays were normally low-traffic days on the second floor, where many of the fiction books were stored. Most students would be on the first floor buried beneath piles of textbooks or nonfiction reference sources preparing for the finals that were only a month away.

Up here was hardly where Darren wanted to spend his Saturday, but Genevieve's voice message sounded urgent. She must have had a lot of information to present to the group, and Darren hoped it wouldn't be so much that they would spend the entire afternoon here sifting through it.

He took a seat at the right corner of the table and retrieved his laptop from its case, tossing the bag onto the floor. While he waited for it to boot, he reached into the pocket of his shorts, located the small black thumb drive, and plugged it into the USB port on the side of his computer. Within minutes, the photos he took at Levenson Asylum were displayed in front of him. He scrolled through them again, anxious to show the others.

The double doors opened and Genevieve entered in front of Ethan. She was carrying a manila folder stuffed with printouts.

"Great, you're already here," she said, laying her folder on the table next to Darren. "Where are Lucas and Reagan?"

"No idea," he answered. "I just got here. You have to take a look at these pictures—"

"We don't have time for pictures, Darren," she told him.

"But—"

She cut him off again, pulling two sets of printouts from the folder and passing them to Darren and Ethan as he took a seat on the other side of the table.

"These are copies of as many variations of what happened at Levenson as I could find online. Some of these are completely different from what we all heard happened."

"Like what?" Ethan asked, flipping through the pages.

"Some people who were actually here when it happened believe the fire was an inside job. They think some of the staff members who weren't on call that night were responsible and pointed everything at Terrance to make him take the fall. Some people think a cult was involved. How do we know which one is even in the right direction?"

"What happened to the official police records?" Darren asked.

"I was on hold with the sheriff's office last night for forty-five minutes while they were searching for them," she said. "One of the deputies finally told me he would have to call me back."

"Don't tell me they lost them," Ethan said.

"Without them we have nothing," she added. "Maybe we should start over. Get somebody else."

The doors swung open again. Lucas entered, carrying his own laptop.

"Sorry I'm late," he said.

"Where's Reagan?" Genevieve asked him.

"She's not coming. She's no longer a member of this group. That's why I'm so late. She just told me."

"Not surprised," Ethan said.

"Give it a rest, Foster," Lucas defended. "She was never comfortable with this."

He went on to explain that Reagan had gone to Professor Owens yesterday evening and requested to be moved to a different group. She was joining Jackson Young and Kaylen Winston, the only group in the class that consisted of four people.

"She said she didn't mention that we were profiling The Hunter. She just told him she didn't feel like this was the best group for her to be in."

"And of course he was eager to move her," Ethan said. "Wouldn't want the F he gives us to affect her 4.0."

Lucas rolled his eyes.

"So now we're down to four people, we've got two weeks to complete this thing, and we're not even sure if this is the case we're gonna do anymore?" Ethan asked.

"What do you mean we're not sure?" Lucas asked.

Genevieve handed him a set of the printouts. "There are far too many different versions of what happened, and the police files may or may not even turn up in time."

"I don't think completely abandoning Terrance Todd is necessarily the answer," Darren said. "The police records aren't off the table. My cousin's a cop. I could ask him to look into it."

"You couldn't mention this yesterday?" Genevieve asked him.

"You were making all the decisions." His reply was self-serving. "Next time, let me talk."

What about his medical files?" Ethan asked.

"My guess is they're still at Levenson," she told him.

"Can't we try to get those?" Ethan continued, commandeering Darren's laptop to do a Google search for Levenson Asylum. "They'll have a list of whatever drugs they had him on and they might even have notes from evaluations and treatments and stuff," he continued. "If there's anything in his files about fire or arson, we can build a motive for the Levenson fire from that, and then all of the survivors' murders are basically the plot from *Final Destination*. After the first few, the rest had to know it was coming."

Darren started clicking through some of the links that came up under the Google search as Ethan continued.

"We can create one of those psychological profiles of this guy and the victims. It still counts as serial, and it's still a truckload of information to use that won't require all this extensive research."

"Have you even *heard* of the law?" asked Lucas. "There is such a thing as doctor-patient confidentiality."

"They're dead, right?" Ethan noted.

"Well, according to some of these legends..." Darren turned the laptop so that the dark screen with bright red text reading *Haunted Places in North Carolina* faced the rest of them.

"Yeah, ghosts don't have a right to privacy, Darren," Ethan said.

"Tell that to Candyman."

"First of all, what are the odds the records are even still there?" Lucas asked. "And secondly, isn't that place condemned?"

"It's either that or start over," Ethan said.

Each of them assessing their options, silence stretched across the room until it was interrupted by Darren's voice.

"Well... I found a map," he said. "Not exactly a blueprint, but from what it looks like, there was a storage space in the basement."

Ethan turned to Lucas. "It'll take us thirty minutes, tops. We get in. If we don't see anything, we get out."

"And hope we don't get arrested for trespassing," Lucas added.

"Okay, just so we're all on the same page," Genevieve started, skeptically. "The four of us are about to go wandering into a burned out mental hospital that for all we know could be haunted to dig up the old records of a suicidal serial killer."

"Bring your flashlights," Ethan added with a smirk.

"I'd rather bring a gun," she replied, gathering her things together.

"Sure, Vieve. Aim a gun at Casper," Darren said, following her out of the room. "One of us'll end up shot."

*

Angst piled into Ethan's yellow Jeep Wrangler along with Lucas, Darren, and Genevieve, who spent the duration of the drive to Levenson trying to fit all the various pieces of the Terrance Todd puzzle into some kind of frame of reference.

"If only we could talk to one of the police officers who were on call that night. Or one of the firefighters that responded," she said.

"Foster, wasn't your dad there that night?" Lucas asked.

Ethan's grip on the steering wheel tightened. "We're not going to involve him in this."

"We might have to," Genevieve said.

"We're not," he insisted. The vivid memory of his father's hand coming hard across his face fluttered with a sting in the back of his mind. "Asking him about anything even remotely related to that fire is like tossing a Molotov cocktail onto a campfire. He's hardly a reliable reference anyway."

"Why isn't he?" Lucas asked. "We're all risking a lot here. You're related to an eyewitness to what actually happened. It's the most viable option we have."

"We're not involving him, Lucas, so drop it," Ethan repeated. "There's a dozen other officials – police officers, even – who'd be just as helpful. Besides, Owens would definitely find a problem with us using my dad as a reference."

"He's right," Darren agreed. "We need someone that none of us is connected to. I could ask my cousin James. He's a cop. Maybe he could ask around at the station."

"The police department isn't so eager to discuss it, Darren. They're not gonna go on the record about any of this." Genevieve shuffled through her folder of printouts before continuing. "Which makes me think there's some truth to one of these stories." She held one up, scanning through the first paragraph. "Here it is. This one says the cops and the fire department practically sat back and watched the place go up in flames."

Lucas reached for the printout as she continued.

"Most of the patients were convicts who the police felt copped an insanity plea just to get out of doing jail time. They didn't think half the patients at Levenson were actually crazy. That fire was their idea of justice."

"So...?" asked Lucas.

"So if that's true, then of course the police are gonna give us the runaround about the files," she said. "They don't want the public to know they pretty much sacrificed the lives of innocent staff members and truly insane people just to serve up some sort of vigilante justice for the ones who were probably faking it."

"Well if that's the case, don't you think they'd be more than willing to corroborate the story that Terrance Todd set that fire and killed all those people?" Darren asked. "He's the perfect scapegoat."

"Then you're saying the *cops* set him up," she said, coming to a terrifying realization. "Which means his suicide was possibly another murder."

"Wait a minute, I'm not saying any of that," Darren said. "Your conclusion-jumping makes me nervous."

Ethan turned onto Grand Street, growing more and more anxious by the direction of this conversation.

"There's a lot we don't know," he said. "I think once we get his files, Vieve, you and I can start putting something together that resembles a psychological profile. Lucas, you work on the Hunter victims. I'll try to talk to my dad and see if he can at least give me some names of some officers or other firemen who were on duty that night. Darren, you've got your video camera, right?"

Darren lifted a small handheld video camera into view.

"Set up some interviews with people who lived around here back then," Ethan continued. "Get them on film, just in case. Even if we get twelve versions of what happened, at least two of them will be similar enough to build on."

"This is getting more and more half-assed by the minute," Lucas said. "We don't know if our suspect might've actually been a victim, we have no way of knowing the police aren't trying to cover up a mass murder, and at least two people in this car think we're on the verge of rewriting an urban legend – which isn't even the assignment!"

Ethan pulled over to the side of the road, bringing the car to a stop. "Somebody murdered all those people. It sure wasn't an accident. A building that large catches fire and only a dozen or so people survive? And all but two of them subsequently get murdered? If the police were behind it, what sense would it make to kill the survivors and set Terrance Todd up when they could have easily brushed any accusations off as the ramblings of certifiably crazy people? This was someone who had a reason to want every person in that asylum dead."

A chill overcame Genevieve. She shuddered.

"I guess that rules out this theory." She reached back to retrieve the page from Lucas, and crumpled it in her hands.

"Any more surprising little nuggets of intelligence, Foster?" Lucas asked. "Or is this your limit for the week?"

"I'm just not in the mood to be starting over," Ethan said,

pulling back onto the road. "Let's hope the files are still in this building and get on with it."

Darren looked at Lucas sitting next to him and held up his video camera. "Ethan with a plan. Maybe we should've got *that* on film."

E I G H T

Hell happened here.

Those were the only legible graffiti-scribbled words Lucas, Ethan, Genevieve, and Darren could decipher as they stood side by side in front of Levenson Asylum. Ethan had parked his jeep on the side of Grand Street opposite the drive entrance. Their walk to the front door of the burned out hospital was preceded by a quick assessment of the mission at hand.

Each of them was armed with a flashlight except for Darren, who held his video camera in front of him as if it could detect a portal that would lead them directly to the medical records they were in search of; his aim to capture every moment on video became less and less a nuisance to the others as he led the group towards the entrance of the asylum. Genevieve carried a rolled up copy of the asylum's floor plan, which they had printed out before leaving the library earlier.

The afternoon was eerily silent, as though even the birds could read those three foreboding words and knew to stay away from the place where Hell happened that night in 1996. Twigs and branches littered the horseshoe driveway towards the front door, each cautious step a thunderous alarm to the dead and dark silence before them.

They finally reached the entrance, and stood staring up at the setting of most of their childhood nightmares. The front steps were cracked by time and bled tangles of vines and weeds. The black double doors at the top of the steps could hardly be seen through boards that had been nailed in random criss-cross fashion across them. One of the larger boards that spanned the width of both doors touted the weathered but still colorful message about Hell. Two large boarded double-pane windows sat on either side of the doors. Single pane windows stretched on symmetrically in intervals along the length and height of the five-story building. Whatever glass remained was blackened by smoke – most of them cracked or shattered, the result of various adolescent dares over the years.

In various spots around the frame of the building, groups of bricks above windows were caked with ash, and wooden panels were lacerated – incisions of rodents and weather. The fire itself had been intense enough to stop the heartbeat of its mammoth victim, but left the charred cadaver erect in its perch – rigor mortis, or its sturdy nineteenth century bone structure preventing it from caving in.

None of them had ever come this close to the remnants of Levenson before today, and when they were younger, wouldn't have even on a dare. Annual Halloween festivities in the town usually included a haunted house or two themed for the tragic event that took place here fifteen years ago. Those were enough to sustain the fear.

Darren was the first to speak. He had his video camera aimed at the top floor of the building, and was panning it slowly from left to right.

"It just occurred to me," he said. "Every successful based-on-true-events horror movie in the past decade or so used found video camera footage. We could get famous!" He glanced over at Genevieve. "Just imagine all the plastic surgery you could afford."

"Funny," she replied.

"We're losing daylight, guys," Lucas said. "Can we just get what we came for and get out of here?"

Genevieve unrolled the floor plan as Ethan started up the steps towards the double door entrance.

"It seems like there was a filing room in the basement," she said. "There might have been some offices on each floor, but nothing large enough to accommodate what would be necessary to hold all the patients' records."

"The basement," Lucas said, sarcasm surfacing. "Of course. Six feet under ground. No red flags there."

"You're not still scared of this place, are you?" Darren asked, turning the camera onto Lucas. "If there's anything in there paler than you are right now, I'd be shocked."

"Turn that thing off, will you?" Lucas told him.

Darren turned the camera to Ethan, and zoomed in on him standing at the door. Ethan hesitated before tugging with feeble force at the boards. None of them would budge. He took a step back, surveying his options as Lucas stepped up to give it a try, exerting more force but with similar results.

Ethan crossed over to the double-pane window to the left of the doors. A section of the glass had been shattered beneath a board on the lower right-hand side. He leaned down, lifted his flashlight and peered inside.

"Looks like this might be our only way in," he told the others. He stepped back and kicked at the board. The wood cracked and a rusted nail fell to the floor. He grabbed one end of the board and motioned for Lucas to grab the other. Together, they were able to pry a couple of the boards from the window, and were left with a space large enough for them to climb through.

Ethan entered the littered foyer first, followed by Darren, Genevieve, and then Lucas. Immediately, their flashlights began sweeping the space, preceding them into the grand lobby. Carpets of ash and dust covered everything from floor to ceiling, and the stagnant smell of smoke did a fine job of making sure they knew they didn't want to spend much time here.

Though a shell of itself, the lobby boasted remnants of what were once grandiose features similar to many of the buildings of it's era. Large marble columns stood on either side of the foyer entrance. A large glass and mirror chandelier lie in a dusty, shattered heap on the floor beneath the area where it once hung. Window-sized oil paintings and portraits speckled the walls mostly in lop-sided disarray. Oversized wicker chairs and tables were piled in front of a room at the far end of the lobby that might have functioned as a registration office. To the left was the most ominous character in the room: a grand staircase against the wall with a right side railing that gaped outward in a fancy curve at the base of the stairs, giving the staircase a triangular look as it ascended *up* into the darkness of Hell.

Lucas started towards the room at the other end of the lobby. Darren slowly followed, sweeping his camera around the room to record as much as possible.

"I doubt they're in there," Genevieve called after Lucas, figuring what he was up to.

"Doesn't hurt to look," he responded. He reached the windowed frame of the room, constructed with panes that opened outward. He slowly opened one of the two panes and scanned the small room, the corner of which had obviously been scorched in the fire. The wall had started to cave in, and all of the furniture had been piled against it in an apparent effort to keep the side wall from tumbling over. Below the window opening inside the room was a desk, on top of which were several stacks of paper, a dried out ink stamp pad, and a rotary telephone – it's receiver dangling by its cord across the opposite edge of the desk.

"I'm going in." Darren opened the other panel and started to climb through the window into the room. Climbing off of the desk, he shot footage from one corner of the room to the other, opening one door that turned out to be a closet, and another which led to a small bathroom.

"Can we move it along, please?" he heard Genevieve call. "This is not the Smithsonian."

She and Ethan were by now standing at the foot of the stairs, studying the floor plans and trying to figure out the best way to the basement.

"Come on Darren," Lucas said, starting back towards Ethan and Genevieve. "There's nothing back there."

"This place is incredible," Darren said, glancing around for a doorway that would lead out. Leaving him further intrigued was the fact that there didn't seem to be one – unless the furniture was all piled where an exit once was.

He climbed back onto the desk and started back out through the room's window. One last glance before exiting snagged his curiosity, and he turned the camera onto the rotary phone sitting on the corner of the desk.

"Who'd care if I took a little souvenir?" he asked himself, reaching in and pulling on the cord to retrieve the receiver.

"Darren, hurry up!" Genevieve called again.

"One sec!" He noticed they were all gathered at the foot of the stairs just as he gave the cord one final yank. The receiver landed on the desk beside the phone. The sudden clank like a gunshot solicited gasps from the others, but Darren's face froze when he saw the unmistakable bloody handprint that gripped the receiver.

He suddenly paid closer attention to the rotary dial on the phone. Two holes were smeared with caked-on blood: nine and one. The realization was a punch to the gut. He instinctively pushed the phone off the desk and hopped out of the window.

"Will you quit messing around?" Ethan called.

"I say we just leave him out here," he heard Genevieve say.

"I'm right behind you," he said, scuttling over to join the rest of them and trying forcibly to defeat the octave fear was pushing his voice to reach.

"What was that about?" Ethan asked.

"Nothing," he answered, defensively. "Which way to the basement?"

Genevieve pointed at an entryway beside them at the base of the stairs. Pieces of a door were still attached to hinges in the frame.

"What are we waiting for?" Darren asked, starting towards the doorway.

"Hold on a minute," Lucas interjected. "Doesn't it strike anybody else as odd that this door looks like it was chopped down?"

"And...?" Genevieve asked, not following.

"According to your floor plans, there are patient rooms down that hall," he continued. "If there's a fire, and your main goal is to get everybody out as quickly as possible, why are you going to spend time chopping down a door instead of just opening it? Evidently, this door was locked that night. From the other side."

"Wait, so you're saying you think the patients had locked the staff out?" Ethan asked, confused.

"The patients didn't. Not if they were all locked in their rooms," Lucas explained. "It would seem to me somebody locked or blocked this door from the other side before or during the fire to keep staff or rescuers from getting in."

"Or maybe to keep Terrance from getting in," Darren said, his eyes widening as he zoomed his camera to get a shot of the hallway in question. "He was on a murder run during the fire too, right?"

The implications of Darren's speculation froze all of them at once. It meant whoever was behind this door locked themselves behind it and stayed there knowing they might burn alive.

"We don't know that vandals didn't do this," Ethan said. "Let's quit jumping to conclusions."

"Lucas started it," Darren replied.

As the rest of them joined Darren at the doorway, they noticed that on the outside wall of the long hallway was a row of single-paned windows. The inside wall hosted a row of patients' rooms – the door to each room flung open into the hallway.

Darren and Ethan followed as Genevieve started down the hall, leading the way towards the end. Lucas trailed behind, glancing into every room as he passed.

For the most part, each of the nine rooms they passed was identical. They were slightly smaller than an average hospital room, with smoky gray concrete walls that eerily resembled a prison cell. Furniture in each ranged from overturned metal twin-sized beds and mattresses to plastic chairs strewn about. The lack of windows made each room look like a dungeon, and the disappearing daylight emanating from the windows along the hall opposite the rooms did little to help.

"Was it even legal to keep people in these kinds of spaces?" Darren asked rhetorically.

"They were criminally insane, Darren," Genevieve answered. "What would you expect? The Ritz?"

She slowly stepped into the tenth room on the hall. The room seemed a bit bigger than the others, but perhaps it was the absence of any furniture at all that lent it greater area. She allowed her flashlight to paint the wall to her right, then the wall directly in front of her.

"What's that smell?" Darren asked, entering the room ahead of Lucas and Ethan.

"I don't know, but there has to be a way to get to the basement from here, or those printouts are--"

The reflections of their lights duplicated in the wall on their left, startling them all.

"What the…?" Ethan started. He took a step back to take in as much of the wall as he could. A large, two-way mirror covered most of the wall, and the darkness of the room would only allow their flashlights to be reflected off the glass.

"Seriously, this smell is killing me," Darren said, covering his nose and mouth.

Genevieve searched the rest of the wall with her flashlight, found a door at the far end, and started towards it.

"Did they do police interrogations here too?" Ethan asked, confused.

Genevieve pushed on the door and was surprised by how easily it gave in, swinging into the room. As she started to enter, her feet stumbled against a cold, cement step in the doorway, and she tumbled to her hands and knees into the room, dropping her flashlight onto the floor. The light landed, it's beam drawn like a magnet to the chair in the center of the room.

"Not interrogations," she said, glancing up into the room, her eyes and breath caught by the sight before her.

"Are you okay?" Ethan asked. He and Darren rushed over to help her to her feet, but her eyes would not – or could not – peel away from the chair. Darren followed her gaze with his camera, the green light of his night vision mode illuminating the horror etched onto his face.

"Is that…?" He slowly lifted his eyes from the camera screen and let them settle on the rotting, wooden electric chair only a few feet from where they stood.

As Lucas joined them in the room, Ethan stood beside the doorway, his gaze and his flashlight beam paralytic. The chair was this room's sole occupant – its stature as foreboding as the asylum itself. Wires and metallic accessories decorated it like a Christmas tree. Speckles of dried blood painted the floor beneath it.

"Okay. So we're done here," said Lucas.

"Let's keep going," Genevieve said, starting for another doorway behind the chair. "I think this might be the door to the basement here."

"Are you out of your mind?!" Lucas yelled. "Look at this!

What did they need an electric chair in a mental asylum for? This is nuts!"

Genevieve started for the door, but nobody made a move to follow. "It's either this, or start over," she reminded them.

Lucas shot an apprehensive glance at Ethan.

"There is no easier way to an A than this, Lucas," he said. He made his way past the chair to join Genevieve at the doorway that would lead them to the basement.

"Darren?" Lucas turned to him with a tone just short of begging.

"Yeah right, like I'm gonna back out," Darren said. "Aren't you trying to be a part of CSI? Just consider it field experience."

Reluctant, Lucas hesitated before starting slowly past the chair to join the others. Darren followed, filming as much of the chair as he could as he passed.

Ethan helped Genevieve push the sliding metallic door as much as it would give, allowing them room to enter one at a time. Ethan entered first, and discovered with a quick scan of his light that the room stretched on for merely a few yards to his left, and maybe eight feet in front of him. To his immediate right, there were two steep flights of stairs. One ascended along the wall across from the sliding doorway up to the second floor. The other, the one closest to him, descended to what was likely the building's basement.

"I think this is it," he called back to the others.

He stepped onto the first step, and noticed the linoleum flooring ended and the steps were made of wood. He aimed his light to the space below, trying to determine how far down the stairs led. When he reached the tenth step, he could see the concrete foundation at the bottom – another ten or so steps. The darkness was total, except for the light from Ethan's flashlight, which darted from here to there in the narrow space. Cinder blocks made up the wall opposite the bottom of the stairs.

"Be careful," he said, realizing Genevieve was just a few steps behind him.

He reached the concrete foundation and shivered as a sudden chill crept up his spine. The basement was huge, and surprisingly not as cluttered as he imagined. A sweep of his and Genevieve's flashlights revealed about a dozen free standing five-drawer filing cabinets lining the wall next to the stair entrance. Ethan and Genevieve exchanged smiles at the discovery.

"You guys see anything?" Lucas called from the stairs. He glanced behind him only to find Darren heading up the other staircase, his camera held out in front of him.

"Darren, can we *please* stick together?" he called up.

"I'll be there in a second," Darren called back. "I just want to see what it looks like up here. I've never been in a mental hospital before."

"Give it another few years," Lucas murmured.

A sudden crack stopped Lucas midway down the stairs. Everyone heard it. Ethan and Genevieve rushed over to the base of the stairs just in time to witness Darren's step collapse beneath him. With no railing to hold onto for support, he tried to leap off of the staircase and onto the top step of the stairs that descended into the basement.

Doing so effectively broke that step as well, causing a crash that left Lucas laying on top of a pile of dust and rotten wood that was their only way back up and out of Levenson Asylum.

N I N E

Still with a firm grip on his camera, Darren landed on his side as the top step gave way beneath him sending Lucas to the basement floor – the boards and nails that comprised the rotting stairs now a pile of debris underneath him.

"Oops," Darren uttered as the dust settled. He lay on his side against the sliding door that led to the room with the electric chair. His legs dangled over the edge where the stairs used to be.

"Darren, you idiot!" he heard Lucas shout.

"Are you alright?" came Genevieve's voice.

"I'm fine," Darren answered.

"Not *you*!" she replied.

Genevieve and Ethan were digging at several beams that lay in the way of getting to Lucas, who was already trying to climb away from the rubble.

"What the hell happened?" Ethan asked, looking up at Darren as they finally cleared a path for Lucas.

"I'm sorry! I was just trying to get some more footage."

"Forget the footage!" said Lucas. "How are we supposed to get out of here now?"

"Relax." Darren struggled to his feet. "I think I broke a rib if that makes you feel any better."

Lucas joined Ethan and Genevieve in the space of the basement. With his flashlight, Ethan drew Lucas's attention to the filing cabinets. Genevieve began inspecting them, trying to find a way to open the drawers.

"Guys?" Darren called down. There was no answer. From where he stood, he could discern their darting flashlight beams, but didn't see any of his classmates' shadows. "What's down there?"

Genevieve finally stepped into the space they had cleared to get to Lucas. She looked up at Darren. "Go back to the main entrance and try to find something we can climb to get out of here."

"By myself?" he asked.

"Going off by yourself is what got us into this in the first place!" she said. "Now hurry up."

"Hey, see if you can grab a couple of those chairs from that room we were in," he heard Lucas say. Then, Lucas peered around the corner behind Genevieve, shining his light up into Darren's face. "They were wicker. You might be able to bring two at once if you'd put that camera down."

"Okay, you know what Lucas, this wasn't all my fault!" he shouted back. "You were the one charging down those stairs like some mad ass cow."

"We're down here, and you're up there. None of us want to be here any longer than necessary. Can you *please* go find something to get us out of here?" Lucas beseeched.

Darren paused, wanting to hurl a remark at Lucas's condescension, but decided against it. "I'll be right back," he said, bitterly.

They faintly heard Darren's cautious footsteps above as he entered back into the room with the electric chair.

"These things are locked and rusted shut," Ethan said as Lucas and Genevieve turned back to him and the filing cabinets. "There's no way we're gonna open them."

"Come on, Foster, your dad's a fireman for crying out loud." Lucas joined Ethan in front of the filing cabinet closest to the stair entrance. "You mean to tell me you didn't pick up anything from him?"

"Like what? An ax? No," he replied, sarcastically.

Lucas turned his flashlight around in his hand, and slammed the back end of it hard against the handle of the top drawer. The handle and a knob beneath it broke, leaving a hole small enough for a finger to fit through. Lucas poked his index finger in, curled it at the tip so that it hooked in, and pulled. With little force, the drawer swung open. Dozens of file folders were stuffed inside.

"Show off," Ethan murmured. The three of them began thumbing through the files.

Immediately, they realized the folders were all filed in alphabetical order by patients' last names. Lucas repeated his method for opening the bottom drawer of the same cabinet, and scrolled the tabs on each folder.

"These are D's down here," he said, his flashlight and eyes lingering on the files in this drawer. "And E's," he finished.

"Then it must be in one of the last ones," Genevieve said.

Lucas watched as she and Ethan headed over to the other filing cabinets to break into them. He returned his attention to the drawer of folders in front of him, lifted one of them out and stood with it, staring at the name on the tab for a moment.

"Here it is!" Ethan proclaimed.

Lucas hastily stuck the folder into the back waist of his jeans and covered it with the tail of his shirt before joining Genevieve and Ethan, who were already flipping through the numerous loose papers in Terrance Todd's folder.

"This is awesome!" Ethan gleaned.

"See how easy that was!" Genevieve started. "All you have to do is trust me, and you can't go wrong."

A sudden thud drew all of their attention to the floor above them. They all looked up at the ceiling, their flashlights revealing nothing but concrete.

"What was that?" Lucas asked.

"Sounds like Darren's having a hard time carrying—" Ethan's answer was abruptly interrupted by a faint yet bone-chilling scream.

"Get out! Get out!" They heard Darren's muffled cry before he broke into a throat-tearing scream that was punctuated by the sudden and loud slam of a door.

The three of them exchanged nervous glances.

"Up to his old tricks," Lucas said with an attempt to sound convincing. "Darren!" he shouted. "We know you're up there messing with us. It's not funny."

Silence responded, and the atmosphere took a sharp and darker turn as if they all suddenly realized where they were – that Hell had happened here.

"Come on, man!" Ethan yelled, trying to mask his own fear. "We got the file, now come get us out of here!"

Still no response. They waited a few seconds in the sinister silence, afraid to not hear anything but equally afraid to hear anything at all.

"Darren?" Genevieve called out.

This time, the silence spoke back. The stillness of a moment like this betrayed itself, and the three of them could hear the very faint sound of something heavy being dragged across an upper floor – drag, then stop, drag, then stop, drag, then stop.

"I'm sick of this," Lucas said to the others. "He wants to play games, let's let him go at it. There's got to be another way out of here."

He looked over at Genevieve, shining his light into her face. He could tell by how wide her eyes were that she was fighting fear. She reached to retrieve the floor plan from it's rolled up position in her back pocket, her hands in a frantic race to overcome the slight tremble that possessed them.

As soon as she unfolded the page, Ethan grabbed for it, knowing she was in no frame of mind to concentrate. He held his light on the page and studied it for a brief moment.

"This is just the first floor," he noticed, pointing his light at Genevieve for an answer. "Where's the floor plan for the basement?"

"We never had one," she replied.

He threw the page to the floor, exasperated.

"Look, nobody expected this would happen," Lucas said. "Let's just follow this wall here until we've gone the perimeter of the room. At least then we'll know if there are any doors. Come on. Stick together."

With his fading flashlight guiding him, Lucas led the trio as they walked against the length of the wall in the opposite direction of the stair entrance and the filing cabinets. Once they hit the corner, they turned left and slowly started along the length of the adjacent wall. Soon after, they hit another corner. For a few minutes it seemed the basement was a square space that had no other rooms or doorways, and they'd be stuck down here until Darren felt like coming back, but then Lucas stopped walking, acknowledging that he could feel air.

"It just got cooler right here. You feel it?" he asked the others.

"Do we *want* to feel it?" Ethan asked.

"Come on." Lucas continued to walk, his arm stretched in front of him against the wall at his side. The concrete was indeed getting cooler, and he could feel a light breeze caress his fingers a fraction of a second before the odor penetrated his nostrils.

The putrid stench they encountered in the room with the electric chair was floral compared to this. It was the kind of smell that would take a lifetime to forget, an odor so pungent it became a taste, and swallowing it choked them.

"I'm not prepared for this," Ethan said between coughs. "I'm going back."

"Wait!" Lucas stopped him. "There's an opening here."

"Wouldn't that be where the smell is coming from?" Genevieve asked, trying to hold her breath as much as possible. "My eyes are watering."

"It could be our only other way out," Lucas said. "I'm not staying down here waiting for Darren to have his fun with us, and then pop up yelling 'Punked ya!' Not gonna happen."

The dark opening ahead was the size of a small doorway, but no door had ever been attached. It led to a pitch black tunnel carved through dirt that curved as it extended beyond what they could see. The three of them walked curiously, carefully, and practically on top of one another, hoping against time that their flashlights wouldn't die.

Five minutes into their trek, the odor became unbearable. Ethan began to lag behind as Lucas and Genevieve marched on, each of them gasping for breath.

"Stop," Genevieve finally said. Lucas kept going. He could sense that something was just ahead. "Lucas, stop!" she shouted.

Lucas stopped and turned around to face her. She had stopped dead in her tracks a few feet back, and beyond her, Ethan was staggering to catch up.

"Come on," Lucas said.

Genevieve's horrified eyes were fixed on the ground between

her and Lucas, her flashlight beam illuminating the dirt floor.

"What *is* this?" she asked, her voice a harrowing whisper.

Lucas followed her gaze to the floor between them, and for the first time noticed the nest of footprints in the dirt. He spun around in all directions, his own fading flashlight beam landing on tracks of footsteps going back and forth. Terrified, he took a few more steps ahead, and found himself in a small cave-like opening. Footprints went off and came in from every direction.

Genevieve and Ethan slowly approached the entrance to the opening and stopped, deciding not to take the few more steps to join Lucas in the cave.

"Who—?" Ethan started, baffled by the footprints.

"Darren?!" Genevieve called out. "Darren, are you down here?"

"They're everywhere," Lucas said, still sweeping his light across the dirt floor. His light finally died, throwing him into a dim glow of the beams radiating from Genevieve's and Ethan's flashlights further away.

"Lucas?" Genevieve called, squinting as his form was abruptly cast in shadow. She aimed her beam in his direction, just as he lifted his finger to his cheek. The sudden panic in his eyes told her that he was too scared to move. He pulled his fingers away from his face and looked at them.

And then she saw it. A smeared drop of red on his cheek.

"Look up." It was a struggle for Lucas to force the words past the terror in his throat.

Genevieve's light remained fixed on Lucas's face, as if his paralysis paralyzed her. Fear would not let them move.

"*Somebody look up!*" Lucas cried out, his words more out of despair than horror.

Ethan slowly raised his light to the ceiling above Lucas. At first all he could see were pairs of feet. One step past Genevieve and into the cave allowed him to get the full scope of the hell that happened *here* – where at least twenty bodies were hanging execution style from the ceiling.

T E N

"…the fuck?!"

It was all Ethan could vocalize as he stood beneath the dead bodies hanging from the ceiling of the cave.

"Wh-what is it?" Lucas asked, trying to read the expressions on Ethan's and Genevieve's faces.

Curiosity overcame his fear. He lifted his eyes just as another drop of blood landed on his forehead. He flinched, returning his horrified gaze to Ethan and Genevieve.

"We gotta get out of here," Genevieve said. She was already taking steps back into the tunnel, and Ethan and Lucas were in a mad dash to follow.

The three of them ran the length of the tunnel until they returned to the dark square basement.

"What now?" Genevieve asked, out of breath.

Ethan scanned the darkness with his flashlight until it landed on the filing cabinets. He handed the Terrance Todd folder to Genevieve and ran over to the first filing cabinet next to the stair entrance.

"Lucas, help me."

Realizing Ethan's objective, Lucas ran over to assist him with tipping the filing cabinet over and pushing it as far as possible into the pile of wood that was once the stairs. Genevieve held her flashlight beam on them as they piled two other cabinets on top of the first, creating a four-foot tall step. They stood a fourth cabinet upright, which gave them another five and a half feet of elevation.

Ethan began to climb onto the three stacked cabinets. His first obstacle would be climbing onto the top of the upstanding filing cabinet; his second would be the diagonal leap from the top of that cabinet to the landing at the top – some three feet above where he'd be standing.

Genevieve turned to Lucas as he watched Ethan make a careful climb.

"What was that back there?" she asked him, finally trying to come to terms with it.

His response was delayed, as if an answer was lost in the darkness.

"You saw the same thing I did," he finally said. He didn't want to hear or see or smell anything else, and he knew that waiting there with Genevieve for Ethan to make it back up to the first floor would only lead to more of one, or two, or all of those. He had to do something.

As Ethan steadied himself atop the last filing cabinet and attempted to assess the options he had for making the leap, Lucas began to climb onto the bottom three cabinets.

"Hold it steady," Ethan said, realizing Lucas was just behind him. "I'm just gonna jump."

"You sure?" Lucas asked. "We could add another one."

"It'll be fine," Ethan answered. He didn't want to stay down there any longer trying to look for a way out. Whatever that was back in that cave was fresh enough that blood was still dripping from it.

He gave himself a count to three, closed his eyes and saw the bodies. The image made his knees shake and his heart speed. He opened his eyes, took in a deep breath, and jumped, his upper body landing in the perfect position for him to pull himself up onto the floor.

Lucas let out a breath of relief, and reached for Genevieve to help her climb onto their makeshift stairs. Once she reached the top, Ethan grabbed her arms and lifted her onto the floor to join him.

Lucas made the same effort and was quickly hoisted up with Ethan's assistance.

"Darren?!" Genevieve called again, the panic buried deep within her surfacing.

"Let's go," Ethan said, taking her hand in his.

He led the three of them back through the sliding door, facing the back of the electric chair with trepidation.

Navigating through the two rooms that would lead them to the main hallway, Genevieve called out again to Darren.

"Where are you?!" Her voice echoed faintly in the distance, an alarm that sent some kind of feathered animal flying from its nest nearby.

The three of them carefully sped down the long hall to the main lobby. Lucas ushered Genevieve to the broken window to exit first, but she stalled.

"Wait!" she said. "We can't just leave Darren here."

Ethan slowly passed his flashlight over the room, the beam landing on the stack of furniture against the room at the back. Nothing had been moved.

"Darren?!" he called. Still no answer. "We're leaving!"

"Let's just go call the cops," Lucas offered. "Get them out here to investigate that... what's down there."

"He's right," Ethan agreed. "What we saw down there is one reason to think what we heard up here was real. Somebody put bodies down there. Recently!"

"And Darren's missing," Genevieve added, tears forming in her eyes.

Ethan pulled her into a hug to calm her down.

"Can we do this in the car?" Lucas asked, reaching for Genevieve to help her climb out through the opening they created earlier.

She slowly turned from Ethan and allowed Lucas to assist as she made her way out of the window. Ethan continued to pan his light across the large room, looking for any sign that Darren had even been there. Then, holding the light steady on the pile of furniture in the back corner, a trickle of dust intercepted the beam, falling from the ceiling. Ethan noticed, and slowly looked up to the ceiling, half expecting to find more bodies.

The high ceiling was bare, save for cobwebs, drastically chipped paint, and layers of dust. A soft thud from above sent another gust of dust to the floor. This time, it was unmistakable.

Ethan glanced over at Lucas, who was preparing to squeeze himself through the opening to join Genevieve on the other side.

"Somebody's up there," he said to Lucas.

Lucas stopped and the two of them listened in silence as another faint thud sounded above.

Ethan reached into his pocket and retrieved his keys. He offered them to Genevieve through the opening.

"Go to the jeep. Call the police," he told her. "I'm going up to the second floor."

"Why?" she asked with a dread in her tone that seemed to answer her own question.

"Just... do it," he replied. He stepped back into the lobby, turned his eyes to Lucas, and waited for his answer

Lucas knew the question, and wanted to say no. But he also knew that if he let Ethan go off on his own, he'd feel responsible if something happened to him as well.

"Let's make this quick," he said, then started for the grand staircase with Ethan close behind him.

*

Genevieve jogged down the drive towards the jeep, clutching Terrance Todd's folder to her chest. She struggled to find anything to think about that didn't remind her of what she had seen in the cave. She darted across the street and fumbled with the keys once she reached the jeep. Somehow she managed to set the file down on the passenger seat and make the 911 call on her cell. She was acting on pure adrenaline, trying to force herself not to think at all, for fear that it would reduce her to tears.

She gripped the phone like it was a lifeline, and waited for a dispatcher to answer.

"I'm at the Levenson Asylum on Grand Street, and our friend... our friend is missing," she managed to say once someone had picked up.

Words were coming at her from the other end of the line, but she could hardly make sense of most of them.

"I'm with my classmates. My name is Genevieve Davis. We

were doing some research out here on a project for school."

She could discern the tone in the operator's voice. It wasn't one of urgency.

"This is not a joke!" she screamed, tears breaking through again. "Two of my other friends are in there now trying to find him. Will you just send someone here?"

She hung up the phone and leaned over the hood of the jeep, wiping tears from her cheeks. Even with her back to the mausoleum, she sensed that it was watching her. She closed her eyes and turned around, determined not to let the monster in her childhood closet dwell there. When she opened her eyes, the sight went like a bullet through her psyche. There against the cloudless, navy-ing sky stood this building, ash like black blood leaking from various crevices along it's frame. Death inside.

She forced herself to think happier thoughts, remembering the comfort Ethan had offered her in their embrace a few moments ago. But the solace turned into a painful reminder that Ethan was not hers to think of like this, and fighting the need to hold onto his comfort right now was proving as hard as a child fighting sleep. Ordinarily, she'd have some other person or matter present to distract her from the magnetic pull he had on her attention. She'd fight back with academic speak, or dress in such drab clothing that it physically reminded her not to care. Now, all of her alternative thoughts were littered with bodies hanging. And suddenly, Ethan's was one of them.

She took in a deep breath, fear washing over her face once again as she took in the asylum. Ethan was somewhere in there, cloaked in darkness despite the cheap flashlights they brought. Two options wrestled in her mind: go inside and convince Ethan and Lucas to come back out and wait for the cops, or stay here and wait alone. A sumo had gone up against a punk.

She started towards the building, her eyes scaling the wall, searching the dark windows for any movement that might indicate where Ethan and Lucas were. She felt pangs of guilt with each step, hearing herself tell Darren to go find a way to get them out of the basement in that tone that gave him every reason to try and play a trick on them. A trick that had evidently backfired... if it was a trick at all.

She climbed the steps that led to the front door and walked over to the broken window. She peered inside, lifting her flashlight to illuminate anything. She could see one of the columns that separated the foyer from the main lobby, and the glass and mirror chandelier in its heap on the floor a few feet beyond it. Shadows eerily danced with the light from her flashlight.

"Ethan?!" she called out. "I called the police!"

No one responded. She tried to push her light in further, but the column blocked her view of the staircase. She panned the beam to the right and caught the back of something tall and black that seemed to *walk* out of her line of vision completely when the light landed. The movement startled her, and she dropped her flashlight into the foyer.

She backed away from the opening and pinned herself against the wall between the window and the double doors. Her breath quickened to a pace that seemed to race her heartbeat. What had she seen? An animal? Just a shadow?

She slowly peeled herself away from the wall, and leaned to look into the opening again. The beam from the flashlight was still aimed in the direction of where she had seen the shadow.

"Darren?" she called, absently thinking what she saw might have been him. "Is that you?"

She carefully stuck her arm into the opening to retrieve her flashlight, but the floor was too far down for her to reach. She gave up quickly, and stepped away from the window. She could hear sirens in the distance and allowed the tinge of relief to infiltrate her gut. She turned and ran back towards the jeep to meet the police when they arrived. Behind her, the glow from her flashlight in the opening rose up, as if lifted by the darkness. The flashlight turned so that the beam aimed out of the building towards her.

When she noticed her vague shadow suddenly appear on the ground ahead of her, she slowed and spun around to face the building again mere seconds after the light from her flashlight in the opening shut itself off.

Nothing to her seemed out of the ordinary. She turned back, and ran the rest of the way to the jeep.

*

"Darren?!" Ethan called as he and Lucas stepped off of the 3rd floor landing. The main hallway in front of them stretched on into darkness to both their left and their right. The wall in front of them boasted two doors. One of them was halfway off its hinges and darkness went on forever beyond it. Splinters of light sneaked past the boards that were nailed against the windows on the far wall inside the room, but it wasn't nearly enough to see anything inside.

"I don't think he'd come up this far by himself, Foster," Lucas said.

The unspoken fear was that Darren hadn't been by himself. They'd both heard him scream while they were in the basement. They'd heard the dragging. Neither of them was willing to verbalize what they suspected.

"What are we gonna tell the police?" Ethan asked, concern overcoming him. "We're responsible for whatever happened to Darren."

"We don't know that anything happened to him for sure, okay?" Lucas said. "For all we know he could have had this whole thing planned ever since we started talking about coming out here. I'll bet you he's somewhere taping this right now, and he's planning to make some kind of embarrassing video and hope that it'll go viral. I refuse to play into this. You stay up here looking for him if you want to."

He hastily started back down the stairs. Ethan started after him, careful not to make any heavy steps. They picked up their pace as they reached the second floor landing. Somehow the anticipation of being almost out of there seemed to give provocation to the darkness; the sense that something here wouldn't let them leave manifested, and their hurried attempt to get away from it made it that much more imminent.

They reached the main floor and darted for the opening. Lucas was the first one to climb out, falling onto his hands in his haste to be out of there. The file folder he lifted from the D's and E's drawer of the filing cabinet slipped from the waist of his jeans onto the porch. He quickly scrambled for the few pages that scattered about and returned the folder to the waist of his jeans. Ethan was a few steps behind him, and started through the opening.

"The police are close!" Lucas noted, as distant sirens pierced the air.

They could also hear the horn of Ethan's jeep honking, and faintly, Genevieve calling toward them "Did you find him?"

Ethan lifted one leg through the opening to join Lucas on the porch. From his perch, he peripherally caught a tiny red laser light on the floor between the stairway and the busted down doorway that separated the lobby from their previously explored hall. He leaned back to get a better look at what might have just been some kind of reflection on a piece of glass. Squinting, he noticed that it wasn't a reflection. The object had a green glow behind it. It was the night vision glow from the screen of Darren's video camera.

"Come on, man." Lucas grabbed Ethan's arm and pulled him the rest of the way out of the opening.

"Darren's—" Ethan started. He realized then that Lucas might have been right. Had Darren been filming them this entire time? Would getting the police involved be the right thing to do?

ELEVEN

An hour had passed, and with each minute that came and went past 10 PM, Havana grew more and more nervous. She sat in her car in the parking lot of Ethan's apartment complex, rereading the last text she had received from him, which told her that he was on his way. Before she had a chance to even consider the thought, she'd pressed the call button on her phone. The ring tones were abruptly interrupted by Ethan's voicemail. She didn't wait for the beep, ending the call with a sigh.

Where was he? She had maybe another half hour before her dad was due back home. He would realize she'd disobeyed his grounding again, and she could only imagine what threats he'd hand out this time.

And here she was, left completely in the dark about why Ethan couldn't meet her two hours ago at the fairgrounds as they had planned. The thoughts that played through her mind ranged from serious to severely serious. In the past year, neither of them had sacrificed a single minute of their appointments. For him to stand her up without warning meant their secret was likely under attack.

She allowed her mind to wander through the album of their previous encounters there. A smile crept across her lips as she remembered their first kiss last Fourth of July. She closed her eyes, and could smell the fabric softener in the blanket they snuggled underneath in the back of his jeep, gazing up at the stars last Halloween. She was still able to sense his chin on her shoulder and almost expected to hear him whisper again as he did that night that this was perfect.

She opened her eyes, and immediately regretted doing so. The truth had no snooze button, and she could only brace herself for the worst. Had Ethan given up on the tip-toeing that was required to maintain their relationship? Had he been approached by some girl at Westmore and allowed his hormones to make the decision to quench his thirst? And if he *had* cheated, could she really blame him – and where would the answer to that question leave them?

She opened the door and stepped out of her car in desperate need of some fresh air. Her father's relentless pursuit of the truth was suffocating her, and it was threatening to cost Ethan his future. Many times she'd chased away thoughts of ending it with Ethan – even if it was for his own good. But they had a handle on each other's hearts, and she knew Ethan wouldn't let go without a fight. He was her first love, and she knew that any guy who would deliberately abstain from sex and go up against her father in lies to protect their relationship was in love, even if the words hadn't yet been said. They didn't need to be said, and if Ethan thought their world would end tonight either by fault or necessity, *she'd* fight it with the sword of those three words. She didn't intend to play fair if her father's war included the use of intimidation as a weapon of mass destruction, nor was she willing to let some other girl take her place. It had been *Ethan's* suggestion for them to abstain, after all. Not hers.

She wiped a tear from her cheek, suddenly realizing one had fallen. She glanced around the parking lot, not unusually crowded for a Saturday night, and spotted Ethan's jeep. Surprised, she did a thorough scan of the lot. Then, turning to head for the stairs that would lead up to his apartment, she ran into him.

"Hey," he said, his voice expectedly devoid of excitement.

She backed away from him to assess his poise, thinking maybe his thoughts could be read like a tattoo, and she'd be able to prepare herself for what she assumed would be heartbreaking for her.

"Sorry I'm late," he continued. "You wanna go in?"

"I can't stay too long," she said. "I have to get back home. Unless—"

She let assumption finish the sentence, not having a clue as to which of the two bombs he would drop.

He nodded. "I really wanted to be there. At the fairgrounds."

"Then why weren't you? Where have you been?" She felt pushed to ask the question, and it left a sour taste in her mouth. He didn't owe her any explanations after all she'd been asking him to risk over the past several months.

"I had a project to work on for class." His eyes avoided hers, and instead, searched for answers that wouldn't beg more questions. "It's just been a really long day, and…"

They both knew he was holding back more than the Hoover Dam. He knew he had his reasons, but she was stopped at a light, waiting for it to turn green.

"That's it?" She felt slighted. At the very least she didn't expect he'd be so vague.

He nodded again. He did feel exhausted, and getting into the whats, hows and whys of this evening with Havana at all would only pull her into the mix, and she was entirely too close to Professor Owens to be aware that his assignment had put himself, Genevieve, Lucas, and Darren all into a mess with the cops. Her relationship with Owens was leaking gas as it was. The last thing she needed was another reason, however slight it was, to resent her dad; finding out about this would send her back to him tonight ignited.

"What's going on?" she asked him. As far as she could tell, he was making it painfully obvious that there was something he wanted to get off his mind.

He glanced at his watch, a subtle way of reminding her that she needed to get back home soon. She picked up his cue, and reeled back. He must have known she was about to dig in.

"If this is important, Ethan…" she started. "If you need to talk, I can risk it with him. I don't care anymore."

"No," he told her. "You should go." He also didn't need to give Owens *the* reason to pull the plug on his graduating this year. With their project on Terrance Todd hanging with all those dead bodies in the basement of Levenson Asylum, there was no assurance his group would even be able to pull together a project at all now.

"I'm just dealing with a lot of stuff right now," he said, deciding to give her *something*. "This project I'm working on... it's problematic."

She squinted as she stared into his eyes, searching for whatever resided between the lines of what he was saying. He wasn't giving her much to work with, and her imagination was quickly filling in the blanks.

He leaned in and kissed her on her cheek, then opened her car door for her.

"I really wish I could have met up with you tonight," he said after she slid into the driver's seat.

"Tomorrow?"

He stared off into the distance for a long moment before answering.

"I don't know," he said finally. "I've got a lot of research to do for—"

"The project," she finished, hating that it sounded like a weak excuse. She closed the door.

He could sense her frustration. He knew she was thirsting for information, but telling her anything meant she'd get involved – no matter how much he'd beg her not to. He bent down to her window and tapped on the glass with his knuckle. She started the car and lowered the window, his apologetic eyes met hers.

She smiled at him, and brought a hand to his cheek.

"I want to be with you," she told him, trying to solidify her commitment to their relationship. "No matter what."

Before those last three words came out, he was sure she meant sexually. The *no matter what* hung between them for a moment. For her, it secured her place in his life. For him, it was a warning that she knew her dad had something to do with the reason he missed their date, and she was about to remedy that.

"Don't cause any trouble," he said, half-joking. He leaned into the car and kissed her, savoring it just in case she did cause trouble and its effect prevented them from ever kissing again.

His cell phone rang, interrupting their kiss. He pulled it from his pocket and glanced at the ID. It was Genevieve.

"I need to take this," he told Havana.

She stopped herself from glancing at his phone's ID screen.

He leaned in and kissed her again, then backed away from the car so she could pull out of the parking space.

She put the car in reverse, and forced herself to check her mirrors to make sure nothing was coming behind her. She pulled out of the parking spot, and tossed a wave at Ethan, who by now had the phone to his ear.

He watched as she slowly drove off, stalling his conversation with Genevieve and giving himself time to think of a way to handle the discussion he knew she wanted.

"You there?" came Genevieve's voice from the other end of the line.

"Yes," he replied.

"I hope you have a plan," she said. She was upset, and she had a right to be.

The two officers that arrived on the scene at Levenson earlier had not been expecting a need to call for backup, and Ethan hadn't given them one. Instead, he'd told them that Darren was just trying to pull off a prank that might have gone a little too far. Profuse apologies followed until Genevieve, unable to gloss over the hoard of hanging bodies as easily, suggested the cops go inside to take a look around for themselves. The two officers exchanged glances that read to the three students that they had much more important things to do on taxpayer money, and Ethan agreed.

The ride home was silent as the patrol car followed Ethan's jeep until they were back within city limits. Ethan was sure any minute the cops were going to pull him over and question them again about wasting their time, and his mind raced to fill in details of the story he had given them. It was the only explanation. There was no way they had just happened to stumble upon a killer's nest. The entire situation was gift-wrapped in classic Darren, and had the police gone inside and landed walk-on roles in Darren's homemade horror movie, they could have all gotten arrested.

"Nothing's changed," Ethan said, answering Genevieve's implied demand for an explanation.

"What if Darren's really missing or hurt in that building? Now we don't even have the cops to rely on for help," she said.

"I saw his video camera," he admitted. It was the first time he'd shared that information with anyone. "It was on the floor beside the stairs. Darren was filming us the whole time. He's probably somewhere going hysterical over how gullible we are."

Genevieve was silent on the other end, struggling to reconcile the idea of those bodies in the basement and the shadow walking out of her sight as she peered in through their opening. Maybe it *was* Darren.

"He had all day yesterday to plant mannequins down there. I don't put it past him. I guarantee he'll be in class on Monday," Ethan finished, hoping he was doing a better job at convincing her than he had convinced himself.

"That immature little snot!" she said. "He probably broke those stairs on purpose to trap us down there. I'm gonna introduce my foot to the front of his throat when I see him."

"Lucas is probably pissed, too. We wasted half the night down there."

"Well at least we have the file," she said. "I'll go through it all tomorrow."

"I'll come over and help," he offered. He figured it'd be a better idea than sitting at home waiting for Havana to get risky by calling or coming over. Besides, he'd already given her this alibi anyway.

"Okay..." she said, a bit surprised that he was offering to come over.

"Is that okay?" he asked, realizing he was imposing.

"No, that's fine," she answered. "That's... That'll be fine." She had forgotten to fight off the smile, and hoped he couldn't hear it in her voice. She rushed to cover it with her default of academic speak. "So we'll read through everything, and come up with a profile."

"Great. I'll let Lucas and Darren know."

They confirmed a 2 PM meeting at Genevieve's apartment the next day and hung up. Ethan considered calling Havana as he started for his apartment, but as much as he wanted to hear her voice, he knew she'd just get frustrated that he still didn't want to get into what kept him from meeting her tonight. Instead, he sent the text message to Lucas and Darren about the meeting at Genevieve's tomorrow, and stared at his phone for a minute afterwards, waiting on - or perhaps hoping for - a reply text from Darren punctuated by the letters ROTFLOL.

No reply came.

*

Lucas's phone vibrated against his nightstand, signaling an incoming text message. He sat in the middle of his bed, surrounded by pages from the file he lifted from the cabinet at Levenson. This was a game-changer, and he would need to spend the rest of the night sorting through all the questions arising like steam from this lake of information.

He began to gather the pages together, and reached towards the foot of the bed to retrieve the empty folder itself. Returning a stack of pages to the folder, he paused, staring at the last and first names on the folder tab: EDGEFIELD, ROBYN.

Reagan's mother.

T W E L V E

"There's a lot you don't know. About your mom."

Jeffrey Edgefield's words had taken up residence in the back of his daughter's mind. Reagan watched vacantly as a fly crawled cautiously across the desk towards Jackson Young's elbow. The small dorm room was it's prison, and he was out in general population now, at risk of being struck without warning at any moment. His best option, she thought, would be to blend in with something and wait for a window or door to open and make a break for it. Instead, he was boldly making himself known, choosing a slow trek down the green mile towards being killed.

Shortly after her father informed her that her mother spent time in Levenson Asylum, Reagan knew better than to proceed down the path to certain danger. She quickly flew towards her metaphorical open window and left the group before she would even get the chance to find out something she wasn't sure she wanted to know. Her father was having enough trouble telling her how desperately he wanted to keep Reagan from finding out anything at all. She couldn't stand seeing him in that much agony, and yielded him reprieve from his discomfort. As badly as she wanted to know what landed her mother in a mental asylum and why he lied for so long and let her decide that her mother was dead, she didn't press him. The fly flew off of the desk and disappeared.

"What do you think?" Kaylen Winston asked her.

It took Reagan a moment to rejoin the conversation. She sat on the edge of a twin-sized bed, facing the desk where Jackson sat scribbling notes in a spiral notebook. Kaylen and Pilar Vasquez were both sitting on the edge of Kaylen's roommate's bed, staring at the screen on Pilar's laptop. Together they were taking turns updating the fifth member of their group, Paul Windley, via instant message since his part-time job prevented him from joining them this afternoon.

"About what? I'm sorry," Reagan replied.

"Giving up on trying to find a female serial killer," Kaylen said. "They're either nurses with a Nightingale complex, black widows, or women who murder their children, and I just don't think I have the stomach for that."

"That's fine with me," Reagan affirmed. "I don't really have the stomach for any of this."

"So we're back at square one," Jackson said, tearing a page from the notebook and crumpling it up in his hand.

"Let's just go back to Richard Chase," Reagan offered. "I just thought it might be something different if we presented a female. It goes against the historical norm."

"I liked it, too," Kaylen said.

"So does that mean we're back to the original Chase assignments?" Jackson asked. "Paul and I are covering the details of each murder because we're the men and can handle it?"

"The man had sex with a corpse, and ate the organs of a two year-old," Pilar said, disgusted. "This was your choice because it was a gore-fest."

It was true. Jackson came up with Richard Chase figuring he would be a lot more interesting to research than some Bonnie *or* Clyde type. Richard Chase was a necrophiliac, and was known as the Vampire of Sacramento, California because of the nature of his murders. He had killed six people back in the late 70's, and in several cases, drank and bathed in the blood of his victims. His story was absolutely disturbing.

At first, Jackson thought it would be exciting to profile Richard Chase because of how intense his murder spree had been. Americans have an unnatural obsession with the sick and twisted. Throw in vampirism and an anti-Nazi undercurrent, and there was some aspect of this serial killer that each person in his group could attach themselves to. Jackson and Paul would detail each of the murders. Kaylen was a World History minor, and had done a paper last semester on Nazi Germany that would help identify cultural or environmental triggers. Pilar was a fanatic of every commercialized pale body with fangs, and a Communications major who could draw life-imitating-art comparisons.

Then, an unexplained twist threw Reagan into their group, and the Richard Chase idea got tossed aside because Reagan, being the Psychology major, didn't want to get stuck doing a psychological assessment of this sadistically dark individual by herself.

"We can all pull together to do that psychological stuff," Kaylen said, typing feverishly to update Paul. "That's the real heart of the project anyway."

She glanced over at Reagan, who was mentally venturing off again.

"Are you okay?" Kaylen asked, starting to worry.

"Yeah, that should be okay," Reagan replied. "Won't be a problem. I can handle it."

Perhaps that fly had been more successful at trying to blend into its surroundings than she had.

"I hope so," Jackson said, just as there came a knock at the door. "There are some sick individuals out there, and you're planning on being a psychologist. Who do you think's gonna be sprawled out on your couch? Muppets?"

Headed for the door, Kaylen shot a glance at Jackson, stifling a laugh. "Some of them have more problems than we do," she replied. She opened the door and greeted Lucas.

"Is Reagan here?" he asked.

Kaylen stepped out of the way, offering him a clear view of Reagan sitting on her bed. Reagan stood, half expecting him to deliver some devastating news about Levenson. It was as if her father's vague information about her mother planted more fear in her than relief of finally knowing something about what had happened. Finding out the rest of the truth would be on her terms, and she was trying to suppress that urge to know. She needed the dust to settle from the one bombshell before she could examine anything internally.

"What's wrong?" Reagan asked Lucas.

"I've been trying to reach you all day," he said. "Your phone goes straight to voicemail."

"I have to take it in," she said. "It's been doing that a lot lately."

"You got a minute?" He motioned for her to join him out in the hall.

She didn't like the sound of this, but followed him into the narrow hallway, closing Kaylen's door behind her.

"If this is about why I left the group, I already told you—"

"I know why you left the group," he interrupted.

"We don't have any right being out there roaming around some burned out, condemned mental asylum."

"We went anyway," he told her. "And before it turned into Darren's House of Horrors, I came across something of particular interest."

He held up the file folder with her mother's name on it for her to see. He waited as her eyes, glossing over, stared at the tab.

"Where did you get this?" she asked. The words were floating on pain. "What the hell are you doing?"

"I found it in the basement along with all the other *patients'* files," he said. "Did you know about this?"

She looked away from him, which confirmed his suspicion.

"How come you never told me?" he asked.

"Because it's none of your business, Lucas! I can't believe you lifted my mom's file."

"I didn't intend to find this," he said.

"Did you read it?"

It was his turn to avoid answering. To her, his silence was betrayal.

"There's nothing in here but pages and pages of notes about delusions and post-traumatic stress, anti-social disorder, post-partum depression—"

"Stop!" she said, suddenly feeling sick to her stomach.

He waited a moment, reading her reaction and suddenly recoiling.

"I'm sorry, Reagan," he said, softly. "I didn't think that maybe this is just hard for you. I didn't mean to upset you, I just... I didn't know your mom died in that fire."

Reagan wrestled with continuing, but the words came out before she could stop them.

"She didn't," she said. The admission seemed more a shock to her than to Lucas.

Giggles from two girls at the end of the hall played in the pause between them. They waited until the gigglers had retreated back into their dorm room. The loud close of the heavy wooden door to their room prompted them to continue.

"What do you mean she didn't?" Lucas asked. "She was one of the survivors?"

"Who else knows about this?" Reagan asked him, hoping to steer the conversation off this track. She knew the detective-to-be in him would keep asking questions that she wasn't ready for.

"Nobody." He knew what she was doing by answering him with questions of her own. It meant she didn't want him to push her, and that meant it wasn't a dead end. "I wasn't gonna tell anyone else until I had a chance to get some answers."

"Well I don't have any answers, okay?" She wanted to be mad at him for bringing all of this to her, but a part of her also wanted to sit down with him and put everything together. She wanted to know everything she'd been deprived of knowing about her mother. Anything she ever thought about Robyn Edgefield was a fabrication of her own imagination. She had killed off her mother in order to deal with her not being around when she was young, and now either because of her dad or Lucas or Professor Owens for assigning this project, an empty casket had been exhumed. All she had in front of her were found pages of severe diagnoses, and an admission from her father that she still wasn't ready to accept.

She looked into Lucas's eyes, and saw in them the same unexpected understanding that comforted her last year as she sat outside of Dr. Kershaw's office with that red D on her exam paper.

This was different, though. As much as she wanted to give in and tell Lucas what her father had revealed, she didn't know what it would do to her. Telling anyone meant she'd have to come to terms with it herself, and that would put her on a course set to collide at some approaching point with a black hole of indisputable truth; a black hole that by nature engulfs all things – even light – leaving nothing but a darkness so powerful it eventually self-destructs. What she was once able to convince herself about her mother, her darkest secret, was going to erupt in a cataclysmic supernova.

"I'm not going to be a source for your project," Reagan told Lucas.

"I'm not asking you to be," he assured her. "I'll be happy with you just telling me you're okay."

She was still noticeably struggling with how much she wanted him to know.

He reached for her hand and entwined his fingers with hers. She obviously needed some kind of comfort. He figured she didn't want to discuss the fact that her mom had escaped during the Levenson fire. That she had been one of the survivors Terrance Todd hunted down and murdered before he and the final surviving Levenson patient were apprehended and taken into the protective custody of County Jail. Reagan would have been seven years old that year. Kids that age easily feel responsible for what happens to their parents.

"She was a victim. It wasn't your fault," he told her.

"Lucas just... please." Her eyes burned into his. "You don't know anything about this, and I'm begging you to leave it alone." She pulled away from him, and reached for the doorknob to Kaylen's dorm room. "If you care anything about me, please just stop this," she said.

She fled to the refuge of Kaylen's room and closed the door behind her. Lucas stood there for a moment, confused in trying to fit her pieces into this puzzle. She seemed to curiously avoid the fact that this madman murdered her mother. Almost as if it didn't happen.

He started for the elevators, determined to follow up on that idea, when his cell phone began to vibrate. He lifted it from his pocket and answered the call.

"Yeah?" he greeted.

"Lucas, where are you?" Ethan asked from the other end of the line.

"I'm on campus," he answered. "Sorry I'm running late. I had to take care of something. I'll meet you all at Vieve's in ten minutes."

"Actually we just pulled up to Furman Hall. Neither of us has heard from Darren yet, and we've been leaving messages for him since last night. Something doesn't feel right, so we're gonna check in on him."

"Okay, well I'm across the street now. I'll meet you over there."

Ethan hung up as he and Genevieve stepped out of her Honda in the parking lot of Furman Residence Hall.

"He's gonna meet us here," he told her.

"I just don't feel like Darren would take it this far," she admitted.

They walked across the drive to the front entrance of the all-male dormitory. A few other Westmore students were scattered about. Two guys that Ethan recognized from the Lacrosse team acknowledged him uncomfortably. Ethan shot back a half-wave.

"I'm so glad I'm not still living on campus," he said. Genevieve picked up a scent of bitterness and followed his half-wave to the two guys.

"What does that have to do with anything?" she asked.

"It's not easy running into old teammates who think you blew your spot on the team on purpose," he said. "They look at me like I wanted to let them down. Like I didn't care."

Genevieve didn't respond. She didn't know how to without showing too much concern, and wasn't exactly sure how much was too much. One extra second of a lingering glance, or a misplaced emphasis could be taken the wrong way – or the right way. She was thinking about it too much, and that wasn't helpful.

"All the more reason to get this project done so we can get across that stage," she said, hoping she had it perfectly masked in senioritis.

Earlier, she and Ethan had scoured through the various pages in Terrance Todd's patient file, and learned that Terrance had been in his early 30s when he was arrested for the murder of his own grandparents. He had been apprehended at the scene of the crime, sitting Indian-style on the couch between his grandmother, the butcher knife still protruding from her neck, and his naked, strangled grandfather. Both victims had been propped up on the couch as if the three of them were watching television together when the cops arrived.

Ethan and Genevieve deduced that Terrance must have wanted to be captured. Though there was no mention of Todd being intrigued by fire, there were suggestions that he absolutely detested people. Perhaps his insanity plea had been his strategic way of getting thrown into a mental asylum where he would carry out his grand-scale plot to terrorize and ultimately kill as many people as possible. Levenson was his theme park, and murder was a grand dame of a roller coaster.

Notes from his psych evaluations were sparse, implying that Terrance Todd was a steel trap, not willing to share what was on his mind. Several pages made mention of numerous orderlies and other patients that Terrance had negative reactions towards or in few cases, run-ins with. They imagined him sitting through each session, staring stoically at the floor or perhaps even the psychiatrist himself, quietly constructing a mental checklist of every individual he wanted to kill, and when the list became too long to remember all the names, deciding everyone there must be on it. A mass murder would do, and it would be slow and epic.

"I wonder if there are any public records from his court appearances," Genevieve said.

"We're not writing a thesis, Vieve," Ethan replied, spinning around just in time to spot Lucas approaching.

"You two been up already?" he asked.

"Waiting for you." Ethan led the way into the dormitory.

They took the first elevator up to the sixth floor and headed towards room 612. The halls were just as narrow as in its all-girl twin dormitory where Kaylen lived. The smell was a little less pleasing, however, and loud rock music was blasting from behind some opened-door on the other side of the floor.

"I don't know how people live like this," Ethan commented.

"It's part of the college experience," Lucas said as they reached the door labeled 612. "I miss living in a dorm."

"No you don't," Ethan told him. "Knock already."

Lucas knocked, and the three of them waited a few seconds before Darren's roommate, Keith, opened the door just enough to poke his head out into the hall.

"Is Darren here?" Genevieve asked, trying to get a glimpse past Keith into the room.

"Dee hasn't been here since yesterday," he replied.

"He didn't come back last night?" she continued, panic rising.

"Dee hasn't been here since yesterday," Keith repeated louder, both arrogant and annoyed at the same time. He swung the door all the way open and allowed them to see that he had been entertaining a lady, as she was staring back at them from underneath the sheets on Keith's bed. Darren's bed was empty, and appeared as if it hadn't been slept it last night.

"When he does get back, tell him Lucas Dutch is looking for him," Lucas interceded. "It's really important."

Without responding, Keith closed the door.

"Who does that at one o'clock on a Sunday afternoon?" Genevieve asked, rhetorically.

"Okay, we need to start treating this like it's real." Lucas's concern was growing as well. "Darren is missing, somebody might be up at that asylum collecting bodies, and the police have officially classified all of this as bullshit. What now?"

"There's a chance Darren might just be out of town," Ethan said. "Maybe he went back to Chicago for some reason at the last minute."

"Without telling any of us?" Lucas asked. They quickly started back towards the elevator. He knew the time for offering explanations was over. The facts needed to be addressed, and the clearest fact of all was that no one had seen or heard from Darren since his screams last night. He also knew stirring up panic right now wasn't going to help anything.

"Until we hear from him, we need to consider the possibility that Darren is missing, and that somebody or some*thing* else was at Levenson last night," he finished.

"Should we go to Owens?" Genevieve asked.

"And say what? *Darren might be dead?* He'll ask us to prove it, and when we can't, he'll fail us for attempting to pull a stunt," Ethan said.

They reached the elevator just as it arrived for another group of guys. They hopped on and rode down in silence, each of them wondering how much of their conversation had been overheard.

Once the elevator let them off in the lobby, they walked out of the building, cautious about discussing anything further until sure they were out of earshot.

They headed straight for Genevieve's car.

"Two things need to happen," Lucas started. "First, we need to find out what might have happened to Darren up there."

"I saw his camera," Ethan said, breaking the news to Lucas.

Other than the image of those bodies hanging from the ceiling, the only thing he could vividly remember was seeing the red light and the green glow from Darren's video camera on the floor by the stairs as he was climbing out of the window.

"We should have sent the police in," he admitted. "At least they would have found the camera and maybe there'd be something on it that would give them an idea of what happened."

"Well, we can't go back and change that," Genevieve said. "The police aren't going to take us seriously."

"My dad will," Ethan said, suddenly realizing it himself. "I'll talk to him. Maybe I can convince him to go back up there with me and get that camera."

"Broad daylight, this time," Lucas said. "And try to pull some more information on the fire. If we know more about what happened that night, maybe we can get a sense of what we could be up against."

"You said we needed to do two things," Ethan reminded him. "Finding out what happened up there was one. What's the other?"

"Vieve was right," he said. "We have to tell Owens."

"What?!" Ethan exclaimed. "What good is that gonna do? He's just gonna blame me, and refuse to believe anything anyway."

"If his student is missing because of a project *he* assigned—" Genevieve started.

"He's going to say we had no right going up to Levenson. That it was our fault. *My* fault," Ethan assured them. "All he cares about is failing me."

"Foster, detour this already!" Lucas said. "The man hates you, but he's not gunning for you. I'm sure he wants you out of his orbit quicker than you want him out of yours."

"It's down to three of us now, and Ethan might be right," Genevieve interjected. "Owens isn't going to give us a pass on the project because Darren might *possibly* be missing."

"I doubt he'd give us a pass even if we asked for it over

Darren's dead body," Ethan murmured.

"But because it's just three of us, we don't have the time nor the resources to start over," she continued.

"You want to continue with the project," Lucas deduced. He glanced from Ethan to Genevieve. He knew they were right about Owens not cutting them any slack over something none of them could even prove, and time was ticking. At the very least, Darren's disappearance tied into their research, so they wouldn't be splitting their limited time between finding him and turning in the project for Professor Owens. Doing one would help them do the other.

"We don't have a choice," Genevieve finished. "Ethan and I already have a good bit of information from his patient records. We'll find out more about the fire, and you've started compiling info on the Hunter murders, right? It'll be tight, but we can still pull this together."

Lucas was quiet. He hadn't been able to look up the Hunter murders because he'd been preoccupied with Robyn Edgefield's patient file. His mind raced back to Reagan's confession. Her mother got out of the building alive that night. A chill slammed into him upon remembering his earlier feeling that the reason Reagan might not have been accepting her mother's murder was simply because it didn't happen. He was at a disturbing intersection. In doing his part of the project, he'd either discover all the grisly details about the murder of his girlfriend's mother, or he'd exhume the horrible suspicion that was buried in the back of his mind – that Robyn wasn't a *victim*.

"I just can't help but wonder..." Genevieve started. "Whatever's going on up there is probably connected to what happened fifteen years ago. If we are dealing with some*one*, what if it was an accomplice? Someone the police overlooked back then."

Lucas's attempts to block out the image of Robyn Edgefield in that role grew even more futile as Genevieve hinted at the possibility that Terrance Todd – a man credited for killing several people right before the fire, nearly a hundred more people in the fire, and then eleven of the survivors before being caught and taken into custody along with the alleged final survivor – might have had a partner!

"Well then we owe it to Darren to find him," Ethan said to Genevieve in response to her accomplice theory.

Lucas glanced beyond them towards McReynold's Hall, the building in which Reagan sat at that very moment, struggling with some truth about her mother that she didn't want anyone to know.

Or *her*, he thought.

T H I R T E E N

If the sins of the father infect the son, what becomes of a son whose father's greatest sin was also his greatest sacrifice?

Terrance Todd never really knew his father. All he knew were the stories his grandparents had shared about their son. For many years, he was being fed an image of a father who went protectively into the Vietnam War shortly before the birth of his son in the early 60's. Communism had threatened to infect the world, but the more fatal infestation was being spoon-fed to young Terrance from a plate of good intentions.

While it was unknown whether or not Terrance grew up under his grandparents' care, and even less was known about Terrance's mother, a vivid picture had nevertheless been painted of the young man who was destined to become a legend. For his father, perhaps leaving to fight for his unborn son's freedom was a sacrifice that backfired, and perhaps never returning was fated, but the feelings of abandonment and expectation left behind took root and cross-pollinated in Terrance Todd – and it multiplied. Psychologists would say the abandoned Terrance resented his father's heroic legacy, and was engaged in constant battle with what others expected of him, being his father's son. It appeared that this projection had radiated an indiscriminate hate in Terrance that bred The Hunter.

Of the few stories Terrance told about his grandparents, a psychologist would underscore the words *no remorse* in the notes collected in his file. The only thing written down about Terrance's mother was *no reaction* – indicating Terrance either loved or hated her too much to speak of her.

It was an afternoon in 1994 when Terrance killed his paternal grandparents and was subsequently tossed into Levenson Asylum. Both murders were symbolic: strangulation, and a knife to the neck. Psychologists suspected that closing or slicing through the throat was Terrance's brutally symbolic way of stopping them from projecting upon him anything more about a man he would never know. In truth, he was the antithesis of the father they gave him.

Sacrifice had given life to sin – father and son.

Had the father survived risking his life, and returned to his son an anger-coated capsule of trauma, perhaps the effect it might have had on the son would have been less catastrophic. Therein lie the difference between Terrance and Ethan. Two fathers revered as heroes. Two sons branded by sacrifice.

Frank Foster had given up most of his comfort in saving the life of that pregnant woman in the fire of 2005. The remarkable incident left him ironically wounded by public expectation. The pressure to be the image others projected onto him was gravitational, and his emotions ebbed towards anger so often it shut him down. He had lashed out at his family on several occasions.

Frank's pride became a weakness. His wife, Janice, had begged him several times to retire from the fire department, but the financial weight of getting Ethan through college was too heavy. When she offered to take on a full-time workload at her family's restaurant to help, he refused. Part of him felt he still owed Ethan for being too proud to apologize for hitting him back then. He knew Ethan had gotten suspended from school for standing up for Frank in an argument with his classmates, but at that time Frank had to be the town's hero first and a father second. He felt he had to reprimand his son because this was not the family image the public wanted to see. Numerous nights since then had found him filled with regret, but the damage had been done and his relationship with his only child had suffered a hairline fracture that wasn't healing.

Ethan, however, knew why his dad had struck him. The rest of the town had Frank playing a role, and behind his back they were giving negative reviews after each show. Gossipers had invented a scandal surrounding Frank's saving the pregnant woman in the fire, yet would rush to applaud him at every chance. Both Ethan and his mom figured after a few months, the celebrity imposition would fade away, and Frank would shed back into his former self. No such shedding occurred. Frank had trapped himself in the duality of being the public hero and a private monster. As a result, Janice and Ethan never figured out how to ease back into normalcy around the house with him, which meant there were a lot of quiet dinners, and days when none of them would all be in the same room together at any given time.

Ethan's decision to live on campus his first year at Westmore was more out of comfort than convenience. Frank had asked him only once if he would rather commute to classes from home, and Ethan hastily turned down the offer, later realizing it might have been Frank's way of telling him that it would be easier on them financially if Ethan could trim room and board fees. Ethan was starving to move out of a house that was quickly filling with awkward tension.

Frank never brought up the subject again. Somewhere inside, he felt like he didn't have a right to. He had made his family uncomfortable in their own home, and there was little he felt he could do about it.

A couple of years ago, Ethan moved out of the dorm and into an apartment complex near campus. Frank wondered where the money had come from to pay for a place of his own, but never questioned his son. He knew Janice and Ethan were having more frequent discussions in private around that time, and suspected Janice had either tapped into her savings account or applied for a loan to help Ethan secure his new apartment. If this was true, the fact that he'd been left out of the decision only made Frank feel worse. He didn't dare to share his suspicions, however. He was going to be left with a tuition bill at the end of all of this, and if Ethan and Janice had found a way to pay for an off-campus apartment without borrowing on the tuition money, he assumed he should be grateful that he wasn't included.

So much had gotten tarnished in the 2005 fire. The Foster

family had been collateral damage, the burden of which felt equally distributed among Frank, Ethan, and Janice: Frank for obvious reasons, Ethan for buckling under the pressure of being a hero's son, and Janice for not doing enough to sustain open communication. The initial and ironic wound of Frank saving that pregnant woman and her baby became an infected sore behind the Fosters' front door, and for Ethan, sterilizing it became harder and harder as the years went by. During his years at Westmore, he'd only come home on major holidays when he knew the grandparents would visit. On only a handful of occasions had he courteously dropped by to give them information that he didn't want to relay to them over the phone, such as losing his scholarship, failing Owens' class, or falling in love with a high school senior. In those instances, part of him wanted to see if he could invoke disappointment from his father, to see if it would push him to hit him again. Perhaps masochistically he thought that any kind of emotional response from his father would be better than this impenetrable wall that had become of him. Another part of him just wanted to let his father know that there was no such thing as spotless, and it would be okay to accept that.

The information he wanted to share this time was different. Ethan needed his dad's help, and asking for it after all these years was going to require braving the turbulence between them.

Janice was sitting in front of dinner at the kitchen table when Ethan entered the back door. His arrival a surprise, she rushed over to give him a hug.

"Ethan!" she exclaimed. "What brings you here?"

"Is dad around?"

"Why? What's wrong?" Concern was etched into her face.

"I just need to talk to him. Is he upstairs?"

He headed for the doorway that led into the living room and started for the stairs. Sunday evenings almost always found his dad napping in the bedroom. He'd have to go to the firehouse for the late shift in a few hours.

"Ethan, please don't upset him," Janice called from the base of the stairs behind him.

"Why would I do that?" he asked her, and continued towards the bedroom.

Frank was propped up against the headboard when Ethan entered his parents' bedroom. He was awake, staring at a floor-model room fan that sat by the foot of the bed. The fan swiveled from left to right, recycling cooler air around the room.

"Is this about graduation?" Frank asked, not removing his gaze from the fan. His tone was one that suggested he anticipated bad news was coming, and it scratched Ethan's mood like nails on a chalkboard. How could four words sound like a life sentence?

"No, Dad," Ethan managed to sneak the words past his offense. "It's actually about the fire."

Frank broke his gaze at the fan and turned to Ethan, his eyes x-raying into Ethan's as if he was prepared to find emotional cancer somewhere beyond them.

"The one at Levenson Asylum," Ethan clarified, suddenly realizing he had brought his dad to the threshold of the wrong memory. In that brief moment, Frank's eyes had read volumes aloud to Ethan. It was clear that Frank had been waiting for it, perhaps even expected a discussion about the 2005 fire was overdue. Ethan, however, needed to focus on Levenson, and began to worry that opening the door to the one fire would create a backdraft that would leave Frank ignited over the events of the other.

He had to proceed anyway. Darren was missing.

"Some classmates and I are doing research on the fire back in '96, and we need to know what happened," he said.

Frank swung his legs over the side of the bed, taking a moment to separate the two fires in his mind.

"You were here, you know what happened," he answered.

"We know what people *said* happened," Ethan replied. "Those stories are like Greek mythology by now. Nobody can be completely sure what really happened. Except those of you who were actually there."

"That guy, one of the patients, set the place on fire, then escaped and murdered a bunch of people to cover it up," Frank confirmed.

"Do you know what happened to the last survivor?"

Frank searched his memory, but grew agitated.

"This was fifteen years ago, Ethan," he said. "What does it

matter?"

"It matters to *me*, Dad.   Thirteen people escaped that night. Eleven of them were hunted down and murdered after the fire. They brought Terrance in along with the last remaining survivor. Terrance killed himself in his cell. Who was, and what happened to that thirteenth patient?"

"Geez, Ethan, I don't remember," Frank said, indignantly.

"I need you to try," Ethan continued. "What we saw up there the other day was... it was the most disturbing thing I've ever seen in my life."

"What are you talking about?" Frank asked, growing concerned. "You didn't go out there to that asylum did you?"

"Yeah," Ethan answered, glad to finally be taken seriously. "We did. And we came across bodies hanging from the ceiling of some tunnel down in the basement. Recently deceased human bodies."

Frank looked at Ethan with skepticism, and suddenly, Ethan was becoming less and less sure that this was a good idea. "Can't you remember anything else at all from that night? Somebody out there today had something to do with what happened back then. This guy is still at it."

"You're telling me you went down into the basement of that place, came across some dead bodies, and now you think a killer is on the loose. Is that right?"

Ethan leaned against the doorframe. Not until now had he realized how fictitious this all sounded.

"Have I ever lied to you?" It was the only card he had to play. He let the question dangle, protected by the invisible sheath of his decision to be honest about why he got suspended in high school back then. They stared at each other, both of them trying not to acknowledge that this was the on-ramp towards a guilt trip.

Frank waited a long moment before continuing, aware that they were bartering trust and forgiveness, and the transaction depended on details he never wanted to reconsider. "I'm pretty sure whoever else they brought in got sent to another asylum after Terrance Todd killed himself," he said.

"Who was it?" Ethan pushed.

Frank combed again through his memory, wanting to come

through for the sake of their relationship. "I don't think they ever released a name," he answered. "I mean they couldn't. For safety reasons. They had to protect him because... they couldn't be sure that *only* thirteen patients escaped."

He could read the fear in his son's eyes, and knew he had to continue.

"Nobody had any way of knowing who all were missing, who all was dead," he said. "That place was littered with unidentifiable bodies, and parts of bodies. I mean, precautions were taken just in case, but the police were counting escaped survivors as the bodies turned up. As soon as they had Todd in custody, the Hunter murders stopped."

Ethan swallowed a lump in his throat. "So they just conveniently decided Todd was the killer."

"But that's a pretty incriminating convenience, Ethan."

"Unless he had a partner."

"No," Frank said, fighting against where he knew this conversation was heading. "Everybody in this town knows Terrance Todd was a loner."

"Nobody in this town knows *anything*, Dad," Ethan said, trembling. "Terrance Todd was set up, and his co-killer – or the *real* killer – is still out there."

"Now wait a minute," Frank tried to pull Ethan back from that conclusion. "It's been fifteen years. *If* there was another person involved, you think they've just been dormant all this time?"

"No, they've been busy." Ethan suddenly felt the emotional grip on his father loosening, and made the split decision to put all of his cards on the table. "I want to be wrong, but a classmate of mine might have been attacked out there. We haven't heard from him since yesterday. We think he might be dead." He paused, gauging the reaction from Frank as it set in.

Frank stood up, avoiding eye contact with his son. He started for the closet, looking to grab his shoes for work.

"Dad, did you hear me?" Ethan asked.

"Just... tell me you kids didn't go out there and do something stupid," Frank said, dropping his shoes to the floor. "I need to know everything that happened."

"I'm telling you everything. Darren had a video camera with

him. He probably recorded everything."

"Have you gone to the police?"

"Yes. They think it's funny," he answered, wondering if he should disclose the fact that he had regrettably given the cops a punch line about Darren playing a prank.

"Of course they would." Frank's response surprised Ethan. He didn't expect his father to agree. He realized why as Frank continued. "They made a mess with this case back then, and as soon as anybody brings up anything about Levenson, they're quick to write it off and save their own asses."

The discussion about either of the fires did in fact erode layers from Frank. Ethan began to understand why his father felt so pressured to be the hero. The police had all but torched the citizens' faith in law enforcement by not following up or informing the public of how many patients had escaped during that fire. They had let psychotics run murderously amok throughout the town without much warning until they thought they were able to say the situation was contained. The public couldn't trust anyone in uniform to be honest and direct about their safety, and when Frank saved that pregnant woman, a bud of hope emerged; and Frank knew how badly the town needed to believe in the authorities again. He had sacrificed his own family's comfort in an effort to restore the comfort of an entire town.

Frank stepped into his shoes and reached for his keys on top of the dresser nearby.

"Are you going to the police station?"

"I'm going to the firehouse," Frank replied.

"What about Darren? What about these bodies? You can't just ignore all of this!" Ethan said.

"Don't go back up to that asylum," Frank said, worried that his advice would go unheeded.

"If there's no way of knowing only thirteen people survived the fire, then you have to believe it's possible that criminally insane people are still out there who weren't killed or captured. Criminally insane is not something you get over, Dad. These people are twisted and dangerous. You and the police sat on this for almost two decades, and now, believe it or not *my* future is on the line. You are the last person and the only person I thought I could ask to help me. Where's the hero when *I* need him?"

Without warning, Ethan had merged into the fast lane of the guilt trip. He didn't want to end up there, but his emotions had taken the wheel. For a few seconds, he thought a fatal crash would occur in their silence, and both of them would end up in critical condition. He didn't realize that Frank already was. The words had cut through him like the jaws of life, scraping tissue and bone. Every ounce of him felt his son's pain.

"One way or another," Ethan finished, "I'm getting Darren's camera, figuring out who those people in the basement were, and finding whoever's responsible for this."

"What do you want me to do? Go with you?" Frank asked, matching Ethan's tone. "You said all you wanted from me was information on what happened that night. I gave you that. If the police won't get involved, what more do you think you and I could do? Believing you isn't enough?"

"No, it's not enough," Ethan said, still trying to avoid a pile-up. He knew he had his father at the edge of a discussion that was long overdue, but he quickly shifted into neutral because there were more urgent matters to consider, and they had neither the time nor the energy to devote to that argument now.

They had made progress, though. These were more words than they had shared together in over a year, and if nothing else, Ethan could at least peripherally credit Owens for this breach in the wall of communication with Frank. Their problems were potholes in a long and winding road, and he still couldn't be sure his father hadn't just filled them in with six years worth of sand and hoped the storms would remain infrequent enough not to create a bigger mess.

"I really don't feel comfortable going out there," Frank said. "Either one of us."

"I just want to get Darren's camera," Ethan reassured. "At least find out if there's somebody else on it. We owe him that."

Frank sighed.

"After my shift tomorrow, we'll go out there and take a look."

FOURTEEN

Havana stood at Ethan's apartment door wearing nothing but a raincoat. The night was crisp and clear with no expected showers, but it was the only coat she owned that would cover her naked body from the knees up.

"Ethan, open up. It's me," she called, vigorously knocking on his door.

Within ten seconds, there was no answer. She momentarily regretted not calling first to see if he was home, but part of her knew that if she had told him she was coming over, he would have made up an excuse for her not to. He was clearly more cautious about her father finding out about them than she was. He figured he had more to lose, but to her, losing Ethan would stop the world.

She rapped at the door again with her opened palm, futile.

"Where are you?" she called.

Part of her knew where he might be, and the idea was like a fist squeezing around her stomach. Girls wanted him, and being in a relationship with him that for all intents and purposes didn't exist meant Havana had to accept the outside flirting. As protective as Ethan was about her feelings, he was equally protective of his status. The few people that knew about them were friends they could trust, and ones that would go to bat for Ethan whenever an interested girl got too bold about how badly she wanted him.

There was only so much fidelity she could expect from him though, particularly when the parameters of their relationship excluded the bedroom. Until tonight, if she wasn't too late.

She dropped her hand to the doorknob and twisted, bracing herself for the reality of it being locked. As the knob continued to turn beyond the point where it should have stopped, Havana realized it was opening. She let go of the knob and allowed the door to swing open into the apartment. Stunned, she found Ethan standing there in front of her in his briefs.

"What are you doing?" she asked him.

His response was a silent, head-to-toe assessment of the body in front of him.

"Well...?" she asked, leaning coyly against the doorframe.

His apologetic eyes met hers and his head shook slightly, an unmistakable no.

A door opened in the hall beyond him. She wasn't sure if it was the bathroom door or the bedroom door. It slowly ceased to matter.

"Who was that?" she asked.

"Sex?" he replied. "Is that all you think it takes?"

"What are you talking about?" Anger and confusion were locked in a duel somewhere between her eyes and her chest. She took a step forward to enter the apartment, but he raised his arm to the doorframe to block her.

"Let me in," she told him.

"It was going to come to this," he said.

She pushed past him into the apartment and started for the bathroom or bedroom door that had opened. A light was on inside. Thoughts were running so wild inside her head that she couldn't remember what room was behind that door.

"Who are you looking for?" Ethan asked.

She spun around to face him, prepared to let loose a verbal wailing, but stopped when she realized he was dressed and holding his key up to the opened door from outside the apartment.

"Get out," he told her.

She sat up in bed with a start, her breath catching in her throat. She could still feel her burning heart reverberating in her chest, having come to the realization before it did that it was just a dream.

"Vana, you're gonna be late for school," she heard her mom call from the base of the stairs.

She threw back the covers and climbed out of bed.

*

Lucinda sat a glass of juice on the table in front of Carter.

"At least consider going," she told him. "You were the one who wanted to move here to get closure."

"I didn't know him," he replied, chomping down the last bite of his pancakes. "We didn't have a relationship. I was already in college when he was born."

"But it's still your brother, and he's missing," she insisted. "I thought the whole purpose of us moving here was so you could reconnect with your family. All these years later and you haven't even tried." Her tone was accusatory.

"First of all, let's clarify what I said and what you *assumed*," he bit back. "I wanted us to move here because I didn't want to be running from what happened to me for the rest of my life. I needed control over the demons to be able to sleep at night. Reinstating relatives from my former life who didn't give a damn to help us even make rent back then was never on my agenda. Bringing them into my life right now would be as counter-productive as this discussion."

"But..." she pressed, carefully. "He could be in trouble..."

"Let's drop it." He got up from the table.

Lewis Carter was born a year after Owen left for college. The late-in-life pregnancy compelled their parents to give Lewis the kind of attention Owen hadn't been afforded in their hippier youth, and part of Owen did resent that. He never saw much of his younger brother or their parents after he'd married Catherine and Daniel was born. He'd spent all of his time in school or working to pay for his tuition and support his own young family.

"All I'm saying is it might be healthy for you to at least touch base with them," Lucinda continued softly. "Your parents are dead. You don't know if they ever knew you even survived your injuries from that fire. What if you've got aunts and uncles and cousins around here that would move heaven and earth to know you're okay? It could tear down that wall you've had up since I met you, Carter."

He had his back to her. "And unleash what?" he asked, afraid the answer was rage.

"Love," she replied. "You never really knew your brother, but what if he wants to know you? The police find your business card in his abandoned car in Durham, and you don't want to figure out how or why he might have had it? You don't think there might be a reason? It could be a cry for help. Forgive me for wanting you to feel *some* responsibility to your family."

"The only family I have is under this roof," he told her, glancing towards the foot of the stairs to make sure Havana wasn't there yet. "And trust me, the responsibility is a full-time job."

"If you didn't try so hard to keep us separated from what happened back then, things might be easier."

He started to reply, but the doorbell cut him off. Lucinda excused herself to go answer.

Carter began to gather his briefcase. His first class started in an hour, and if he left now he could escape Lucinda's paleontological dig into his reasons for not wanting to talk about Lewis, and possibly take the need-to-clear-his-head scenic route to Westmore.

Lucinda returned to the kitchen ahead of Genevieve Davis.

"You have a visitor," she told Carter, and resumed her place at the stove to finish breakfast.

"I'm sorry for barging over unannounced, but I really needed to talk to you Professor Owens, and it couldn't wait until class tomorrow." Genevieve's nerve was fading fast, but she knew this was her only window of opportunity to possibly salvage her GPA.

"Let's go into the other room, Miss Davis," Carter said, ushering her back across the threshold that separated the kitchen from the living room.

"Darren Gabriel is missing," she blurted out once they were in the living room. She didn't exactly know where to start, and felt she didn't have enough time to explain it all. "We thought at first it was a prank, but none of us nor his roommate have heard from him since Saturday."

His silence prompted her to continue. "And I'm starting to worry about our group project. Now, without Darren or Reagan, we're down to three people. We're at a serious disadvantage."

"Are the cops involved with this Darren situation?" he finally asked.

She hesitated. "Not exactly."

"You said he's missing."

By now, she was running on only the fumes of the courage she'd arrived with. "We were out at the old burned out asylum. Levenson? We're doing our project on Terrance Todd."

"Really?" he replied. She expected more of a reaction than this, and waited until it was obvious that he wasn't going to give her one. Terrance Todd and the Levenson fire was the bone buried in this town's backyard, and it was surprising that he wasn't going to address that.

"We were all up there when Darren disappeared," she continued. "Maybe we shouldn't have gone up there by ourselves, but we had a great lead on some good information for the project."

"It's dangerous up there," he told her. His voice seemed cold.

"We can't switch gears now," she said. "Not with just the three of us working on it. Unless we had more time."

"More time," he repeated. She could feel him reading her. "Ethan Foster may be able to manipulate you, but I'm not that stupid."

"Excuse me?" she asked, confused and offended.

"It's not beyond him to convince Darren Gabriel to skip town for a few days while you all convince me that he's missing so that you could get some sympathy and an extension. He's lazy, he's a liar, and he's going to fail my class if this project is not turned in on time."

"That's not what's going on," Genevieve started. "The *only* thing Ethan cares about is getting an A on this project."

"Then I suggest putting an end to these games and getting to work."

"We are at an unfair disadvantage. All I'm asking for is an extra week." Genevieve tried again to reason.

After a long pause, Carter conceded. "Alright. I'll give you an extra week."

"Thank you," she replied.

"But *only*," he added, "if you give me everything that's going on between Ethan Foster and my daughter."

She paused, deliberating with her conscience. Here was a

chance to feed Owens information that would break up Ethan and Havana, and place her strategically on the sidelines in wait for a vulnerable Ethan. The pros of blabbing everything right now to Owens seemed to outweigh the cons of Ethan possibly finding out she dealt that blow and never forgiving her. As much as Ethan needed an A on this project, she needed it too, and an extra week to complete it meant an extra week of working together in very close quarters day and night to insure they'd graduate this year. Ethan would graduate.

Professor Owens had raised the bet, and Ethan was on the table. He called her hand, and she looked down at her cards with a smile.

"Well—" she started.

"I didn't know we had company!" interrupted a voice from the stairs behind Owens. Havana descended, entering the living room with her eyes locked squarely on Genevieve's. "Everything okay?"

"All fine," Carter said. "Miss Davis just had some concerns about her project."

"Well Daddy, you don't want to be late for your *actual* office hours," Havana said, tossing a hint at Genevieve.

"You're right. I should get going." His car was parked in the garage off the kitchen, so he started back in that direction. "Stop by and see me later?" he added with a pat on Genevieve's shoulder before exiting.

"For what?" Havana demanded once Carter was out of earshot.

"Havana," Genevieve sighed.

Havana's left eyebrow shot up in skepticism.

"How long were you listening?"

"Long enough to know that you were ready to ruin Ethan's chances of graduating. "

Suddenly, Genevieve was glad Havana entered when she did. She hadn't realized until just then the realistic repercussions of what she would have told Owens. Of course Owens wouldn't have given Ethan an extra week's extension and a diploma for sneaking around with his daughter.

"I wasn't going to tell him the truth," she lied. "Ethan is a friend of mine, he's got a lot on the line."

"Including a relationship," Havana added. The dream she had earlier crept back into her mind. Someone else was in Ethan's apartment. Another woman. "Or is *that* why?" she asked.

"What?" Genevieve tried to brush off the insinuation as absurd, but Havana was getting too close to the truth. Any closer and she'd have enough ammunition to take to Ethan and put even their friendship on ice. She didn't want to risk that either.

"I've seen the way you look at him," Havana continued. "So what, you're older and smarter. And maybe you're able to give him things I can't right now, but that does not give you the right —"

"I don't know what you're talking about," Genevieve said, trying to avert. "I have to get to the library."

Havana wanted to believe Genevieve, but whether it was the dream or the way Ethan had been acting when she last saw him, something was in the way of her satisfaction. She grabbed Genevieve's arm as she reached for the front door.

"You and Ethan have been friends for a long time, but you would tell me if something was going on that I should know about."

"You and Ethan are fine," Genevieve said, starting to see the cracks in Havana's security. "Right?"

As she turned to leave, Genevieve's cell phone rang. Retrieving it from her pocket, Havana noticed Ethan's name on the screen. It sent a flash of red behind her eyes.

"I'm on my way to the library now, are you headed there?" Genevieve said into the phone.

Anger seized Havana. This project that had Ethan so distracted the other night was one he was working on with Genevieve, and her father had assigned it.

"What do you mean you're going back?" Genevieve was asking Ethan.

Suddenly convinced her father's suspicions had led to this, Havana realized it wasn't beyond him to go this far to put hers and Ethan's lie to the test. If Genevieve's attraction to Ethan was obvious to Havana, surely her father had noticed it, and was capitalizing on it by grouping them together on a big end-of-the-semester project. Was he meeting Genevieve here this morning for updates? Were they in on this together?

Nothing was making sense quick enough. Bits and pieces of the conversation between Genevieve and her father just now were struggling to get past the recollection of last night's vivid dream that was looping in the front of her mind. She remembered hearing her father calling Ethan lazy and a liar, and Genevieve defending him.

Then I suggest putting an end to these games and getting to work. She'd heard her father say.

All I'm asking for is an extra week, Genevieve had said.

Give me everything that's going on between Ethan Foster and my daughter. It was the last request from her father before Havana intervened. Genevieve was up to something, whether it was some scheme cooked up with her father, or if her actual feelings were involved she couldn't be sure. It could have been both.

"I'm gonna meet you there," Genevieve said into the phone. "I'm on my way right now."

"You're meeting up with him?" Havana asked her once she'd ended the call.

"At the old Levenson Asylum. Not the Motel 6," she replied. "We're working on a project together, Havana. That's all."

"I know," Havana said, reaching for her wallet. "I'm going with you." Enough was enough. If her father was going to mastermind a plot to expose or corrupt their relationship by using Ethan's friends against him, this game was over. It was her move, and she had his pawn cornered. Sure that she'd convinced Genevieve to keep her mouth shut for Ethan's sake, the only other base she needed to cover was if Genevieve was planning to seduce him. Showing up with her at a condemned mental asylum would definitely piss Ethan off to the point where he'd hold her responsible for getting his girlfriend involved in something this dangerous.

A flame can't burn on ice.

Check.

F I F T E E N

Pain was a migratory animal – traveling from the head, to the heart, to every other joint and muscle in the body, and for Lucas, the only anti-inflammatory to treat it was sweat.

He'd spent two hours already in the campus gym, the past twenty minutes running for dear life on the treadmill. Endorphins were like morphine, and they were kicking in to alleviate the pain of knowing that the truth Reagan was about to confront would be because of him.

There were 23 newspaper articles published about the Levenson fire. At the end of Terrance Todd's reign of mayhem, the papers listed the names of the eleven victims that escaped the fire but had been hunted in the horrific aftermath.

Until he'd been tasked to research the circumstances surrounding the Hunter murders, Lucas assumed Robyn Edgefield would either be one of those eleven, or the thirteenth survivor who was captured along with Terrance Todd – the twelfth. In the 23 newspaper articles he read and reread last night, none of them mentioned Robyn Edgefield among the victims.

Three truths plagued him: Since Robyn Edgefield's file was among the records kept at Levenson, she was indeed being treated there. According to Reagan, Robyn did not die in the fire that night. And according to the newspaper articles, Robyn was not one of the eleven survivors who were murdered, and the thirteenth survivor was locked away in another asylum.

Lucas stepped off of the treadmill and wiped the sweat from his forehead with a towel. He'd been running from deductive reasoning, and it was suddenly catching up to him: If the only person who remains unaccounted for in all of what's been happening at Levenson recently is Robyn Edgefield, who else could possibly be responsible?

He ran through the idea that it could have been a gang whose territory included the burned out asylum they had broken into. It would certainly explain the mass of footprints and hanging bodies in the basement cave.

He was trying to steer clear of a catastrophic conclusion for Reagan's sake, but her sudden evacuation from their group and reluctance to share anything about her mother or Levenson had swelled into a tidal wave of suspicion.

Clearing his head had been an abandoned goal this morning, and now the only thing he could think to do was the inevitable. He had to get the whole truth from Reagan. If her mother was in any way connected to the clear and present danger at Levenson, trying to protect Robyn by not divulging her involvement was doing more harm than good.

He hurried to the locker room to change out of his workout clothes, grab a quick shower, and head to Reagan's. The more he thought about how to approach this issue with her, the more nervous he became, and several times he came close to talking himself out of it.

The drive to Reagan's house seemed longer than usual. He was stopped at every red light, which seemed on some symbolic level to indicate that he should heed the same signals with Reagan. But he loved her too much to let her take an emotional fall thinking she was protecting her mother.

He loved her.

It was the first moment he'd realized those feelings were in play. There was a fragile element in her eyes that she guarded with her life – as if should anyone see it, the find would split her open and reduce her to a pile of vulnerability. Part of him thought he was the only one who knew it was there, and now he was afraid telling her those three words would set time in reverse and drop him off at 398 days ago, when she hardly allowed herself to talk to him.

Five minutes from now, he would pull into her driveway with questions that might turn love into an irrelevant matter.

*

Loneliness had been a power player in her game since day one, and Reagan was up against its stiff competition. With a mother who'd gone off the deep end and a father who was for the most part only physically present after that, abandonment issues were, to say the least, at the root of every relationship she'd ever had. She always created a way to keep from getting too close or falling too deep, many times without even trying.

Lucas was no different. As hard as he was trying, and as hard as she tried herself, she was always afraid that it wouldn't last long. The past year had been a surprise to her. She'd half-expected Lucas to give up on her after the first month of pursuit, but when he didn't, she found herself determined to care against her better judgment. Nothing inside of her wanted to trust herself with him, and part of her was still an army surrounding that wall.

Alone in the house, she sat on the edge of her bed, silently staring at an old photo of her as a newborn in her mother's arms. Both of them were sleeping peacefully in the photo, Robyn's lips resting against Reagan's tiny head. She wondered now more than ever what had happened, and the only words that kept ringing in the back of her mind were ones Lucas had found listed in Robyn's medical folder from Levenson: postpartum depression.

Part of her wished she could talk to her, to find out what happened at that critical point that turned Robyn into who she was today. There had to be more than one contributing variable, and only half of Reagan wanted to know. She was tip-toeing around the entire issue with her father. Jeffrey had been involved in this metaphorical earthquake, and revisiting the fault was obviously difficult for him. Still, her life until now had been a jigsaw puzzle, and fabrications had filled in the places where chunks were missing. Someone was to blame for that.

Distracted, she didn't hear the doorbell until it chimed a second time.

"Rea, are you in there?" She could faintly hear Lucas's voice calling from outside.

She stuffed the photo underneath her pillow and headed into the living room to answer.

He stood in the doorway, carrying his manila folder with copies of news articles.

"Can I come in?" he asked.

She stepped away from the door allowing him to enter. "Do I know what this is about?" she asked him.

"Probably," he answered. "First of all, I apologize for going through your mother's file."

He could tell she was already shutting down in front of him, her defenses starting to set like a security alarm.

"For what it's worth, I still haven't told anybody else about her," he continued. "But you have to understand what this looks like."

"I thought I asked you to get out of this," came her cold reply.

"Darren's missing." It was the punctuation that preceded a brand new paragraph in this argument. "When we all went up to Levenson the other day, he never came out. Nobody has seen him since. He could be dead, Reagan, and for all we know, whatever happened to him is connected to what went on up there fifteen years ago."

"Oh come on," she said, not wanting to believe what he was telling her.

"You think I'm joking about this?" The question came almost as if he had been betrayed. His tone reminded her that he was not the type to play a game like this.

"Are you sure Darren's not just fooling around?" She was scared, and even more afraid of where the conversation was headed.

"I didn't want to tell you this," he continued, "but we also found about twenty bodies down in that basement. Dead bodies, literally just hanging around down there."

"And you think that has something to do with what happened fifteen years ago?" she asked him.

"We're dealing with the criminally insane," he answered. "Murderers were locked away up there for years. That was the last home a lot of them knew, and now it's an abandoned mansion that this entire town is too scared to even drive past. Evidently, it's the perfect place to hide bodies."

She felt sick. He took notice of the change in her demeanor and pushed on, determined to go for broke. This situation had escalated far beyond his need to selfishly protect their relationship.

"Back in '96, the newspapers listed twelve people who survived that fire, including Terrance Todd." He held up the manila folder for her to see. "Here are their obituaries. The thirteenth survivor has been in custody ever since. Up until the other day, nobody knew that Robyn Edgefield also survived that fire. Not even the newspapers. She was the only patient who was there that night who remains unaccounted for, and *somebody* has turned that burned out asylum into the Bates Motel."

"So right away you think my mom's responsible," she spat. "My *mother*."

The irony of her statement after his hung between them for a moment.

"I want you to trust me," he said, preparing himself for where this was going.

She looked up at him, the pain he was causing her wasn't his fault. It was referred pain, shooting to her heart and her mind from someplace in her past where her mother was inflicting wounds.

"Keeping quiet about what happened to her isn't making me think she's not involved," he continued.

"She's not." Being forced to confront her internal dilemma, she was losing a fight with her will to hold back tears.

"You know that for a fact?"

"Yes."

"How?"

"Because she's at Glendale." She was upset with Lucas for taking away her decision whether or not to face the fact that her mother was in another asylum only an hour away, but at the same time grateful. Peering over the edge of the diving board had to be scarier than hitting the water.

"Glendale?" he asked. She had pulled him into the deep end of the pool along with her, and now submerged, the perception he once had was disoriented. Robyn wasn't involved? Was she the thirteenth survivor?

"Apparently, on the day of the fire, Mom was being transferred to this other institution in Wilmington. Dad said it was such a quick decision that they had to get her out immediately."

"So quick that she was transported without her file?" Lucas was struggling to get his bearings. "What happened?"

"That's all I got out of him," she said. "I didn't ask him anything else. He has such a hard time talking about it. I couldn't even tell him you found the file."

"Okay, I gotta talk to her," he said, starting for the door.

"Why?" She was still scared. "She wasn't the thirteenth survivor, Lucas. She wasn't there during the fire and she had nothing to do with those murders – if she even knew about them."

"Why was she being transferred in such a hurry? Why on the day of the fire?" he asked, rhetorically.

She rushed over to the door to stop him from leaving.

"Please don't do this," she begged. "It's only a class assignment to you. This is my mother."

The plunge into the truth about Robyn Edgefield's whereabouts had them both trying to reach the surface to breathe. He understood Reagan's hesitation to dig any deeper into what had become of her mother. It was another layer of her defense. She defaulted to protect the little girl who had to convince herself that her mother was dead, and was trying to block out the reality that something was amiss in the way Robyn Edgefield's transfer to Glendale was handled.

"This isn't just a class assignment anymore, Reagan," he said. "We've got a murderer on the loose, and if your mom isn't involved, and any of this is at all connected to the Levenson fire, then what if that makes her the final target?"

He was appealing to her basic human instinct, even if she had no reason beyond blood to feel protective of her mother. He had seen so far that it was enough.

"Maybe we should go to the police," she said after a moment. "Take them to the bodies."

"We kinda screwed up that opportunity," he admitted. He knew he was asking a lot of her, but if this killer was in fact still active, they had all seen too much of his handiwork to be granted exemption, and each of them were clearly identified on Darren's camera. Any information from Robyn was necessary and urgent if Lucas had any intentions of protecting her and Reagan. "All I ask is that you trust me."

She wanted to, unwilling to take the chance that her mom might be in danger. She tried to ignore feeling somewhat responsible for her mother's postpartum depression. She knew it was not her fault, but because Reagan was born, Robyn ended up at Levenson and then Glendale – and the fact remained that almost everyone associated with Levenson was dead, and a brand new act was taking place fifteen years later according to Lucas.

"Fine," she said. "Let's go."

S I X T E E N

FAYETTEVILLE, NORTH CAROLINA – 1989

"I don't understand how this could happen."

Jeffrey Edgefield sat across from Dr. Leona Murray, fighting to keep the pieces of himself together. He was a dump truck of used emotions.

"She'd been getting better," he said, reaching over to grab his wife's hand. Robyn Edgefield sat vacantly in the chair next to him. He squeezed, his prayers for any physical response reduced to the habit of false hope.

"Why don't you tell me the first time you noticed something was wrong with your wife?" Dr. Murray asked him.

He let go of Robyn's hand and wiped his mouth, fidgeting to keep from falling apart.

"It was like a switch, you know?" he started. "It was like somebody had flipped off all the lights. But it only lasted a few weeks. Maybe a few months."

"When?" Dr. Murray asked again.

He rubbed his eyes, trying to pretend he couldn't recall. But that night was as clear as the day before this one.

"We were living in Greenville at the time. I think it was... three years ago," he answered, slowly continuing. "There was one night, she came home from her shift at the hospital a few hours earlier. She's a nurse. She had long shifts. Emergency room nurse."

He stopped, seeming to streamline that night in his memory.

"She was fine when she left that morning." His shift in time meant he could get to the point more easily if he was allowed to incorporate nostalgia. "We had this thing where if she left the house before I did, she'd leave our next meal menu on the kitchen table and expected that I'd have it in the oven for her when she got home. That morning, I got up the same time she did. We were practically racing each other to get ready. We..." he stalled. His eyes were staring at the memory, and it was so vivid a smile formed on his lips. "We shared the shower."

He sat back in the chair and cleared his throat with a grunt of an exhale.

"I got a call from a buddy of mine, and that's how she was able to leave the house before me," he recalled. "She left a menu. She wanted grits, eggs, link sausages, toast, and one cigarette for me."

Dr. Murray's expression shifted to reveal her confusion. Jeffrey caught it.

"She only let me smoke a cigarette after we had sex," he explained.

He glanced over at Robyn next to him, and the realization seemed to hit him all over again.

After a moment, he continued. "She wasn't due back home until the next morning. Around dawn. I was in bed when I heard the front door close. It was just me in the house, and it was still dark out. I got up and went to check the door, and found her sitting on the coffee table in the living room. Like I told you, it was like somebody turned off the lights. She wasn't... "

"Did she say anything?" Dr. Murray asked. "Did you try to get her to the hospital?"

"She said she couldn't do it anymore," he told her, glancing again at his wife. "She only said she couldn't do it anymore."

"Meaning her job, correct?"

He nodded, the guilt over not getting her more help back then was crashing against him.

"I tried to get her to see somebody," he said. "I kept asking her to go talk to a therapist, but she wouldn't even... she couldn't even talk to me."

"And this lasted for...?"

"A little over a month, and then she started to come out of it. A year later, she even wanted to leave Greenville, and that's when we moved here. I figured it must have been some type of pre-mid-life crisis or nervous breakdown or something."

"Did you ever try to find out what happened during her last shift at the hospital?" Dr. Murray asked.

He nodded again. "I figured that had to be it because she wouldn't discuss it. The hospital called a few days later to find out what happened to her – why she just walked away. I didn't have any answers. I asked about her shift. There hadn't been anything too far out of the ordinary. A couple of car accidents, and there was a house fire that night. Some guy and his kid came in with terrible burns. The kid died." He paused, trying to remember how he felt. "I just figured that could break anybody, to see that. To be there, and not be able to save a child."

Dr. Murray looked from Jeffrey to Robyn, full of sympathy. Robyn hadn't lifted her eyes from the corner of Dr. Murray's oak desk since she was seated. The poor woman had all but given up.

"What am I supposed to do?" Jeffrey asked. "She was fine for the past two years. She'd been coming back to me. And now you're telling me that having our daughter brought her back to this? That you have no idea how long this will last?!"

"With postpartum it's very hard to say," Dr. Murray said. "It could be three more months. It could be a year."

"This is an important time in our daughter's development to bond with her mother, and just look at—" he couldn't finish, feeling himself sort through the remnants of anger, sadness, and even hope that were somewhere inside.

"You don't want her on medication," Dr. Murray said, thumbing through pages in front of her.

"She would never agree to take meds," he told her. "She'd been getting into these naturopathic remedies."

"Then there's one other option I could suggest," she continued. "It's an experimental therapy program they're about to start."

"Experimental?"

"Yes, which means it has a fifty-fifty shot of working, but it involves no drugs and it's a very intensive treatment."

He glanced over once again at his wife, taking a long moment to consider bringing this mother back home to their three-month-old daughter.

"Now, it's being conducted at Levenson," Dr. Murray continued, sensing his deliberation.

"What is that? An institution?"

"Asylum." She braced herself for his reaction. She expected it would be the same reaction she'd gotten from several other patients she had recommended for the program.

"As in *mental* asylum?"

She had prepared well. "It's one of the leading facilities for treatment in the state, and the only one offering this kind of program."

He shook his head, his eyes pinched shut in an effort to will away this option.

"She needs to be at home with our daughter."

"What can she do for your daughter?" Dr. Murray asked, sensitive to his dilemma. "If she spends another year in this condition, it's another year of you sitting beside her, emotionally and physically exhausted. How will little Reagan benefit from that?"

"I can't," he said. "I got her out of this once before. Everyday for weeks, I made her grits, eggs, link sausages, and toast until one day she asked where was the cigarette. I can do it again."

"Okay, but you understand the postpartum might be feeding whatever that event was three years ago, or vice versa. It may be a much tougher process this time."

She hated playing the devil's advocate, but there was a helpless baby depending on the strength of at least one of her parents, and she needed Jeffrey to see that Reagan's well-being trumped every other consideration.

Jeffrey blinked, freeing a teardrop from the captivity of his eyelids. If only love could as easily break Robyn free from her desolate prison. But Dr. Murray was right. It had taken everything in him to hold his marriage together before, and now he had Reagan to consider.

"How long is the program?" he asked.

"It's a year. Maybe less. Maybe more," she said. "But you will have unlimited visitation. I can even reach out to a few contacts up there who can help you find an affordable place to sublet while she's there."

Jeffrey sighed, succumbing to another pound of anguish on top of what had already been anchoring inside of him. He wouldn't be able to subject himself or their daughter to visitations, but he also couldn't just ship the love of his life off to another part of the state alone. He slowly nodded in response to Dr. Murray's offer, hanging on to the speck of hope that remained unburdened by anguish – that soon Robyn would be herself again, even if only for a moment long enough recognize her daughter.

He stared past Dr. Murray and out of the big window behind her desk overlooking Fayetteville. He would be near Robyn, but unwilling to explain to Reagan where her mother had gone just in case Robyn never came back. He didn't want their daughter living with the same failing hope he'd had to endure, and alongside a sacrifice like this, he would have to vow never to be too far from Reagan.

S E V E N T E E N

It took a little over an hour for Lucas and Reagan to arrive at Glendale Institute in Wilmington. As soon as they left Reagan's, he'd gotten a text from Ethan that said he and his dad were on their way back to Levenson this morning to look for Darren's camera. It wasn't Ethan's best idea, but given where he and Reagan were going, he knew he was in no position to argue. It only provided little comfort to know that at least Ethan was up there with a man who was one of the authorities.

Glendale was a daydream compared to the darkness of Levenson. It looked like a six-story hospital, with a packed parking lot that surrounded a large fountain out front.

Walking through the electronic doors of the main entrance reminded them of one of their newer academic buildings on campus – marble floors, fluorescent lighting, and warmly painted walls. A large reception desk was stationed straight ahead, and on either side was a hall housing the east and west wing elevator banks.

They approached the receptionist, presented identification, signed in, and received their visitors' passes. They were directed towards the right elevator bank and told to go up to the third floor.

It was a slow ride up in the spacious elevator, and Reagan's discomfort was visible.

"Hey," Lucas said, reaching for her hand. "Are you sure you're okay with this?"

She nodded. "I just wish I could tell my dad we were here."

She knew her dad would have pulled out every stop to prevent her from coming up here – especially without him. But she also knew that after their last talk, his emotions were all over the place, and this was nothing he'd probably ever be ready to face.

The elevator stopped and a second set of doors behind them opened. They stepped out into a large waiting room area, with a glass-walled room stationed at the far end of an aisle in front of them that divided the area in half. Chairs, coffee tables, bookshelves, and magazines gave the space a very comfortable feel. Halls on the left and the right of the elevator bank ran parallel to each other. A bright EXIT sign at the entrance of the hall to their right hung over a door that undoubtedly led to the stairs.

They started up the aisle in front of them towards the glass-walled room where several women in white nurses outfits were writing notes, gathering folders, or taking calls.

"We're here to visit Robyn Edgefield," Lucas said to a woman sitting on the other side of one of the opened glass panes that separated the room from the waiting area. The woman stopped writing and glanced up at the two of them.

"Your passes?" she asked.

Lucas and Reagan offered their passes to her, and she took them with a slight smile before turning to a computer beside her. Typing feverishly, she spoke, not taking her eyes off the screen.

"I have you registered for thirty minutes," she said. "Will that be enough time?"

Thirty minutes rested in Reagan's mind for a long moment. She would have half an hour to meet the woman who gave birth to her. *Would* that be enough time?

"That'll be fine," she heard Lucas say.

"You'll need to remove any and all items from your pockets including cell phones, wallets, pens, coins, and paper. You can leave them along with your purse, jackets, jewelry, belts, and sweaters in one of the bins to your left. Attach one of the colored stickers located in your bin to the front of your visitor's pass beneath your name, and have a seat in the waiting area. Someone will be with you shortly." She returned their passes to them along with a clip, which they used to fasten the passes to their shirts.

They began to do as instructed, removing all of the mentioned items and storing them in selected bins located on a large rectangular table to the left of the glass room.

"Do you think she's dangerous?" Reagan asked, looking to Lucas for comfort.

"It's just protocol," he said. "It looks like a really nice place. I'm sure she's well taken care of and is probably used to short visits."

"Visits from who?" she asked, verbalizing the sudden guilty realization that here her mother hadn't had anyone to come see her for the past fifteen years. She was convinced her father had talked himself out of ever visiting for the simple fact that he couldn't take it, and not doing so had possibly even added to the gauntlet of emotional torture he endured at the mention of his wife.

"I'm sure he's been up here," Lucas said, reading her thoughts. "As much as you said he loves her, I don't think he could stand to not ever see her again."

"But to see her here?" she noted, uncomfortably. "All I keep imagining is that they've got her restrained in some strait-jacket or confined to a bed back there."

Her imagination was still filling in whatever missing pieces she came across with the most horrendous pictures. It was the only way she could prepare herself for the actual image.

"I don't know what she did to land her here, or what she's done to keep her here," Reagan continued.

One of the nurses emerged from the room with a clipboard and approached the two of them.

"You can follow me," she told them.

She led them towards the door beneath the EXIT sign and turned left down the long and narrow hall. On the right side of the hall were doors every ten feet or so, all of them brandishing odd numbers beginning at 301. As they passed door numbered 309, the wall on their left turned into a balcony, and light from the other side poured into the hallway.

Reagan stopped to peer over the edge of the balcony, stunned to see that below was a beautiful courtyard, complete with green turf, small trees and bushes, and a colorful array of flowers. Sunlight poured in through a glass roof, and several patients were with visiting family members.

"This is our atrium," the nurse said, allowing them a chance to take it in. "The west wing has one too, but it's the cafeteria. I like this one better because of the flowers. I've spent five years working here, and I have to say they are the best form of treatment."

She walked a few feet further down the hall and stopped in front of door 313.

"People hear mental institution, and they have a certain perception of what one should look like," she said. "I like to think of them as a haven. People are only dangerous if they feel threatened."

Reagan's heartbeat slowed, and the pulsing in her ears receded. She'd been one of those people with a skewed perception, and had categorized a mother she'd never even known for spending twenty years in one. Maybe this was her mother's haven. Maybe this was where she felt safest.

"Here we are," the nurse said, sliding a key card into a slot above the doorknob of room 313. A soft buzzing sound alerted them that the lock had been turned. "If at any point she becomes agitated or upset, there is a yellow call button next to the door."

The nurse pushed the door open and stepped aside for Reagan and Lucas to enter.

Robyn Edgefield sat in a wooden chair in front of a small window with her back facing them. Her gray hair retained a faint hint of its formerly brown hue, its ends split against her shoulders. The room itself was less than what the front lobby and atrium had led them to expect. The eggshell-colored walls were coated with some kind of firm foam padding that pretended to be décor. The beige carpet boasted several stains, some of them large, but most of them diminutive. Some of the spots had been bleached and were brighter than the carpet itself.

Against the left wall was a 3-foot high twin-sized luxury-looking mattress that sat on the floor. The head end of the mattress was slanted up slightly. There were no pillows or blankets.

A square magnetic board was mounted on the opposite wall, and was littered with photos of Robyn with Jeffrey. One photo Reagan immediately recognized was the photo of Robyn asleep with her newborn daughter in her arms.

"Mrs. Edgefield," the nurse said politely, "you have visitors!"

Robyn didn't turn around.

Reagan looked to the nurse, her eyes asking if this was normal. The nurse nodded, and allowed the door to close, leaving Reagan and Lucas alone with Robyn.

Lucas rested a supporting hand at the top of Reagan's back, rubbing gently as if to let her know that she could take her time. He was eager to hear Robyn say anything about Levenson, but more than that he wanted to hear her say Reagan's name and recognize who she was.

"Mom…" Reagan said softly. "It's your daughter."

She slowly took a few more steps into the room, cautiously approaching Robyn's chair.

"It's Reagan," she uttered, faith in acknowledgement quickly diminishing.

Silent seconds passed before the wooden chair creaked under the weight of the frail woman pulling herself to her feet.

Reagan stood back as Robyn slowly turned around to face her daughter. Her weathered face made her look ten years older than her actual age. The first things her wet eyes landed on were Reagan's, and the two sets locked for a moment long enough to push a tear from Robyn's.

She wasn't sure if it was recognition or simply Robyn remembering that she even had a daughter, but Reagan held onto their gaze until sorrow pulled Robyn's eyes away.

"Is he dead?" The question narrowly escaped from its prison of helplessness. Her voice was raspy from seldom being used.

"Who?" Reagan asked, confused.

Robyn looked over at the magnetic board of photos. If regret were a scab, her eyes would now be dripping blood.

"Daddy?" Reagan asked. "No." It was a gut-wrenching realization for Reagan that Robyn might have assumed the only thing that would bring her daughter here was news of Jeffrey's death. "That's not why I'm here."

Robyn walked over to the photos, almost as if rediscovering all of them.

It was turning into a lost cause – both her agenda as well as Lucas's. Reagan couldn't be sure her mother wasn't locked in a time warp that only consisted of the days before her bout with postpartum and whatever madness that led to. She turned to Lucas, hurt, and he took her in his arms. At the very least, she could stop wondering about the condition of her mother's mind.

She still needed closure. To walk out of Glendale, she needed to feel there was truth to her belief that she did not have a mother anymore. By knowing that she had covered every possible attempt to find out anything about Robyn, she'd be able to detach herself from the psychological string that tethered her to this void of abandonment. She would have room to learn to trust.

Out of the corner of her eye, she saw Robyn lift her hand to the board of photos, resting her palm on the photo of a mother and her baby. It was the one gesture that reversed closure, re-enforced that psychological string with cable wire, and started filling that void with love.

"You were so tiny," Robyn said.

Reagan smiled. Whether Robyn really remembered or not was inconsequential. She knew Reagan was her daughter, and the affection she showed towards the photo was all Reagan needed to see.

"Mom, we don't have a lot of time," Reagan said, "and there's something I wanted to talk to you about." She remembered Lucas was there, and corrected. "Something *we* wanted to talk to you about."

Robyn turned back to face Reagan, and then looked past her at Lucas.

"This is Lucas," Reagan introduced. "He's a very special friend of mine."

"Mrs. Edgefield," Lucas greeted. "It's nice to meet you. I know it means a lot to Reagan."

A Mona Lisa smile formed on Robyn's face, and none of the three of them knew if it was pride, approval, or even understanding. But Reagan sensed it was a sign to continue.

"We had a couple of questions about Levenson Asylum," she said.

Robyn's smile came under sudden attack by a ghastly expression that pulled her eyes wide open with fright.

"I'm not going back there!" she said, her raspy voice cracking as she strained to give it more volume.

"No, Mom," Reagan said, reaching to calm her down. "It burned down years ago. Don't you remember?"

"Remember?!" Robyn struggled to swallow, her dry mouth strangling the life out of her desperate pleas for them to understand her fear. Neither Reagan nor Lucas had ever known pure terror until now. "I wish I knew how to forget! That place..." she said.

Afraid that contact would trigger Robyn to scream, Reagan stepped back as her mother pressed herself against the wall and slid backwards toward the corner of the room.

"That room!" Robyn said, still gripped by fear. "The blood! Those bodies! It was *him*..." She formed the fingers of her right hand into a claw, clutched the left side of her forehead, and began a slow, deep scratch around the side of her head towards her right ear, as if she was trying to scratch the frightening image out of her head. "It was him," she repeated. "It was death."

Blood began to seep from the scratches in her forehead made by her fingernails.

Reagan rushed over to the yellow call button by the door and slammed her hand against it.

"We're leaving," she told Lucas.

"I told them not to go up there," Robyn continued, frantically pointing at Lucas with her bloodied fingers. "I told them... but they didn't listen. I didn't want to see it."

"See what?" Lucas asked her.

"I wasn't supposed to go up there," she cried. "I wasn't supposed to see that, but I did. I didn't want to, but I saw it. I saw all of it, and nothing would make it go away..."

Reagan pounded on the yellow button again.

"No..." Robyn continued. "I didn't just see it. My whole body *felt* that place." Eerily, her entire countenance subsided from frantic to hopeless in the breath she took before adding, "Still does."

It was Robyn's sudden personality shift that made Lucas shiver. The door to the room opened, and a male orderly entered to assess the problem.

"What happened," he asked.

Reagan and Lucas stared at Robyn as she pressed herself against the corner of the room, blood streaking down her face.

"They don't want to hear what I say about that room," Robyn continued, her subdued temperament inexplicably back to how it was before the mention of Levenson Asylum. "That's why I don't say it anymore."

She looked at Reagan and Lucas, something unrecognizable behind her eyes turning sly. "He knows I know," she whispered. "And oh what happens to those who know..."

Lucas tossed a concerned glance at Reagan, who was wiping a tear from her cheek.

"Don't let him come," Robyn said, slowly starting for the mattress and suddenly aware of the curtain-less window. "I pray... maybe he wouldn't because he knows that if he does, they'll know. They'll all know."

"Know what?" Lucas asked, disturbed.

Robyn sat down on the mattress, her posture perfect, her vacant eyes shifting towards the window. "You will see," she slowly sang in a lullaby-like refrain. "You will see."

E I G H T E E N

It was a cacophony of screams that Frank could still hear fifteen years later. He never expected to find himself back at Levenson after the fire had been put out, but here he was, crawling through a broken window behind his son, about to walk through scenes from a gruesome nightmare.

"The camera was over by the stairs," Ethan said, noticing as his father waded in the memory of that night. He suddenly realized he'd been so against using his father as a resource for their project that he'd neglected the notion that Frank could very well be ready to volunteer information simply by being out here.

"You okay?" Ethan asked.

Frank turned to him and grunted. "Nobody was prepared for this," he said, the firefighter in him pooling every brute fiber of his being to combat an inferno of emotions.

"Do you remember the call?"

Ethan didn't want to push too hard fearing Frank would bail, calling it silly to be up here trespassing in search of a video camera. The only reason he felt Frank hadn't already backed out was because he felt he owed Ethan something. Either that, or part of Frank held this fire partially responsible for what had become of him – for better and for worse.

"Six engines came out here," Frank said. "You couldn't tell the sky even existed from all the smoke. It was like walking right up to the devil's doorstep and staring him in the face."

Somewhere in Frank's mind, he heard sirens and commotion get louder and louder. He could smell flesh cooking despite his gear.

"It was so many people," he continued, and started towards a hallway on the left. "Scotty and I... we came through here first because..." He was either struggling to remember why or waiting for the channels of images to settle on one. "This woman, she had to be a nurse, was on her hands and knees, crawling from back here. She was on fire. She was a ball of fire crawling along here, and she was screaming 'Unlock! Unlock!' and she was trying to point down this hall. That's when Scotty went in."

He looked down the dark hallway, all the doors on both sides were still closed.

"I stood here and watched this woman burn," Frank continued, "and at one moment – the one I'll never, ever forget – she screamed through the pain of turning her head and looked up at me. I yelled for somebody to bring a fire blanket, but... *everybody* was screaming. She looked me square in the eyes... and lost hope." He glanced over at Ethan, heartbreak reverberating throughout him as the memory splashed into a pond of his emotions. "I saw the moment this woman decided to die."

"You weren't responsible for that," Ethan said.

"You don't get it," Frank replied. "That's what I was trained to do. I was supposed to save this woman's life. I was supposed to risk my own, and as soon as she collapsed, I couldn't move. I was surrounded by complete pandemonium. Smoke, and flames, and heat, and the screaming was like throats were on fire, and I couldn't move."

Now Ethan knew why his dad had hesitated to come back here.

"I never saw Scotty again after that," Frank said, sounding as if he'd gotten past the wall of emotion and was himself again. "I thought he went to get into those rooms, but I guess not. He must've—"

A wave rushed over Frank, and suddenly he was watching through smoke the images of several men emerging from the hall and battling their way towards the entrance that night.

"Scotty had to have unlocked the doors," Frank said. He vividly remembered Scotty going down the hall at the woman's request to unlock the rooms, and could vaguely remember noticing patients come from that direction. Why had they all been told later that Scotty's body was found at the end of that hall? Why were all of the doors still closed?

"Dad?" Ethan summoned for his father's attention. He had another idea. Credibility was all the police department needed in order to take them seriously. "You don't happen to know if there was another way to the basement, do you?"

Ethan headed towards the hallway on the other side of the lobby that led to the basement, and stopped when he reached the foot of the grand staircase. He searched the area, certain this was where he last spotted Darren's video camera.

"What...?" he asked himself, spinning around and sweeping the floor with his light in confusion. It was gone. He started down the hallway, thinking perhaps a squirrel or raccoon might have carried it off into one of the opened rooms.

Shining his flashlight into the first room on his right, Ethan noticed it was more spacious than any of the other patients' rooms they had seen in the building. This was no ordinary patient room. It was a nursery.

Stuffed, moth-eaten teddy bears had been gnawed apart by critters. A rusted tricycle lay on its side, its seat and one of its back two wheels missing. Three wooden cribs, one of them noticeably uneven, were lined against two of the walls. Another crib lay in a pile of pieces against another wall. Children's drawings speckled the walls randomly.

The thought was a bear gnawing at him. Did they keep kids here, too? Had doctors in the earlier part of the 1900s, not knowing what else to do with disfigured babies, sent them to live here in the company of sadistic murderers?

He forced himself to consider that perhaps this room was for parental visitations, and moved on, checking each of the remaining rooms for the animal, its nest, and its prize, but the search produced no evidence. He returned to the entrance to the hall.

"You're not gonna believe this—" he said, stopping as soon as he saw Frank was no longer standing in the lobby. "Dad?" he called.

Figuring in the five minutes he'd been away looking for

Darren's camera, Frank might have been overcome by the horrible memories and opted to leave the building, Ethan ran over to the front windows and tried to glance around the yard as much as the boarded windows allowed.

"Dad?" he called again, waiting several seconds for no response.

He returned to the lobby area, and remembered Frank had been rambling about another fireman going down the other hallway.

"Dad, you back there?" Ethan headed towards the other hallway's entrance. Despite the morning hour, the boarded windows and layers of ash, soot, and dust still cast the gut of this burned out lobby in darkness. He stopped at the threshold of the hallway, and pointed his flashlight towards the other end. All of the doors on both sides were still closed, and the hallway was empty. He walked slowly down the hall, turning each locked doorknob he passed, and shining his flashlight through the small square windows at eye level on each door. He hoped that one of the doors would open and he'd find his father inside a room, still trying to figure out what must've kept poor Scotty.

As he reached the end of the hall, he found mounted on the far wall a small metallic cabinet, much like a safe that protruded from the wall. His curiosity lifted the light to the box, and he noticed its door was ajar. He tapped the end of the flashlight on the inside of the door, and it slowly creaked open. Inside was a lever similar to that of a fire alarm. On top of the lever was the word *Lock*, and beneath the lever was the word *Unlock*.

Ethan dropped the light, feeling stupid that he'd even gotten caught up in this mystery.

"Dad, I think I figured out what that nurse was talking about," he said.

But no response.

"Come on, Dad," he said again, finally glancing down to where his light had landed on the floor.

In the carpet of dust and ash were two fresh sets of footprints. One set was his own, headed in this direction. The other set seemed to come out of the last room on this hall. The room right next to him.

He reached for the doorknob of that room and slowly turned. It was still locked. He pointed the light once again through the small window, but could only see the wall on the opposite side which housed a boarded up single-pane window. He brought the light back to the floor and experienced a sudden and total recall of terror. Lifting his light to the ceiling, he forced himself to look up. The ceiling was bare.

He followed the second set of footprints down the hall, across the back of the lobby, and towards the foot of the grand staircase where a small puddle of blood had formed out of nowhere.

"How'd I miss this?" he asked himself, confused. His heart began thumping to the rhythm of panic. The blood looked fresh. Dread overcame him as soon as he noticed a right footprint had left a bloody stamp on every other step headed up.

And Darren's camera lay facing the lobby against the wall by the hall entrance at the foot of the stairs, exactly as he had noticed the other night.

The red light in the top corner of the camera indicated it was still recording.

*

"This is the dumbest thing I've ever done in my life," Genevieve said, bringing her car to a stop next to Ethan's jeep on Grand Street.

Havana climbed out of the car and stared up at Levenson. "It would have been smart for you to come out here by yourself?" she asked.

Genevieve slowly got out of the car, completing a text message to Ethan that told him she was on her way inside and that Havana was with her. At least if he had a heads up, he might abort this mission and be already on his way out before they even got inside.

She hadn't been intimidated by Havana's threats to ruin her friendship with Ethan if Genevieve refused to let her tag along, but Genevieve gave in anyway. She knew Ethan would be upset with her for bringing his girlfriend into this, but poor judgment tied right in with every other self-deprecating attribute she donned to remind herself not to fall for him.

Maybe Havana had a reason to be insecure, but Genevieve

knew that reason wasn't her. Ethan was happy with Havana. They were clearly in love and were used to fighting against the world to be together. She felt like she needed a chance to cover up whatever scent of a crush Havana had picked up on – if not for the sake of Ethan's feelings, their friendship, and her future, for the protection of her own. Having Havana along today would assure both girls that Genevieve was not trying to split up the couple. Ethan would never look at her as anything more than a friend, and it was beginning to hurt reminding herself of that. Her only salvation was to get through to graduation and follow her plans to move to Europe. Any romantic feelings at this point were just going to be obstacles in the way of a plan she'd had mapped out for the past four years.

"Do you think he found Darren?" Havana asked.

"I haven't gotten any messages from him, so no," she replied.

"Let's go in."

"Maybe we should just wait out here for a while. It's been an hour since he called, I'm sure he and his dad have searched every inch of that place by now."

Genevieve was hoping that was the case. She wasn't thrilled when Ethan told her he was coming back up here to look for Darren's camera, but when he said his dad was coming with him, she figured he wanted to show the bodies in the basement to someone who could go to the police and be taken seriously.

Havana was already heading across the street as Genevieve's hopes started giving way to concern. She didn't want to take the chance that something might have happened to Ethan.

"Wait up," she yelled. She reached through the opened backdoor window and retrieved a flashlight from the seat, then sprinted across the street to catch up with Havana.

The two of them made their way quickly up the horseshoe drive and through the broken window of the building.

"Have I already gone on record as saying it's not safe for you to be here?" Genevieve asked once they were standing in the dark, haunting lobby area.

"Yes," Havana answered. "But you still haven't told me why you all chose Terrance Todd. Wouldn't this have been a mass murder and not a serial killing?"

"Our focus is on the eleven survivors who were murdered after the fire," Genevieve clarified. She had hoped giving Havana details of their project would be the way to talk her out of coming along, but it only piqued her interest even more.

The lobby area was empty and eerily silent. Assuming Ethan and his dad had found their way down to the basement, Genevieve took the time to pay more attention to the details in this room. The combined light from her flashlight and the small amount of sunlight that had broken in before they did allowed her to notice several faintly discernable ash handprints on the left wall. She stared at them, remembering the dark shadow she had spotted – or thought she'd spotted – the other night. The memory fired like a bullet, and her entire reaction to seeing the shadow came back to her. She shifted her gaze to the foyer where she had dropped her flashlight before running to Ethan's jeep and calling the police.

The flashlight was no longer there.

Maybe Ethan found it when he got here.

She noticed Havana was standing at the foot of the stairs, trying to get a photo of something in front of her with her phone. A sudden flash went off.

"What are you doing?" she asked her, annoyed.

"Putting this on Facebook," Havana answered. "I'll tag you."

Genevieve rolled her eyes as she approached, wondering what would convincingly distinguish these stairs from any other grand staircase. She immediately spotted the pool of blood.

"Where did that come from?" she asked, knowing this blood was not here the other night.

Havana read her reaction, and struggled with the horrifying implication.

Genevieve lifted her eyes to the stairs and finally noticed the bloody footprint that left several marks on the stairs. She pulled her phone from her pocket and quickly checked it, praying that she'd received a reply text from Ethan.

She had no signal.

"Oh my God…" Genevieve said. The words came out of her as if she already knew Ethan and his dad had suffered the same fate as Darren. Something inside of her fought it, determined to believe that somewhere in this burned out building Frank and Ethan had found Darren and were discussing the details of what had happened to him. That belief was losing this battle.

Havana didn't like the sound of that. "Ethan?!" she called.

"Shhh!" Genevieve pulled her back from the stairs. "The last thing I want to be is hunted and strung up—" She stopped herself. The bodies in the basement had been one detail she had neglected to fill Havana in on. "We don't know who did this, or where they are now."

"I don't know where *Ethan* is now," Havana pointed out, scared the blood might be his. "I'm going up there." She started up the stairs.

"Are you crazy?" Genevieve pulled her back. "Ethan *and* his dad were here together. If something happened to them, what makes you think you can survive it?"

Havana stared at her for a moment. "I guess you don't care about him after all," she said, knowing whichever response she got from Genevieve would be a problem. Right now, she needed the crush to be real.

The comment was exactly what Genevieve wanted and didn't want to hear. It stung more than it pleased her, however, and she decided she didn't have time now to think about what she needed to prove. She cared, and she hated that she couldn't walk out of this building and back to her car.

"Ten minutes," she told Havana. "If we don't find anything in ten minutes, we leave."

She and Havana started up the stairs, careful not to step on the bloody footprints as they ascended. They reached the landing, and turned to start up the second flight. Halfway up, the footprints faded.

"Stay quiet," Genevieve said, stepping in front of Havana to lead the rest of the way.

They stepped onto the landing of the second floor. A quick pan of her flashlight showed Genevieve that the hall extended to her left and her right. A couple of doors decorated the wall in front of them, and Genevieve noticed a large photo hanging between them. She approached, steadying her flashlight on the soot-covered black and white photo of Levenson around the time it was first built in the early 1900s. Nurses and male orderlies were lined up dressed in their white uniforms in the yard with the asylum towering in the background. That none of the people in the picture were smiling gave the photo its unsettling aesthetics.

Havana gasped suddenly, startling Genevieve who clutched her own hand to her mouth to stifle a scream.

"Something just crawled across my foot!" Havana whispered, frightened. "It went in that direction." She pointed down the hall to her right, and Havana aimed the light towards the floor, slowly guiding it down the hall until it came to rest on a nest of rats a few feet away, scavenging something she couldn't identify.

"Gross..." Genevieve said. She turned the light back to the wall in front of them, and took a few steps towards the left wing of the hall. Coming across another door, she noticed this one had the word *Medical* etched into it. Next to the door hung yet another large, smoke-stained black and white photo from the same era. In this one sat an older man sitting at a big oak desk, wearing a white doctor's lab coat. His black eyes had been staring directly at the camera, which made them seem to watch the hallway.

At the base of the photo, a nameplate was attached. The name was illegible beneath a layer of soot and dust. Genevieve gently wiped her fingers against it to be able to read it: Dr. Theodore Sweeny, Asylum Administrator.

Just as Genevieve removed her hand from the frame, the photo snapped at a hinge, and became detached from the wall. It dropped to the floor with a loud crash, the frame shattering. Startled, both girls jumped back against the opposite wall, and then listened for any indication that someone else had heard the crash below.

"It's been ten minutes," Genevieve whispered to Havana, whose eyes were still glued to the wall where the photo once hung.

Genevieve followed her gaze with the flashlight, and saw that the photo had been covering a small square hole carved into the wall. They stepped forward to get a better look inside the cubby, and were both terrified to find inside were several dusty 1940's pistols and about a dozen boxes of bullets.

"What..." Genevieve started, scared that she already knew the answer. "What did they need guns for?"

Something was not settling well with her about how this

asylum had been run when it was operational. First the electric chair in a hidden interrogation-like room, and now a secret stash of pistols?

A distant, abrupt thud above them removed her from her train of thought.

"What was that?" Genevieve asked.

"What if it's Ethan?" Havana didn't wait for Genevieve to respond. She reached into the cubby and grabbed one of the pistols.

"What are you doing?!" Genevieve didn't want to admit she'd had the same fleeting thought to take one of the pistols. Now that Havana had made the decision that they needed to be armed, Genevieve knew she didn't want to get shot by a trigger-happy teenager. "Here," she said, offering Havana her flashlight in exchange.

Surprisingly, Havana didn't put up a fight to keep the pistol.

Genevieve leaned into the beam of the flashlight and checked the chamber of the pistol. Three bullets were loaded. With one flip of her wrist, she locked the chamber back into place and then glanced up at Havana, already prepared to address her surprise.

"Westerns," she said, answering Havana's unasked query.

She led the way towards the next flight of stairs and ascended until they reached a similar layout on the third floor. The sound they'd heard seemed more distant than this, so they continued up. When they reached the fourth floor, she noticed there was a final flight of stairs up that led to a door.

"Nobody's here," Genevieve whispered to Havana who was still only an inch behind her.

"I don't believe that and neither do you," Havana answered, stepping forward to take the lead up the stairs.

Climbing up the narrow stairway reminded Genevieve of the stairs that had crashed in the basement. Not wanting a repeat event, she slowly inched past Havana once they'd neared the door at the top.

"Don't make any heavy moves," she warned. "And keep the light on me."

She reached for the doorknob and turned. The knob twisted all the way around easily, but the door seemed to be jammed shut.

She gave herself some leverage by positioning one foot on the step beneath the top one, and thrust her shoulder against the door. After the third attempt, the door flew open into another dark hallway that extended to her left and her right. The odor was the first thing she noticed, as it reminded her of the smell from the basement. The lack of any windows cast the area in a smoky darkness.

"What do you think is in there?" Havana asked, pointing the flashlight towards a single door across from the one they'd just entered.

"An attic, probably." It was Genevieve's best guest, and unspoken hope that would placate Havana's curiosity. She could hardly tolerate the smell, and having come across what they'd seen the last time she'd encountered this odor, she didn't want to explore any further if she didn't have to.

Havana started towards the other door, ignoring Genevieve's attempt to head back down. She slowly rested her hand on the doorknob, working up her courage to enter – half-expecting to find Ethan and his dad and Darren tied up or worse when she entered.

"I'm not gonna give up on him," she justified. It was a pill coated in conviction to make it easier for both herself and Genevieve to swallow. "We've been fighting for each other since day one, what makes anybody think we'll stop? I know everybody thinks the way we feel about each other isn't serious, or it won't last, but the fact that I can't walk out of here without him proves you wrong."

Genevieve could tell Havana was near tears, bracing herself to find the guy she loved dead. It was the moment she knew how she could prove to Havana and reaffirm to herself that she was somewhere in the bleachers – a simple spectator to their relationship, with no stakes in the game whatsoever.

"I'll go in," Genevieve finally said.

"No," Havana replied. "I don't need you to do that."

"I know how to use the gun," she argued. "If someone…" She hesitated, losing nerve. "I know how to use the gun."

She stepped up to the door, inching Havana aside.

"Is anybody in there?" Genevieve called, taking the doorknob in her hand. "If this is a joke, it's time to stop. The cops are involved."

There was no response.

Havana stepped back, allowing herself a better position to give Genevieve as much light as possible.

Pushing the door open, Genevieve held her breath and stepped into the square room. A small, completely boarded window on the opposite wall kept any light from entering the dark space. The far wall to her left was the only other thing she noticed, and it was a sight that was scraping against her bones.

"I need the light," she said, reaching her hand out to Havana.

"What is it?" Havana asked, trying to get closer for a better view.

"You stay out there!" Genevieve said. She grabbed the flashlight from Havana and stepped further into the room and closer to the left wall.

"Is it Ethan?" Not being able to see what had Genevieve so terrified seemed worse to Havana than the prospect of finding out Ethan was in there, mutilated. The sound of a piece of glass crashing on a floor below startled her, and she instinctively crossed the small hallway to slowly close the door that lead back down the stairs. She wasn't sure what good it would do.

As Havana's focus shifted to concealing their whereabouts, Genevieve ventured further into the room, unable to comprehend the images haphazardly covering this wall in front of her. Photos unblemished by smoke or water, but stained or caked with burgundy-black blood. Photos unlike anything they had seen hanging on the walls on floors below. These were color photos of nearly thirty faces. All of them bruised, scarred, burned, or slashed up nearly beyond recognition. All of them dead.

Horrified by the grisly collage and trembling, Genevieve dropped the flashlight and brought her hand to her face. The light hit the slightly slanted floor with a clank. It's beam of light rolled across the wall behind her like a beacon sweeping across the shore, and crept slowly past a shadowed figure standing in the room behind the opened door. One of its arms was extended, slowly pushing the door closed.

The light rolled on until the gravity produced by the slant of the floor brought it back along its path. This time it landed on the figure, who was dressed in a long, black overcoat and a black fedora hat that obscured much of its face. The shadow was several feet in front of the now-closed door, approaching Genevieve.

Completely unaware of what was behind her, Genevieve was still under the horrific hypnotic spell of what she had seen on the wall when in one swift movement, the figure pounced.

NINETEEN

Havana heard the thud of something hitting the floor inside the room, and turned back to the door only to find it was now closed. She thought she could faintly hear the sound of a struggle.

"Vieve?" she called.

Another thud, and then a loud, single gunshot broke the silence.

Startled, she cautiously reached for the doorknob, pausing only to recognize the decision she was about to make. As soon as her hand touched the knob, the door flung open and a disheveled Genevieve stood there, her face a recipe of pain, terror, and shock.

"Go!" Genevieve screamed, trying to balance enough to escape the room herself. Her ankle had been twisted as soon as whatever or whoever had landed on top of her, and though the unknown figure had endured a firm kick as Genevieve struggled to get away, she had only managed to fire the pistol into the darkness as they wrestled. The figure was quick, and there was less than a second to run.

Havana swung open the other door that led back to the stairs, and raced down.

"What the hell is happening?" she yelled up to Genevieve as she reached the landing.

Genevieve appeared at the doorway to the steep stairs, her panting and crying stifling her need to scream. Ignoring the searing pain in her ankle, she stepped as quickly as she could down onto the first step, but her sprained foot never touched the second one. A force sent her hurling through the air above the stairs.

Her body landed like bowling pins onto the bottom steps, tumbling until her head came to a crack against the wall at the landing in the fourth floor hall. Havana stared at the sight in front of her. Blood was splattered and pouring down the wall from Genevieve's head. Her shoulder was in such a form that it was certainly dislocated. Her lifeless eyes only half closed.

A gasp of fear escaped from Havana's lungs, and she covered her mouth with her hand to silence herself. What indeed was happening? She had to know. Had Genevieve lost her footing and slipped? Was she pushed?

The top stair creaked under weight. Havana leaned forward as slowly as she could to get a glimpse without giving herself away. From her angle, she couldn't see the top two stairs. A second later, she didn't need to. She saw one foot, then another, and the bottom of an ankle-length black overcoat slowly descending the stairs.

She ran quietly towards the next flight of stairs down, and took them two at a time until she'd reached the third floor hallway. She couldn't be sure whoever that was wasn't still on her trail, nor did she want to find out. She glanced in both directions down the hall, spotting at the far end of the left wing what appeared to be a fire exit – a door that would lead to a second set of stairs. She made a break for it, praying the door would not be locked or sealed shut, as going back to the main stairs now wasn't an option. Surely whoever that was would be on the third floor with her at any second.

She reached the door, took a breath, and leaned her weight against it slowly just in case it made noise.

It began to open, and as soon as there was enough space, she slid into the dark stairway, and turned just in time to run into Ethan.

She gasped again, her heart pounding out of her chest.

"What the hell are *you* doing here?" Ethan was equal parts scared and irate. He had been staring at the playback screen on Darren's camera on his way up the stairs and hadn't noticed the door opening. When he saw a woman's form slip in, he thought it was Genevieve.

"Ethan..." Havana started. Multitasking to get control of her breathing, get out of panic mode, and try to put into words what had happened to Genevieve was something she couldn't master. "We gotta get out of here. Where's your dad?"

She grabbed his hand and was starting to lead him back down the stairs when Ethan resisted.

"Where's Vieve?" he asked, panicking.

Havana knew she had to tell him something, and the truth was the only way she'd get him to understand her urgency to get out of this place. "Something happened to her up there."

"Was she shot? Was that what I heard?" Ethan asked, reading Havana's tone.

"We don't have time for this!" Havana was trying not to raise her voice above a whisper, but she almost didn't have a choice. "She's dead, Ethan. We ran into whoever that was in the attic, and... she died."

"You saw somebody?" He already knew they weren't alone. Somebody else was up here with a macabre agenda. The proof had been left for him on Darren's camera.

"Yes!" Havana's answer was something of a screamed whisper. "Now can we please just go call the cops?" she begged.

It was Ethan's turn to deliver the breaking news he wasn't even ready to accept himself. "I have to find my dad," he told her.

She could tell he was holding back, and it frightened her.

"Why would you split up?" she asked, confusion wrestling with panic.

"I walked away for five minutes, and he was gone," he continued. "And whoever grabbed him left footage for me." He held up Darren's camera. "There was blood on the main stairs. I followed it up to the second floor, but then I heard the gunshot and didn't want to walk into a trap," he finished, explaining why he was in the fire stairway.

If he didn't already know, Havana couldn't tell him Frank was probably dead. She needed to get them out of here though, and she only had one appeal.

"We don't know where this guy is," she started. "All we do know is what he's capable of, and it's nothing you and I can take on by ourselves."

"What was in the attic?" he asked, sidestepping her logic.

"Ethan, please…"

"I begged him to come out here with me. I laid a guilt trip on him about how I needed him to be my hero for a change, and I never even—" he swallowed the facts in front of him, trying to refuse to admit or believe them. "I owe him an apology."

Havana knew the history between Ethan and his father. She knew all about the distance that had been between them and how badly Ethan hated that he couldn't seem to do anything about it. Half of the reason he needed to finish college this year was because he felt his dad would be disappointed and burdened with having to help pay for another year – even if Ethan didn't ask for it. Frank's moral obligation had always been his first priority.

Ethan started up the stairway towards the fourth floor, and Havana promptly followed. They quietly emerged from the fire stairway into the fourth floor hall. Ethan handed Havana his flashlight, and he kept Darren's camera on in front of him – not recording, but using the night vision feature to see through the darkness better.

Havana immediately spotted the area across from the attic stairs where Genevieve had landed. The bloodstain was still on the wall. She pointed the light at it and whispered Genevieve's name in Ethan's ear.

"Maybe she came to," Ethan suggested. Havana gripped the tail of his shirt in her hand and pressed her forehead to his shoulder. She'd seen Genevieve lying there, and she knew what Ethan hoped hadn't happened. Genevieve had been moved, and that wasn't to say that maybe Frank was the one who moved her.

They approached the narrow attic stairway and carefully started to ascend. Havana was sure the rapid pounding of her heartbeat would give them away, and she thought for a moment that she could even hear Ethan's in his chest as well.

They reached the door at the top of the stairs and Ethan slowly opened it. Havana remembered Genevieve had been carrying a pistol that was nowhere to be found. There were significant chances that whoever had done this was now armed – if they weren't already.

Both of them were too afraid to speak as they stepped into the short hall that separated the stair door and the closed door that led to the small attic room.

Something moved at the end of the hall to their left, and Havana closed her eyes and pressed herself tighter against Ethan. He angled the camera in that direction, and the green images on the playback screen included one of a lifeless body lying face up on the floor in the middle of the hall.

Ethan took the flashlight from Havana and motioned for her to stay put. He started inching closer to the body, sweeping the light around to ensure that no one and nothing else was there.

As he got closer, he recognized the clothes that outfitted the body, then the body itself. It was Darren!

He was dead; blood had soaked through the front of his shirt.

On the ground beside him was a pistol.

T W E N T Y

The video display showed a barely visible Frank standing at the end of the hall that opened into the lobby, talking to someone else further away and off screen. Whoever was holding the camera stayed at a twenty-foot distance.

"I thought he went to get into those rooms, but I guess not. He must've—. Scotty had to have unlocked the doors." Frank could be heard speaking on the screen, but more to himself than to whoever was listening.

Frank turned away from the camera, seemingly distracted by more reflections from that night, and started walking towards the grand staircase in the lobby. Perhaps he was about to follow whoever he had been talking to. The cameraperson stalked silently behind Frank until he reached the stairs, and then suddenly, a gloved hand wielding a heavy rock came down hard over the back of Frank's head, the camera capturing as he dropped quickly to the floor at the foot of the stairs.

The camera angle began to shift, as whoever had been recording set the camera down in a particular spot next to the stairs. The only discernable feature to be made out of the videographer was its shadowy black overcoat that reached far past the figure's knees. The screen went dark as the too-close figure struggled to lift Frank's body. Then, two feet started up the stairs and out of view.

Moments passed before Ethan's voice was heard. *"You're not gonna believe this,"* he'd said, pausing a moment before finishing. *"Dad?"*

*

Ethan closed the playback screen and shut off the camera. He was sitting with Havana in his jeep, still parked on Grand Street outside of Levenson Asylum. After finding Darren, they'd ran out of the building for their lives, determined not to wait around for the killer to attack again.

"We need to go to the police," Havana told him. "We can show them this video."

"Of what?" Ethan asked, exasperated. "We can barely make out that it's my dad. The cops are just gonna think this was something we put together to make them look like a bunch of idiots to follow up on a story out here."

"Where they will find Darren's body!" she insisted.

"If its even still there!" It wasn't his intention to snap at her, but he felt responsible for all of this because he'd lied to the cops the first time. Not only that, he felt responsible for his dad being a victim. He felt responsible for Darren and Genevieve being victims.

"Do you think Vieve fired that shot?" he asked, the image of Darren lying next to the weapon throbbing in his memory.

"I don't know," Havana said. "All I know is she had the gun."

"If she fired the gun, then there's residue on her hands," he said. The realization was a jigsaw puzzle of more questions. "Would he be trying to make it look like Vieve killed Darren? Why else would he leave the gun laying there like that?"

"Let's just call the cops," Havana said.

"We can't!" Ethan retorted. "And have them hunting Vieve as a murderer?!"

"Vieve is dead." It was a cold truth, and Ethan was within the limits of denial.

He squeezed his eyes shut, trying to get a grip on this reality. "This has gotten out of control," he said, for the first time regretting not pulling the plug on this assignment when Darren first went missing. "This was supposed to be the one assignment that had everything practically laid out in front of us, where Owens wouldn't have been able to say we didn't do enough. All of a sudden getting killed over it is a coin toss!"

Frustrated, he started up the jeep before continuing. "He does everything in his power to hold me back, to stop me from actually doing good with something. It's like he wants me to fail at life. Is it ever gonna change?" He pulled off, heading back towards home.

"I'm calling the police, Ethan." Havana reached for her cell phone and started to dial, but Ethan grabbed it from her and abruptly ended the call.

"What are you doing?!" she asked.

"The police are going to tell your father all about this, and if he finds out you were up at Levenson Asylum with me cooking up what the cops already think is a trick, you can kiss our relationship *and* my freedom goodbye."

"We have to do something," she pleaded.

"I will," he said. "Owens wants a serial killer. I'm gonna give him one. *This* one."

*

"You just got a text message from Ethan," Reagan said, picking up Lucas's phone from the console between the front seats. "Want me to read it?"

"Yeah," Lucas said. He checked his mirrors and then proceeded to merge into the lane that would allow them to get off at the next exit and lead them back to campus.

"He says meet him at his apartment."

"Call him," Lucas told her. "Put it on speaker. We're backing out of this." He glanced over at Reagan who offered him a slight smile of gratitude.

"Thanks, but Darren's still missing, and my mom clearly thinks the killer she saw up there fifteen years ago is still around," Reagan told him, sending the call to Ethan.

They'd left Glendale shortly after Robyn had calmed down and retreated back into the quieted self she was when they'd arrived. Everything she'd told them slithered uncomfortably up and down both of their spines. They weren't sure if Robyn had developed a split personality – though the nurses didn't seem to think so. Her outburst was as confusing and new to them as it had been to Reagan and Lucas.

Then there was the matter of what she said she'd seen in "that room," and why she continued to feel threatened that "he knew." Who was *he*? Reagan and Lucas were under the assumption that "he" could only be the killer, and the mention of Levenson Asylum had thrown Robyn back to that night. She had seen something, or had seen him do something – perhaps murder someone – before setting the fire. Perhaps she'd seen him set the fire.

It was the only explanation Lucas could think of as to why Robyn might have been transferred to Glendale in such a hurry. She must have grown incredibly erratic after seeing whatever she saw up in that room – to the point where Levenson had absolutely no other option. Whatever the case, seeing what she saw had saved her life.

However, it still unnerved Reagan to see her mom go in and out of the past like she did. She'd been speaking as if she was in imminent danger, having noted that she thought the killer was coming for her, and yet she knew she was no longer at Levenson. It could have simply been the case that Robyn was having delusions of Terrance Todd still being alive and coming after her, but given the fact that Darren was missing and Lucas seemed sure that someone else was killing and collecting bodies at Levenson, Reagan had brought up another theory to Lucas: What if the guy Robyn saw that night wasn't Terrance Todd? What if it was the thirteenth survivor? What if *he* was the real killer?

The theory opened up a brand new terrifying field of play, and it was one Lucas couldn't invest time in given the deadline for the project, so he offered to help Reagan figure it out if she came back to their group and they all got a different killer to profile.

She didn't give him an answer. Instead she took his offer to mean that he might have shared her theory about the thirteenth survivor, and she needed to find out who and where this person was. They needed to find out *now*.

Ethan greeted after the second ring. "Where are you?"

"We're headed back to campus," Lucas said. "I've got you on speaker. Reagan is with me."

"I'm here with Havana," Ethan said, pulling his jeep to a stop across the street from the Owens' house. He switched his phone to speaker so Havana could listen. "We just left Levenson."

The hesitation in Ethan's voice was unmistakable.

"What happened?" Lucas asked.

"We found Darren," he confirmed. "He's dead."

Assumption had been a pebble in Lucas's stomach compared to this boulder of knowledge. When Darren was just missing, there'd still been a small chance that this was all one of his practical jokes. Now knowing for sure that he was dead made Lucas feel like they were all in some way accomplices.

"The police...?" Lucas asked, knowing the answer.

"No, and there's more," Ethan replied. "Vieve is missing."

Lucas slammed his brakes, provoking a pick up truck behind him to honk furiously before swerving to pass and move on.

"And so is my dad," Ethan finished, figuring he should give all the news at once. "I found the camera, and whoever attacked my dad has it on film. All of Darren's footage is erased."

"Wait a minute," Reagan spoke up. "You've got this guy on video?"

"Trust me, it's not enough to show the police," Ethan said. "Given how they feel about us."

Lucas pulled his car over to the side of the road to continue the conversation.

"So what happened to Vieve," he asked.

"We went in together," Havana said. "It's a long story, but somehow we ended up in the attic, and she was attacked by this guy. I'm pretty sure she's... I'm pretty sure she's dead."

"Up in the attic?" Reagan repeated, catching Lucas's eyes. Neither of them could forget about the room Robyn had referenced.

"Any idea who could be doing this? Maybe a family member of one of those victims you're researching?" Ethan asked.

Lucas peered at Reagan, their eyes communicating whether or not to share her theory.

"My mother was at Levenson that night," she blurted. "She wasn't there when the fire got started, so she wasn't counted as one of the survivors. But she thinks... well *we* think we're dealing with the thirteenth survivor."

"Wait a minute, Lucas, you knew Reagan's mom was there that night and you didn't tell us?" Ethan asked, irate. "Do you know the only reason I roped my dad into this was because you all thought it would be for the good of the project?!"

"Pump your brakes, Foster," Lucas said. "It wasn't my place to put Reagan's business out there like that."

"Well why didn't Reagan speak up before ditching our group? Or was that why you ditched us?" Ethan asked.

"None of that matters," Reagan replied.

"It doesn't matter?! *My* dad could be dead right now!" Ethan shouted.

Havana placed her hand against the back of his neck to calm him down. There was a long silence.

"What's her name?" Ethan finally asked. "Where is she now?"

"Why?" asked Lucas. "So you can go track her down? Not gonna happen."

"I am entitled to research," Ethan said. "Look, I promise I won't track her down. Enough people have died already because of this."

Lucas sent Reagan a look that told her she didn't have to give up any information if she didn't want to. She spoke anyway.

"Robyn Edgefield," she said. "She'd been a nurse before she got admitted into Levenson a few months after I was born. She was being transferred to another institution the day of the fire because we think she had some kind of episode after she encountered something up at Levenson. She kept rambling about 'that room up there,' so it might have been the attic. She might have seen the killer."

"Where is she now?" Ethan repeated. Part of him felt upset and the other part guilty that Reagan's mom had been admitted into Levenson for probably endangering people's lives and escaped all of this completely unscathed, when his dad was there to save lives and it might have just cost him his.

"That's enough," Lucas said. "I'm sorry, but knowing everything about Robyn Edgefield is not gonna change what may or may *not* have happened to your dad. He's a fireman. He knows how to get out of a dangerous situation."

"What if he can't this time?" Ethan asked. "We can't file a

missing persons for 24 hours, and God only knows what could happen by then. I have to catch this guy."

"We both agree," Reagan said, speaking for Lucas. "I'm coming back to the group, and we'll all figure out what's going on up there. I may have an idea of how we can find out who that thirteenth survivor is."

"How?" Lucas asked.

"Let's go back to your place," she told him. "I'll make a few calls."

Lucas told Ethan he'd give him a ring later with any updates, and the two of them ended the call.

"This is the plan?" Ethan asked, skeptical. "Just the three of us playing Scooby Doo?"

"Four," Havana said.

"No." Ethan's adamant refusal caught Havana off guard.

"You need all the help you can get," she argued.

"You are in high school! I'm not gonna be responsible for you like this. I have too much on my mind."

"And it's my fault," she said. That he couldn't respond told her she'd found truth. She'd fought to have this secret relationship with him, and refused to make things easier by breaking it off the minute her father started suspecting. It was the reason Owens was so tough on him now.

Of course, he could have broken it off with her himself, but he truly cared for Havana. At the very beginning, he may have been doing it out of spite – to have something of Owens' and delight in the professor not being able to figure it out. But along the way, Havana became his comfortable place. He didn't have to prove himself with her as he had to with Owens. He didn't have to retreat emotionally as he had to with his parents. And most of all, Havana had become his support, his motivation, and the secret weapon of his heart.

"I'm involved, Ethan," Havana continued. "I don't care anymore. This is important. If we can't do anything about my dad, at least we can do something about yours."

"No. If something happened to you..." He looked into her eyes, pleading with her to just this once listen to him. "I need you the most."

She stared at him a moment, trying to decide whether or not to smile. "If this is your lame way of telling me that you love me, Ethan Foster…"

He returned her gaze, a serious look on his face. "I thought you knew that already."

The curl on her lip disappeared, and her eyes pinned love in his. She wanted to kiss him. She wanted to be with him, regardless of the consequences. He could have asked her for the moon right then and she would fly.

"Don't let me interrupt," came a voice from behind them.

Abducted from their moment, they both tossed their glances at the sidewalk where Carter was standing on the curb, disgust etched into his face.

Ethan exhaled a dejected sigh.

"Get out of the car." Carter glared angrily at Havana.

She opened the door and started to climb out of the jeep. "Before you say anything Daddy, let me talk."

"More lies, Havana?" he asked.

"Professor Owens, it's not what you think," Ethan started. He climbed out of the jeep and rounded the back to join Carter on the curb.

"Oh it's exactly what I think. You two ditch school and run off to play 'Daddy Doesn't Have a Clue.'"

"It's not like that," Ethan tried again, scrambling to stay calm in order to salvage whatever he could of either relationship once the dust settled. "Havana and I—"

"We're in love," Havana declared, boldly planting her gaze on her father. She'd had enough of this. "So whatever you and Genevieve Davis were talking about this morning, it's over."

"Wait," Ethan said, now struggling to catch up. "What are you doing?"

"I overheard Daddy and Vieve in our living room this morning," Havana told Ethan, not taking her eyes off of Carter. "Tell me you weren't trying to bribe her into breaking us up, Daddy."

"That had nothing to do with you, Havana," Carter replied. "But I guess it should have."

"Wrong." She wanted a jumpstart on his temper. She had a

right to be angry, too. "You weren't gonna be satisfied until you found out, well here! *I'm* telling you. Ethan and I are together. We've been together since last summer, and he has done nothing but try to get you to see that he's not the lazy, lying failure you seem to think he is – those were your exact words this morning, right?"

"Yes, and entirely appropriate. Now get in the house," he ordered.

"Not until you tell me why it matters so much to you that Ethan is the guy I want to be with."

"Look at you," Carter said, disdain dripping from him like sweat. "You've been running around trying to cover this up for months, lying to everybody, skipping school, putting your mother and me through hell wondering where you are at all hours of the night, and you stand here *bare-faced* demanding to know why it matters?!"

Havana suddenly realized she hadn't thought the argument all the way through, and regretted momentarily that she might have done Ethan more harm than good. But then she remembered the moment before they were interrupted just now, and remembered why she wanted to come clean to her father about their relationship.

"Neither of us wanted to sneak around," she told him. "Regardless of how hard he was trying, for whatever reason you were firing shots at his future already. We didn't want to give you more ammunition. But if you're gonna fail him anyway, why keep hiding this? I'm tired of being scared of you. It was wrong to lie, and I'm sorry, but your threats and your bullying pushed us to it."

Ethan knew either Havana or Owens was waiting on him to speak up, but he had nothing to add. In fact, part of him was suddenly relieved that this was out in the open now. Havana was right, if Owens was going to fail him for this, then there would be no need for him to obsess about the project anymore, and he could focus entirely on finding out who was responsible for whatever was going on at Levenson.

Havana continued, taking a step towards her father. "Why do you need to make it so hard for him? You don't know half of what he's been through, or what he's going through."

"Oh I know exactly what he's going through," Carter said, glaring at Ethan. "And it's gonna get worse."

Was Owens talking about Ethan's shot at passing the class, or something else? Ethan wasn't completely sure and it terrified him given what he *was* going through.

"What does that mean?" he asked Carter in a tone mixed with anger and suspicion.

"The reason Genevieve Davis came to see me this morning was to ask for an extension on your project," Carter told him. "She said Darren Gabriel is missing."

Ethan thought he saw a smirk on Owens' face, but in a blink it had faded.

"There will be no extension," Carter continued. "And the next time you take a field trip up to Levenson Asylum, go alone."

Chills paralyzed Ethan. Sure, Genevieve probably told Owens their project was on Terrance Todd and that they had been doing research up at Levenson, but the way Owens' threat – if that's what it was – came across just now, it was as if he *wanted* Ethan to go up there alone, even when he'd been told (or knew?) that Darren was missing.

Or was he referring to keeping Havana away from there?

He tried his best to push the ideas that were running rampant throughout his mind aside for the sake of clarification. "Genevieve is..." He let the rest of it hang there, watching Owens' reaction. Did he already know Genevieve was dead?

Owens' stoic expression did not refute Ethan's fears. His dark eyes could have hidden the entire history of life.

Or the past few days of death.

Ethan needed to provoke a reaction. He needed to make Owens smirk again before he could start down a recklessly theoretical path of suspicion. Owens was waiting on him to say something, and he had to choose his words carefully.

"Genevieve is against the wall." Ethan waited for Owens' reaction. The slightest flinch or smirk would signal that Owens knew Ethan was alluding to the truth that Genevieve was dead.

Owens tilted his head slightly, his eyes locked on Ethan's.

"I doubt that," he replied.

T W E N T Y O N E

The tug of war with horrific speculation had ended in a standoff, and Ethan had been figuratively gunned down by his own unshakeable suspicion. Owens didn't explode, as expected, upon finding out the truth about his relationship with Havana. He didn't ask any questions about Darren. Genevieve was a brief waltz of a conversation, and it seemed Owens had let Ethan lead. All the landmines were triggered, but none of them went off.

He couldn't wrap his brain around it all at once, and wrestled with everything that had happened outside of Owens' house as he drove toward Lucas's apartment complex. Logic wanted him to think that Owens believed Darren wasn't really missing, and Genevieve was alive. Perhaps Owens was simply trying to call their bluff, believing they were just trying to get their extension on the project. It was clear that he was tired of Havana's disobedience, and his tank of tolerance with Ethan had been empty since last year. Maybe this was Owens at the end of his rope, and he was set to fail Ethan no matter what just out of spite.

That was logical. The gnawing feeling in his gut replayed the images of Owens' I-dare-you temperament, and the double meanings of every sentence he uttered about Genevieve.

She's up against the wall.

It was a direct reference to where her body had landed after she was, according to Havana, knocked down the stairway.

I doubt it.

Vieve was never a desperate student. And she wasn't still slumped against the wall at Levenson when Ethan and Havana left.

*

"I have good news, and I have bad news." Reagan entered the living room from Lucas's bedroom and joined him on the couch. He finished typing out a sentence on his laptop before giving her his full attention.

"I just got off the phone with Glendale, and we were right," she continued. "Whenever a patient was being transferred from Levenson, they would get placed at Glendale."

"Which means odds are likely that's where the thirteenth survivor was sent after Terrance Todd committed suicide," Lucas said.

"Odds are definite," Reagan confirmed. "The bad news is they wouldn't give me this patient's name, of course. After I told the people in the Records Office that my mom was unnerved at the prospect of running into anyone from Levenson – which that orderly who came in could attest to – I got them to dig around a little bit and get this, that patient was released from Glendale ten years ago."

"So they're out roaming the street? This is definitely our guy."

"All we need to do is identify him," she said, acknowledging the mountain of a feat that would be. "What are the chances there'd be fingerprints on Darren's camera?"

They both took a moment to consider alternative ways to finding out the identity of Survivor #13, and all roads led them straight to the local police.

"What if we tell them we've seen some stranger lurking around up there. They'd have to follow up on it, right?" Reagan asked. "Especially if we told them we know for a fact this guy is out of Glendale."

A frantic knock at the door interrupted Lucas's response. He yelled that the door was open, and Ethan entered.

"Just in time, Foster," Lucas said, rotating his laptop towards Ethan. "We're up to six pages on Terrance Todd. Medical records and newspaper articles alone. Plus, I did a Nexis search and found out a ton of information about how he slaughtered his grandparents. And so far, I've found that seven of the eleven Hunter victims were found blind-folded. Could be a signature—"

"Blind-folded?!" Reagan turned the laptop to face her, reeling from this bit of information. She immediately remembered Robyn noting earlier how she wasn't supposed to see it, and her raspy, child-like lullaby echoed hauntingly in her ears: *You will see, you will see.*

"I thought the same thing," Lucas said, reading her mind. He turned to Ethan to explain. "Robyn Edgefield kept talking about something she saw, and that he comes for those who know, or something like that. We think she was talking about the thirteenth survivor – the *real* killer. The one who let Terrance Todd take the fall. The one who is still out there."

"I'm sorry," Ethan said, confused. "Then why are we writing this report on Terrance Todd if you don't think he killed all those people?"

"Because we have no way of finding out who this person is unless the police get bored," Lucas answered. "And right now, this thirteenth survivor scenario is just our assumption. Besides, the cops and everybody else in this town believe Todd did it. It's a clean case, and there's tons of stuff to include for this project."

"So wait." Ethan shifted his gaze to Reagan. "Your *mom* thinks this killer is still out there?"

"If you're gonna make some joke about her being in the loony bin, then save it," Reagan said.

"No, I agree with her. I just don't think it's this thirteenth survivor ya'll are obsessed with. Yesterday, my dad said none of the officials working that fire could be sure only thirteen people survived. They were just trying to prevent mass panic, so when the murders stopped with Todd's suicide, they basically told the press thirteen and crossed their fingers that another body wouldn't turn up."

"No disrespect to your father, but it doesn't make any sense that the cops would put a cap on the number of victims," Reagan said. "And it's just a bit too convenient that it ended up being thirteen, don't you think?"

"Wait a minute." Lucas started digging through the manila

folder of printouts Genevieve had given him. "Remember that first day we went out to Levenson, and Vieve was going through all the different versions of what people said happened. One of them was this story that people thought the police didn't give a shit and basically let the place burn because it was full of criminals who had unjustly copped an insanity plea." He pulled out a printout with details of the story and handed it to Reagan.

"You think a *cop* might be the killer?" Reagan reeled, reconciling all the inexplicable aspects of the case that would make sense under this new theory. Why the cops weren't taking any of the current events seriously. How the murders conveniently stopped when Terrance Todd and Survivor #13 were apprehended. The unquestionable must-be-guilty suicide. Todd was snuffed out and then framed. By the police department.

"No, it's not the police. It's not the thirteenth survivor!" Ethan was frustrated by the possibility that his next statement would be met with ridicule. "It's Owens!"

The silence was stale. Neither Lucas nor Reagan knew what to say.

"I know it sounds ridiculous, but hear me out," Ethan explained. "They moved here in '95 – a year before the fire. Havana always said he was very distant back then. He was always gone for days or weeks at a time until sometime after the fire. We all know he's got anger issues, and flips out on people like me for no apparent reason."

"You're dating his daughter," Lucas said, amused.

"Which we came clean about today, by the way, and he practically sent me off with a pat on the back!" Ethan knew there was no convincing them. He could tell by the incredulous way they were looking at him. "It doesn't faze him that Darren is missing. He knew we were up at Levenson today. He knew details about what happened to Vieve. He didn't come right out and say it, but I could tell he knows she's dead."

Lucas paused for a moment. "I'm gonna say it," he started, looking intently at Ethan. "Only because you need to hear it."

Ethan rolled his eyes. He knew what was coming.

"We're talking about a man who expressly hates you, and who holds your somewhat hard-earned college degree in the palm of his hands. You're in love with his daughter. Getting him out of your way will make things easier for you, and pinning these murders on him is one calculated way to do that."

"What if I'm right?" Ethan asked, still not expecting a real answer. "Just *what if* I'm right? What if he killed those eleven people, and when Terrance Todd got arrested, he decided that was his perfect out? What if by doing this project – for *him* – we got a little too close to the truth, and he had to kill again to keep this secret? When Havana and I found Darren's body today, he was laying face up in the middle of the hall with a bullet in his chest. There was a gun laying on the floor beside him. I'm telling you Owens hinted to me today that he knows what's going on. He knew Havana and I were up at Levenson because he was there! He killed Darren. He killed Vieve." He glowered. "My dad…"

He didn't try to hide the fact that he was upset. He suddenly wasn't sure he wanted Lucas and Reagan to believe him. Part of him wanted them to convince him that this was crazy – that there was no chance any of this was possible.

"I guess we shouldn't rule out anything," Lucas said.

It wasn't what Ethan needed to hear. He'd just given a prosecutor's closing statements at his own trial, and the jury was buying it.

"But what do you suggest we do?" Lucas continued. "Ask him flat out if he's a serial killer?"

"Let's be careful here," Reagan chimed in. "We're tying our college professor to a string of murders based on a flimsy collection of insinuations and coincidences."

Another knock at the door caught them all by surprise. Ethan walked over to the door to answer it, and found a police officer standing on the other side.

"Does Lucas Dutch live here?" the officer asked.

"I'm Lucas." Lucas stood up, apprehensive. "Is something wrong?"

"That's what I'd like to know. I'm James," the officer introduced. "I'm Darren's cousin. My family hasn't been able to get in touch with him for the past few days. When he didn't show up for Sunday dinner like he normally does, my mom started to panic."

Lucas and Ethan exchanged glances, both wondering where this was going to end up.

"I promised her I'd drop by his dorm room after my shift this afternoon, and his roommate told me you'd been the last person over there asking about him."

Ethan could tell Lucas wasn't sure how to respond. Was this an investigation? Even if it wasn't yet, it was bound to be one.

"I know where he is," Ethan spoke up, deciding to take this opportunity for what it was. "We tried to tell you guys what happened, but none of the cops took us seriously."

James looked at Ethan, confused.

"I'm Ethan Foster. Darren was working on a class project with us up at Levenson Asylum." Ethan stalled, not sure how to continue. "You should get up there and see for yourself."

"What exactly am I gonna find?" If he wasn't here on official police business when he arrived, James was transforming from cousin to cop right before their eyes.

"Look, whatever the cops thought was finished fifteen years ago has been rebooted. Someone is up there." Ethan was having a hard time telling a cop that his own cousin was dead. "People are dying."

James looked at each of them one at a time, trying to fill in the blanks of what he was hearing.

"What does Darren have to do with this?" he asked them.

"He's dead, Officer," Ethan said. "He's dead. And so is Genevieve Davis. And so is my father. Now please tell me you can help us catch the guy who's doing this."

"I'm gonna need you to come with me," James told Ethan, reaching for his handcuffs.

"What?!"

"You just told me that three people are dead," he said. "You can either come down to the station with me for questioning, or we can all wait here while I call for backup."

"You've got to be kidding me!" Ethan exclaimed.

"I'm not kidding," James said. "And if you had anything to do with what's happened to Darren, take *this* seriously, Levenson will be a Bed and Breakfast compared to where you'll end up."

"We'll both go," Lucas said. "We're not under arrest, right?

We'll tell them what we can, and see if they can at least send some cops down to Levenson to check it out."

"What about you?" James asked Reagan. "Are you a part of this?"

"She's never been to Levenson," Lucas said, trying to usher James and Ethan towards the door. "Once we tell you who we think it is, maybe you can get them to the station, too," he said, directing the hint at Reagan. He winked at her on his way out the door, hoping she understood what he was trying to tell her to do.

*

Carter stood at the door to Havana's bedroom, banging his fist against it angrily.

"Havana, open this door!" he shouted, the words and actions like a sucker-punch to his memory, making him that much more furious. "Open the damned door!"

There was no response.

He suddenly thought maybe she'd climbed out of her bedroom window and took off in a defiant attempt to go be with Ethan. The thought sent heat pulsating throughout him, and he stepped back against the wall opposite her door. Before he knew what he was doing, he'd lifted his foot and kicked at the door with such immense fury that it cracked and fell open.

Havana jumped from her bed, startled by both the crash and her father's entrance. His dark eyes glowered at her, a mix of disappointment and pure anger. For a long moment, neither of them said a word, and it only added to Havana's discomfort.

"I'm already grounded," she said, struggling to keep the sarcasm in her tone from biting.

Lucinda appeared at the broken doorway, aghast by the scene.

"What on earth..." she managed to say, teetering between the decision whether or not to enter.

"You think I set rules for fun?" Carter finally asked his daughter.

"Yes," she replied. "There is no reason for you to be this upset about me going out with Ethan. He respects me. He loves me. He makes me happy."

"You haven't deserved happiness," he growled. "I know you skipped school today to go running around on your little excursion with him. I stayed home from work today knowing I'd catch you two together. You've been sneaking around, lying, doing whatever you want, and you turn around and expect us to let you have your fun?! Where do you get the nerve?"

"What fun?" she retaliated. "Ethan is all I want, and if you would get out of the way, and stop trying to hold him down just to spite me, I wouldn't have spent the past year lying and sneaking around. Yeah, a hell of a lot of fun that was."

"Havana," Lucinda spoke up calmingly.

"He's an amoral, irresponsible slack-ass, and you're my daughter," Carter said. "There's only one place this relationship's gonna end up, and I'm not gonna stand here and watch that happen."

"What are you talking about?" Havana asked, boldly keeping her eyes on his. "He has done nothing but try to live up to your standard. He wouldn't even touch me out of respect for you. If that's amoral or irresponsible, then maybe I should go find a nice rapist."

She was irate, and knew she had no right to speak to her father like this, but he hadn't given her one legitimate reason why he was so against Ethan, and she knew it was because there wasn't one.

"You want to know what else he's done?" she continued. "This project you've got them doing on serial killers, they might have uncovered an active one right in our own back yard. You want to know why we were up at Levenson today? Because people are in danger right now, Daddy. Darren and Genevieve are dead, and Ethan is still going on with this project just to prove to you that he's not what you think he is. His own dad could be dead for going in there with him today."

"And there you go, frolicking into this danger right beside him," Carter said. "I'm supposed to be okay with that? Suppose you had gotten killed. Or is that the sacrifice you're willing to make for this true love of yours?" He waited for her to respond, knowing he had given her something real to think about. "You would die for him?"

She softened, but realized her true feelings as she spoke the words: "I would die to protect him."

"That makes you stupid," he told her. "And you will not go back up to that burned out building again. Do I make myself clear?"

She didn't respond.

"Murders," he continued, scoffing. "You honestly think if people were being murdered up there, the cops wouldn't be all over it by now?"

"They don't believe it," she answered. "But it's only a matter of time now that we've found someone who might actually know who this killer is. If it's the same guy, Reagan said her mother might have information."

"*Reagan's* mother?" Carter asked, illustrating the absurdity of how interconnected this seemed to be.

"Robyn Edgefield," Havana said. "She used to be a nurse a long time ago. She was there the night Levenson burned down."

Carter froze. His face flushed, sucking all of its color into a drain that led to the pit of his stomach where it churned.

"She knows exactly what's going on," Havana continued. "And as soon as Ethan finds a way to get her to talk to the police, you can believe he's gonna hand over this killer."

Carter's eyes caught hers, and he immediately identified her determination.

"Flunk him then," she said, almost daring him, and then left him alone in the room.

†ᴡᴇɴ†ʏ †ᴡᴏ

GREENVILLE, NORTH CAROLINA – 1986

He remembered the midnight sky, dancing with flashes of red and blue. The urgent, demanding voices around him. Then blackness. He remembered the emergency sirens wailing, and himself strapped to a blood-stained gurney, his nose and mouth covered by a plastic mask that blew painful air into his facial orifices, then blackness. He remembered screaming in agony as they hoisted him off of the gurney and onto an operating table, and the sensation of needles puncturing muscles, and cloth attached to skin being separated from epidermis and dermis. Then blackness.

He awoke lying on his side, surrounded by the sounds of machines. Everything audible was magnified. He could hear beeping, dripping, humming, whirring, and even the hallway chatter, which made him aware that he was close to a nurse's station. He knew he was in Intensive Care.

Owen Carter pried his eyes open. When he blinked, a tear fell onto the pillow, and left a red stain as it trailed down towards the sheet. He wasn't crying. Opening his eyes had drawn blood. The morphine dulled the pain, but didn't alleviate it completely, and did absolutely nothing to numb the excruciating shock of being alive.

He couldn't move. He was propped up on his side, and had nearly a dozen wires or IVs attached to him. The florescent lights were off, but the one over his bed was bright, and gave him enough light to make out the pea green walls of his hospital room.

No one was here visiting. No one was waiting for him to wake up.

The explosion came back to him first, and his memory started rebuilding itself backwards. He'd frantically tried to open the bathroom door, unaware of how out of control the fire in the tub had spread. He heard Daniel crying on the other side of the door. He'd yelled at him. He'd smashed his fist into the mirror. He'd vomited in the sink. He'd poured chemicals into the tub. Pine Sol. He could still smell Pine Sol.

His memory stopped there, and refused to fill in the rest for now. It seemed like it had happened years ago, but a calendar on the back of the door facing him told him at least the month was still the same. He lifted his palm to his face. He needed to see what was there and what wasn't, since he could hardly feel anything. His palm looked fine, but as he rotated his wrist he found that the backside of his hand was terribly scarred. He followed the scars up the length of his arm, patches of skin missing in places. He felt a tear breach in his eye, and forfeited the fight to will it away. It fell, the salty fluid a string of fire across his cheek. Perhaps he only felt it burn because he knew it was there.

For whatever he didn't know was there, he felt nothing. There had been a vacancy in his heart for years, and loss simply didn't register. Those who had stopped caring about him only taught him how to stop caring. He remembered a wife, Catherine. They'd never been in love, and he knew the only thing in her heart for him was expectation. She expected his money. She expected his success. She expected him to be a man he wasn't sure he knew how to be. He'd rarely seen his father be a man – at least a sober one. He married Catherine for their son, Daniel, who deserved two parents who could support each other when the chips were down. But the chips had been depleted, and Catherine still expected a successful doctor and supportive husband who was always available to their son. Expectation kicked his ass and tossed a lighted match on hers.

The memory filled in and solidified. Their argument. The stairs. Her body in the bathtub. The fire. The explosion. All the scenes came together like a nightmare, and panic punctuated it.

What did they think happened?

The door to his room swung open before he could theorize, and a young raven-haired nurse entered. She had a calm demeanor that implied sympathy. It eased him a little. As she approached his bed, she locked her eyes to his. Her sorrow was a laser beam that pierced into him.

"You're awake," she said. "Are you in any pain?" As she reached up to check his IV, her nametag met him at eye level. Robyn Edgefield. Nurse.

He gave a slight shake of his head to indicate he wasn't.

"What..." he murmured, surprised that even though his mouth was dry, it didn't pain him to speak. "What happened?"

He could tell she was struggling for words. Not knowing what she wanted to tell him made him afraid that cops were waiting in the hall to arrest him for murdering his wife and son in that fire.

"You have..." she started, choking back tears, "such a brave little boy."

Wait, what?!

It sat on his chest like a brick. What had Daniel told them? Did he tell the police he'd found his father burning his mother's body?

"Mr. Carter, " she continued. "There's something you need to know." She could barely remove her eyes from his, and they seared into him. "We've done something we shouldn't have."

He had no idea where this was going, but he knew Robyn Edgefield could hardly pull herself together to tell him. Whatever she had to say, he knew it was serious enough to not just be a blip on the radar. He knew from the way she looked at him that this would be the woman who would headline a shift in the course of his life.

"What happened?" he repeated, insistently.

The door to the room opened again, and a slightly overweight doctor entered. Robyn glanced over at him, and the stern expression he gave her made her back away from Owen's bedside.

"Robyn, what have you told him?" the doctor asked.

"I haven't said anything yet," she answered. "But he needs to know. You have to tell him before this goes any further."

"Before what goes any further?" Owen asked. "What happened to my son?" The beeping heart monitor sped up, racing to match

Owen's anxiety.

"Just calm down, Mr. Carter," the doctor said. "I'm Dr. Harold Ashley. I've been overseeing your son's… situation."

"What situation?" Owen asked, upset that he still hadn't gotten any answers. He glanced over at Robyn in the corner of the room. She had her hand covering her mouth, her wet eyes drooping in sorrow. "Tell me," he demanded.

"He's stable," Dr. Ashley said. "For the moment."

"I want to see him," Owen said, making a feeble effort to sit up.

"We can't do that," Dr. Ashley told him.

"Why not?"

"We can't move him right now, and you've sustained second and third degree burns in some areas we can't even treat yet. We can't let you out of this room."

"It's a miracle both of you survived," Robyn uttered.

Dr. Ashley looked over at her again, and Owen tried to study their nonverbal communication.

"Give us a minute?" Dr. Ashley asked her.

"No," she answered, resolutely.

"Be a nurse and do your job, Robyn," he said. "Let me do mine."

She waited a moment, assessing her role here. "You tell him the truth," she said. "All of it." She stepped out of the room, purposely not allowing the door to close all the way behind her. She left it open just enough for her to eavesdrop and make sure Dr. Ashley didn't wrap the unspeakable truth up in a fancy package for this boy's father.

Dr. Ashley waited a moment until he was sure Robyn was gone before he spoke.

"Your son is in critical condition, Mr. Carter," he started. "When they brought him in, when they brought both of you in tonight, we were looking at burns so severe we thought for sure we were going to lose you both before we could even begin treatments for shock."

"But you didn't." For a moment, Owen couldn't mask his panic.

"We lost him for a minute…" Dr. Ashley said, struggling. "And then, by some miracle we found a heartbeat again. It was very weak. It was going in and out, really, so I administered an experimental drug – an injection I've been working on with a colleague here. It's like electroshock therapy without the shock. It's designed to have the same effect as caffeine on the heart, only a bit more powerful and immediate and over a shorter duration. We didn't expect that it would cause a mild cardiac episode."

"An episode? You mean he had a heart attack?" Owen asked, offering Dr. Ashley the words he was clearly trying to avoid.

"A very mild one," Dr. Ashley continued. "But then he started to have convulsions. Oxygen flow to his brain had stopped in that moment we thought we'd lost him, and the treatment must have jumpstarted his heart much faster than we anticipated. I'm not sure."

"So what's the situation now?" Owen asked.

"His vitals have dropped again. Drastically," Dr. Ashley admitted. "We know the serum works. Now I can dilute it and inject him again, but I can't be sure it won't have the same effect or, without a blood transfusion, combine with what's already in his system and make things worse. Time is very critical right now. We'd just need your permission."

Owen stalled a long moment, staring at the wall beyond the doctor.

"I don't want to rush you, but we don't have time to waste," Dr. Ashley said.

"You need my permission…"

"Yes."

"You didn't need my permission the first time?" There was a detectable bite to Owen's question.

"You've been unconscious until now," Dr. Ashley said. "We weren't sure… *I* wasn't sure you'd wake up in time. I needed to save him."

"But you didn't know if it would save him," Owen said. He had Dr. Ashley right where he wanted him. "And you went ahead and administered an experimental treatment on my son without any approval."

"I brought him back." Dr. Ashley was fighting the urge to crumble against his own unspoken admission of guilt. While it may not have been the ideal circumstance to test his serum, protocol would have wasted time and turned this into a much more tragic conversation. Ethics aside, he thought he'd made the best decision.

"And injecting him again without a transfusion..." Owen inquired. "This could...?"

Dr. Ashley stared down at Owen, the truth grim. "It could kill him," he said. "But I could dilute it by seventy percent, and it would be like a static shock. Very small."

Owen brought his eyes to Dr. Ashley's, and with unmistakable intent, the words came out: "Kill him."

Dr. Ashley twisted his face in confusion. "I'm sorry?" he said, begging for clarity.

Owen kept his voice low, but annunciated. "I said kill him."

Dr. Ashley's search for words was short. Thoughts became verbal before he could even process and filter them. "I can't do that. I can give him a diluted amount just because we know it could work. I'll bring him back again."

"To *this*?!" Owen was seething. "You said the burns are severe. What kind of life will that be to live and look like that? Years of hating himself and blaming himself for what happened? He's not even eight years old yet. He won't be able to handle all the surgeries it's going to take to make him look normal again – if he ever could. Saving him would be a mistake. I mean, having him go through that would be a mistake."

Dr. Ashley stared at him in disbelief. "I can't even believe you're suggesting this. I can't... I *won't*."

"You already did," Owen said. "You almost killed my son once without my permission, why the sudden hesitation knowing I'm armed with a malpractice suit?"

"This is your child," Dr. Ashley beseeched. He knew his earlier indiscretion had him now at Owen Carter's mercy. "Why would you want this?"

"Time is ticking," Owen replied. "We don't want another miracle, now do we?"

Dr. Ashley backed away from the bedside slowly, waiting for Owen to retract everything he'd just ordered, blaming it on the drugs. What father would do this, even if their reasons were as justified?

Owen watched threateningly as the doctor headed for the door.

Daniel would remember everything and send him to prison for murder. Catherine was dead, and there'd be no one to take care of him, and no one would be able to handle the surgeries, least of all Daniel himself. This was the best thing to do. Put Daniel out of his misery so that Owen could be free of his own. The lone survivor of this American tragedy – the night someone broke into their home, and left his family for dead. He'd have everyone's sympathy, and no one would question it if he decided to leave town and never look back.

Dr. Ashley yanked open the door and rushed out of the room. Robyn Edgefield appeared from around the corner. She'd heard it all, and watched as Dr. Ashley headed into Daniel's operating room. Seconds later, orderlies emerged from the room as if they'd been told to evacuate. He was going through with it.

She couldn't think anymore. She knew what was going on around her, but couldn't wrap her mind around it. It couldn't be. She reached for the doorknob of Owen's room, and slowly pushed it open – just enough to see Owen Carter, still laying on his side, a hideously burned face surrounding dark eyes which stared directly into her, unblinking, unflinching, uncaring.

She jumped back, squeezing her eyes shut and pressing herself against the wall to be out of his line of sight. Malevolent darkness had escorted Dr. Ashley out of Owen Carter's room, and part of it lingered tauntingly just inches in front of her. She could sense it breathing on her, but made the bold choice to open her eyes anyway. Drenched in pure terror, she met the glare of this translucent manifestation and saw it shift into her own reflection – a Robyn who would have to live and die with this inside.

And suddenly she became the reflection, trapped in the portal of a dark dimension with no exits. She caught one last glimpse of the old Robyn and let out a grievous, endless cry for the loss. She was from henceforth a prison cell, and the inmate inside had marked her with screams no one would hear but her.

TWENTY THREE

Ethan rested his head on the same table where he had hours ago first implicated his girlfriend's father as a suspect for murder. It was going on midnight, and he'd been hashing and rehashing all of the last five days with officers and detectives since earlier this afternoon. Finally, he'd been left alone for the past hour or so, forced to wonder if any of this would make a difference.

He hadn't seen Lucas since they arrived at the police station and both of them were led off into different interrogation rooms. It didn't worry him at all, because he knew whatever Lucas told them would line up with everything he'd told them himself. From the insane class assignment, to losing Darren at Levenson, to the bodies that were hanging in the basement – it was all out on the table as well.

He was still hanging onto the hope that Reagan had picked up Lucas's hint and somehow managed to convince Professor Owens to come down to the station with her. With each passing hour that hope diminished, and now it seemed like the only shot Ethan had at being believed. But what would that accomplish? He already knew Owens had a special way of admitting something without actually admitting it, and there was simply no incentive for him to come down here – other than to throw his own stones at Ethan, casting further doubt on the credibility of his suspicions, and possibly even pointing a finger at him as this alleged murderer.

Whatever happened, getting Owens down to the police station

was going to be the first hurdle. Once he was surrounded by cops, he'd be confronted with the fact that he was a suspect who fit the profile of a serial killer. How would he talk his way out of that, and how soon would it be before he made his first mistake?

He surprised himself, having retained some education about the operations of a killer after all. There was a certain degree of tragic Greek irony in the idea that perhaps the self-righteous teacher had in fact taught his most reviled student how to bring him down.

The door to the small room opened, and an officer Ethan recognized from one of his earlier rehashings stepped aside to allow Lucas to enter.

"What's going on?" Ethan asked. "Is he here?"

"No," Lucas answered. "But Reagan is, and she's not alone." He stepped into the room followed by Reagan and Havana.

Ethan's face dropped. "What are you doing?!"

"You can all wait here," the officer said. "Ferguson is on his way back from Levenson. He's gonna want to talk to all of you." Without any further information, he left the room, closing the door behind him.

"Are you alright?" Havana asked Ethan, taking a vacant chair beside him.

Ethan looked up at Lucas and Reagan, wondering how much Havana knew – if she knew they were all suspecting her father of murder.

"I wasn't gonna stay home," Havana continued. "When Reagan showed up and told me you were down at the police station, I knew I needed to be here. I can tell them what happened to Vieve."

"I think we need to be careful about what we talk about in here," Lucas said, nodding towards a huge mirror on one of the side walls.

"Where's your dad?" Ethan asked Havana.

"Who cares?" she shrugged. "He flipped out after you left. I've never seen him so angry. He actually kicked down my bedroom door! But let him have his tantrum, this is more important. And if he can't realize what risks you've taken just to prove yourself to him, then we don't need his approval anyway."

It seemed she wasn't aware. Ethan glanced up once again at Reagan, who discreetly shook her head to confirm it for him.

"I tried to tell him you're putting everything into this project and how determined you are to find this killer. He didn't want to hear any of it, so I left. When I got back home, he was gone."

"I'd called all of his numbers, and ended up going to his house when I couldn't reach him," Reagan told Ethan. "That's when I ran into Havana."

Havana tossed a confused look at Reagan. "You were there for *him*?" she asked, puzzled. "Why were you looking for my dad?"

Reagan's gaze traveled from Havana to Ethan. She didn't want to be the one to drop that bomb, so she'd lied about the reason for her visit when she knocked on the door of the Owens' residence and Havana answered.

Ethan waited a long moment, scrambling for the best way to answer Havana. "He knew we were up at Levenson today," he said, cautiously. "Maybe he was there. Maybe he saw something."

Havana's brows furrowed as she studied Ethan's eyes to figure out what he wasn't saying.

"The good news is the cops went down to Levenson," Lucas chimed in, deciding to rescue this situation. "They're bound to find something that can prove everything we told them is true. Even if this guy somehow managed to get rid of all the bodies, there was blood all over that place, right? If they find the tunnel and the cave, one drop of blood is all it'll take."

"What cave?" Havana asked Lucas, confused.

"I just hope they find my dad," Ethan said, clinging to the only ounce of hope he had left. Earlier, one of the officers surprised him by bringing his mother into the interrogation room. They'd watched as he told Janice what he suspected had happened to Frank, figuring if Ethan was lying, he wouldn't have been able to tell her. Perhaps it was the moment when he sat here consoling his fragile mother that the officers on the other side of the two-way mirror decided to check out Levenson.

The door to the interrogation room opened again, and a stocky Detective Ferguson entered clutching a folder stuffed haphazardly with papers. On his heels was Darren's cousin, James.

"Well…" Ferguson said, exasperated. He tossed the file onto

the table with a loud splat. "Hell happened up there alright," he said, referring to the graffiti he'd undoubtedly seen upon entering Levenson.

"The cave?" Lucas asked him, bracing for the answer.

"First of all, one of you better start explaining to me why my guys pulled twenty-five freshly dead bodies out of that place," Detective Ferguson demanded. He was well into his fifties and well-seasoned on the job, but all of them could tell from his demeanor that he had never encountered anything this horrific in his life.

Shock permeated Havana, and she turned wide-eyed to Ethan, wondering if there was a reason none of them had ever mentioned the cave or the two dozen additional dead bodies to her following what happened to Genevieve. His eyes met hers and quickly deflected to the table, letting her know that this secret was merely a baby skipping ahead of its mother.

"That's what we'd like to know!" Lucas said, responding to Ferguson. "I told you we went up there for a class project, and ran into this."

"Ran into this?!" Ferguson repeated, dumbfounded. "Son, this is not a traffic jam."

"We tried to tell you," Lucas continued. "We called the police on Saturday when Darren went missing—"

"And you said he was playing a joke," Ferguson said. He reached down and threw open the folder, crime scene photos splattered the table. "Does this look like a joke to you?" he shouted.

James stepped forward to pull the detective aside. "Why don't you let me talk to them for a bit? I'm sure Forensics are on their way here."

Without a word, Detective Ferguson hulked out of the room, leaving the folder and photos on the table.

When they were alone, James started gathering all the photos together and stuffed them back into the folder.

"Is there anything you can tell us?" Ethan asked him, carefully approaching the subject.

"Darren's dead," James admitted. "They found his body, and like you said, he'd been shot. They found Genevieve Davis with a cracked skull. She's dead, and her car, which you said was still at the site, was nowhere to be found. They found your father with…" James paused, thinking better than to give those details. "He's dead."

Ethan's world stopped. He wanted to blame himself for guilting Frank into even going to Levenson. He wanted retribution.

"I want his blood," Ethan growled through gritted teeth. "I want him to pay for this. Every day. For the rest of his life! I don't care how you have to do it, but you get him here. I want him to face me, and tell me what the hell I ever did to make him want to ruin my life like this."

Havana placed her arm around his shoulder to comfort him, but he jumped to his feet, pulling away from her and knocking his chair to the floor.

"Don't you dare say it's because of this," he told her. "It's deeper than that, and you know it. You don't just murder this many people because your daughter is in love with someone you don't like."

The baby secret was alone no more. Its mother had appeared, and she was bold and brazen.

"My dad?!" Havana stood up, offended by Ethan's accusation. "You think my dad did this?!"

"We don't know that," James ordered, equally heated. "Everything is speculation at this point. Even if that was a reason for him to off Frank Foster, there is no motive for Darren or for Genevieve. I want to find this guy too, but you have to let us do our job."

"The man doesn't care about a motive!" Ethan shouted. "He's spent the past three weeks in class talking about how motives are basically inconsequential. He's doing this to prove his point."

"Foster, chill," Lucas said, trying to wrap his brain around all of this as well. "What about the attic?" he asked James. "What did they find up there?"

James shuffled through the papers in the folder and pulled out several printout photos. "This."

He dropped the photos onto the table, allowing the four of them to check them out. There were pictures of a wall in the room, covered with dozens of blood-smeared close-up photos, faces of deceased victims.

"We've identified some of them as the people from the cave in the basement. The others we're not sure," James said.

"This is unreal," Reagan said, wondering to herself if what her mother had seen the night of the fire had been anything like this, or were these victims' photos now covering up something even more sinister on that wall. She couldn't tell, but knew that if Ethan was right, and Professor Owens was responsible for this, then his reign of terror dated back much farther than however recent those dead bodies were in the basement.

Another officer knocked on the door as he opened it, and handed over a small stack of papers to James.

"They're running ID's on the bodies from the cave. Here's the first batch. Captain said put this with Ferguson's folder," the officer instructed.

"Thanks Perez," James sighed. Within the past couple of hours, his life had become a carousel. He still needed to tell his family about Darren, and deal with the loss himself.

"Fifty bucks says most of them are more survivors from the fire," Ethan said. "Survivors you never knew about because you capped it off at thirteen just to make it easy. He'd probably been torturing those poor people for years," he argued. He felt he owed it to his father.

"We can only hope that's the case," Perez said to James on his way out. "Otherwise we're gonna be closing a lot of missing persons cases from the past few years. Oh, and they're gonna rush the lab reports on that DNA in case we wanted to uh..." he glanced at the others in the room before finishing, "add anything."

As Perez left the room, James turned to the four of them. He knew he had to explain.

"They found some skin cells under Genevieve Davis's nails," he said. "We might have the killer's DNA."

"Why didn't you tell us this?!" Havana demanded.

"Because the four of you think you're playing Clue," he replied. "And we're not gonna have you getting in the way of an investigation."

"So what did he mean 'add something'?" Ethan pressed.

"Standard procedure," he said. "We can swab you to eliminate you as suspects."

"What about Owens?" Ethan asked, knowing it would scratch a nerve with Havana.

"Whenever we get a hold of him, we can bring him in and swab him too," James said, trying to diffuse Ethan's anger.

"And what if you don't get a hold of him in time?" Ethan continued. "He just said they can get a rush on these lab reports which normally take what, a few weeks? None of *us* are going to come back a match, but you're going to wait to go after Owens, and give him another two weeks minimum to either open fire at Westmore, or relocate. And start over."

James knew Ethan had a point, and debated how he could effectively placate Ethan and simultaneously get him out of their way.

"I can do it," Havana blurted, numbly. The more Ethan built his case against her father, the harder it became for her to reject it. All of the instances of his dripping disdain and exponential rage collected in her mind as evidence sorted chronologically from way back then to earlier this evening. It was possible. "I'm his daughter. It wouldn't be a perfect match, but if it's close then that's enough to get a warrant, right?"

"Why don't you discuss that with Detective Ferguson," James told her, fighting against every instinct to show empathy. "They're gonna sideline me on this investigation because of Darren, but until we know who did this to him, don't think that I'm on your side. I'll let them know ya'll are ready to be swabbed." With that, he pulled open the door and stepped out of the interrogation room and into the open area of the frenzied police station.

"Oh, here's one more." Perez approached, thrusting one more page on top of the folder in James's arms. "Another vic from the basement. This place is chaos, can you believe it?!" Perez did little to hide his excitement. "This might be the biggest case of our careers. Play your cards right, and I bet you some of us are going to be looked at to make detective after this!"

"Yeah, some of you," James said, desolate. He knew it wouldn't be him. He glanced at the paper he'd just been given and confusion swept over his face. "Are you sure about this one?"

"What's wrong?" Perez asked, leaning over to be sure.

"We got a fax about this guy a few days ago," James said. "They found his car abandoned in Durham."

"Lewis Carter," Perez read.

James searched his memory for more details about the missing persons report he'd intercepted on Lewis Carter. Something had stood out about it, but he couldn't remember what it was.

"Doesn't ring a bell to me," Perez continued. "But if this guy got picked up all the way out in Durham, this serial killer could be a statewide operation. That's even bigger than... well it's even bigger than the Levenson fire itself."

TWENTY FOUR

"Why won't you let me take you back to your apartment?" Havana asked Ethan as she pulled into her driveway. "This isn't exactly the best place for you to be right now."

"I can call a cab once I make sure you and your mom are safe," he answered. It worried him that no one had yet been able to get in touch with Professor Owens, and he dreaded the thought of Havana staying here tonight, even if there were only a few hours left before dawn. "Besides, I think I'm gonna go to my parents' house tonight."

"Are you okay?" she asked him, concerned about the emotional ramifications of his begging his father to accompany him to Levenson.

He didn't want to confront how he felt out loud. "I'll be a lot better if I can unfold myself out of this car," he joked. "Sweetie, you gotta get rid of this Beetle. Nobody drives these anymore."

She smiled as she watched him climb out of the car. "Everybody's driving jeeps," she cracked back at him.

She turned off the ignition and got out as he reached her side of the car. For a moment standing there together, both of them knew the fight they were facing with her father. It didn't matter to her. She meant what she'd told him during their fight earlier. She would die to protect Ethan.

"I'm sorry," he told her. "About all of this. None of us expected any of this."

"I know." For the first time, she was fighting back tears. "I just keep thinking about all those times he'd lash out for no reason. Times I'd seen him turn into somebody I didn't even recognize. All the things I've never known about him." She leaned back against the side of the car, staring at the lawn behind Ethan. "There was a moment at the station when we were getting swabbed... I thought about how angry my dad was last night, how much he hates you. If he could do this to innocent people, why wouldn't he go after you? What if the reason he went after them and not you was because for him, you being murdered wasn't enough? What if he was planning to set you up?"

Ethan had thought the same thing earlier, and now, hearing it out loud made him appreciate not having handled the gun they found lying beside Darren's body. If Owens wanted to set him up, Ethan wouldn't make it easy.

"Think about it," she continued. "If you got killed, you'd just be one of those poor victims. But if you were the killer, they would condemn you. You'd be branded for life."

He pulled her into his arms to comfort her. He didn't want to feed her anger and risk obscuring her judgment tonight. She needed to be on guard and thinking logically in case her father returned. "They'd have a really hard time connecting me to the murders from 15 years ago," he said, reminding her that this case had spanned over a decade.

"Unless they maintain that those were committed by Terrance Todd and these new ones are a copycat. I mean, you *are* doing this project, and you're trying awfully hard to convince everyone that he's the killer. It wouldn't take a genius to figure out why your life might be better without him around. What if he's trying to frame you to make it look like you're framing him?! Why would he—"

"Sweetie!" He interrupted quickly, stepping back and taking her face in his hands. "Your imagination! It's supposed to turn me on, not turn me *in*!"

"That's not funny," Havana told him.

"I'm not laughing," he replied. "If you think I'm capable of something like this..."

"You're asking me to think my father is!"

They stood in silence for a moment, the stillness of the spring night invaded by the ghosts of winter as a chilly breeze sent shivers through the trees.

"Let's wait for the results to come back from the lab before we start trying to figure it all out." He took her hand in his, and led her towards the front door.

A dim glow behind the curtains alerted them that a lamp was on in the living room. At this hour, it worried Havana. She fumbled with the keys in her hand and tried to steady her nerves as she opened the door. Lucinda was seated on the couch, nursing a glass of wine.

She looked up at them as they entered.

"Havana, it's four in the morning," she said, justifying why she wasn't asleep. "What are you doing? You know how your father gets. *Why* are you doing this? Just to provoke him?"

Lucinda wasn't a regular drinker, and Havana could immediately tell that her sobriety was starting to slip. She reached over and took the glass from her mother.

"Relax, mom," she answered. "I was at the police station."

Dread came over Lucinda. "Is that why they were here earlier looking for Carter? Kicking in a door is *not* abuse, Havana!" Lucinda cried. "I can't even believe you went to the cops over that. And now the government is involved…"

"Where's Daddy?" Havana asked, struggling to get some answers before her mother lost sobriety altogether.

"I assumed he was out looking for you," she replied.

"Not if he knows the cops are after him," Havana countered. "He probably ran away."

"Ran away? He didn't run away," Lucinda said. "He's always done this. Ever since you were little. Don't you remember? It's just one of his trips to get away. Clear his head."

"And all these years, you've never asked him where?" she asked her mother.

"It was always someplace different," she said. "And he's always in a better mood afterwards, so I figured it was therapeutic. I didn't question it. I don't know why all of a sudden we need to."

Ethan and Havana exchanged glances. Homicidal therapy. That was a new one.

"What's…what's going on?" Lucinda asked them again, almost

begging to be told everything was fine, even though somewhere behind her glazing eyes she knew it wasn't. Ethan could see that part of her was unnerved, as if she was forcing herself not to produce critical pieces of this jigsaw puzzle. If she couldn't find them, perhaps it was because they didn't fit into the picture of her marriage.

Rather than risking Lucinda having a breakdown, Ethan took over the conversation. "They're questioning a bunch of people from Westmore about some things that have been happening lately. I'm sure the cops are just covering their bases. The sooner they talk to him, the sooner this can all be over for us. He hasn't mentioned anything to you in the past few days that might help us find out where he's gone?"

He was getting desperate. If Professor Owens saw the mob of cops up at Levenson, felt the walls were closing in on him here and had to get away for another "therapy" session, it was probable that another victim was bound to surface. Only this one couldn't be added to the rest of them in the basement of Levenson.

"The last conversation we had was this morning, before one of his students showed up," Lucinda answered.

"You mean Genevieve," Havana clarified.

Lucinda nodded. "He left for work right before the two of you left here together," she continued.

"He said he stayed home from work all day because he was trying to catch me and Ethan together," Havana said, confirming Ethan's suspicions even further that Owens had either followed them into Levenson, or had been there waiting.

"I didn't see him again until you both came in earlier tonight fighting," Lucinda finished.

"What did you talk to him about this morning?" Ethan asked.

Lucinda paused for a moment, trying to remember. "His brother."

It was a curve ball neither Ethan nor Havana expected.

"Police in Durham called and said his brother was missing. They found his car abandoned and one of Carter's business cards in the glove compartment. Is that what it is?" Lucinda asked, suddenly realizing it herself. "Does that have anything to do with why the cops are looking for Carter?"

Ethan didn't respond, afraid that this brother might be the latest victim.

"I never knew Daddy even had a brother," Havana said, thrown by the revelation. "Did you know?" she asked Lucinda.

"He kept us so separated from his family," she answered. "I tried to get him to open up. I tried to get him to go down to Durham. He didn't want anything to do with it. He didn't care." She looked defeated. "I think maybe he resented them for some reason after what happened twenty years ago."

Havana's theory about the killer was now split into three, a result of the unrelenting instinct to love thy father. If there was a chance he was the killer, there was also a chance he wasn't, and now there was a chance he was a target. This mysterious uncle of hers who may have had a reason to hate his neglectful brother, suddenly had a motive and possibly an agenda if Carter's business card was to be considered. It wouldn't discount her dad as their prime suspect, but nobody knew anything about this brother of his, and if he wasn't a victim then he sure as hell was a person of interest.

"Do you know anything about Dad's brother?" Havana asked.

"Only his name," she answered. "Lewis Carter."

"His brother's last name is Daddy's first name?" Havana asked, confused.

"No," Lucinda corrected. "When we first met down in Miami, Carter's name was Owen Carter. He changed it after the fire."

"Wait, what fire?" Ethan asked her, his pulse quickening in bewilderment.

"The fire that killed his first wife and their son."

And there it was. A link in Owens' history to fire – the connection so clear it essentially comprised a helix in his DNA.

"I gotta go," Ethan said, starting for the door.

"Now?" Havana asked.

"Yes." Trying not to alarm her, he gave her a quick kiss on her forehead as he opened the front door. "*Please*, Havana... stay here with your mom. She's not in any frame of mind right now to be alone. If he comes back before I do, do whatever you have to do to go straight to the police. Promise me."

She didn't know what was going through his mind, but she

trusted him, and nodded her acknowledgement. "Take my car. Mom's is in the garage. We can use that if we need to." She pulled the keys from her pocket and tossed them to him.

He left the house and started towards her VW. He had to find Lucas so they could put their heads together and figure out who the hell was Owen Carter, and deal with the nagging hunch he had that Terrance Todd was nothing more than the Levenson patsy.

TWENTY FIVE

It was dawn when Ethan pulled his jeep into Jeffrey Edgefield's driveway. He had gone straight to Lucas's apartment after leaving Havana, and found Lucas and Reagan had fallen asleep on the sofa. It had been a long night for all of them, but the information about Owen Carter and his secret life had caffeinated Ethan, and they didn't have time to waste in trying to figure it all out.

A quick Internet search produced several news articles about the tragic, unsolved 1986 break-in and attack, which resulted in a fire that killed Catherine Carter and sent Owen Carter and their seven year-old son to Mt. Victoria Hospital in Greenville for treatment. One of the articles included a solitary quote from the attending doctor, Harold Ashley, about how unspeakably tragic it was to lose a young mother and her child in such a way. What led the three of them to Jeffrey's driveway was the realization that Reagan's mom was a nurse at Mt. Victoria around that time. As far as they could piece together, it was possible that Robyn helped treat Owen that night, and perhaps he played a part in her breakdown, particularly if he was the one she "saw" and recognized at Levenson in 1996. In order to get those answers, Jeffrey would need to pay his pain a visit.

"Are you sure you don't want me to come in with you?" Lucas asked Reagan, stepping out of the passenger side to allow her to get out of the backseat of the jeep. She had her opened laptop with her as she got out.

"I'm sure," she answered, handing him her laptop. "You two keep trying to reach out to Dr. Ashley just in case I can't pry my dad open about what happened."

Lucas climbed back into the jeep and they watched as she approached the front door and entered the house.

"Do you really think he'd know if Robyn recognized Owen Carter?" Ethan asked him.

"Who knows what he knows," Lucas answered. "The man has been repressing it for decades, so whatever it is, it's relevant."

Reagan stepped into the front hall and immediately smiled at the aroma of bacon and eggs. She started for the kitchen, and found her father standing at the stove.

"Morning," she greeted.

"Just in time!" He smiled at her, motioning for her to take a seat at the table. "I made enough figuring you'd pulled an all-nighter prepping for finals."

"I'm not staying long," she said. "Lucas and Ethan are outside waiting for me."

"Oh? Heading up to the library before class?" he asked.

She hesitated, bracing herself for his reaction. "Heading up to Mt. Victoria."

He didn't answer, but reached to turn off the stove.

"Did you hear me?" she asked.

"Why are you drudging this up all of a sudden?" he asked her. "Your mom was just ill."

"I know," she said. "Postpartum." She stepped closer to him so she could speak to him in a softer tone, hoping it'd make him more comfortable. "But that was 1989. I want to talk about 1986."

He needed to deflect. "You expect me to remember the difference between three years from twenty years ago?"

"*These* three years... yes," she answered. "I need you to think back, Dad. I really need you to think hard. Did Mom treat a patient who was burned in a house fire back in '86? His name was Owen Carter. He was rushed in with his son."

Jeffrey closed his eyes and could still see his wife sitting stoically on the coffee table in the middle of that night. The night the lights went out in Robyn. He looked over at his daughter, wondering how she could possibly have ended up in that vicinity.

"What does that have to do with anything?" he asked.

"The short version is it all ties in with the research we've been doing on the Levenson fire," she answered, deciding again that giving sections of the truth might make him feel in control and more willing to share even though she had the upper hand.

"It was the last case she worked on," he said, caught up in the memory. "The kid died, and I figured it was the moment she'd decided that she couldn't be around it anymore. Death, I mean. As much as she loved children. As much as she wanted you, whatever darkness she had seen that day never left her alone."

"That night at the hospital... it contributed to her breakdown," Reagan said, reaching for clarification.

Jeffrey nodded.

"She got better, and then got pregnant and we lost her again. She was at Levenson for what was supposed to be a year-long treatment for her illness," Jeffrey said. "After the year, she'd gotten dependent on the comfort of that place, and didn't want to come home." Sadness washed over him as he confronted the notion that his wife felt safer within the walls of an insane asylum than within the walls of their home together. All these years he had to deal with knowing she felt he couldn't protect her when that was all he wanted to do.

"We think Owen Carter was at Levenson that night and she recognized him. Did you authorize her transfer to Glendale?" she asked, pushing the subject while she had him there. "Did they tell you what happened?"

"No one knew what was going on. They called and said she was hostile and they had to remove her. I never got to see her before..."

"Have you seen her since?" she asked, curious to know if he ever visited her at Glendale.

He fought with his inner demon. "I couldn't," he admitted, shamefully. "I didn't want to risk her not recognizing me, or me not recognizing her. I couldn't take that."

She placed a hand on her father's shoulder comfortingly, remembering how Robyn reacted to the photo of herself holding Reagan as a baby. "She recognizes you," she said, her way of also telling him that she'd visited Robyn and it would be okay if he went to visit her too.

He reached over his shoulder and patted her hand with his, determining not to turn around to face her. One look into her eyes would pull tears out of him like a faucet.

She slipped her hand from beneath his and left the house, finally understanding why Jeffrey was so protective of her. She also felt more empowered than ever before. Owen Carter had crossed paths with her mother, and it had altered Reagan's life forever. As long as he was roaming around, Robyn remained in captivity, and it was time to set her free.

She got back to the jeep and Lucas stepped out to let her climb inside.

"Just as we suspected," she said. "My mom treated Owen Carter the night he and his family were pulled out of that fire."

"So we can take a photo of Owens up to Glendale, show it to your mother, and if she recognizes him, we can prove he was at Levenson," Ethan suggested.

"We're not gonna do that," Reagan said. "I'm not putting my mother through that. If she panicked once before, it might provoke another episode. I'm gonna call Glendale and request that they move her to another hospital. Since we now know Owens is capable of stalking people, we can't be sure he isn't trying to track her down like she told us, and she's the only living link to Levenson."

"So what do we do now?" Ethan asked.

"Dr. Harold Ashley," she replied. "Where is he?"

"Unfortunately he retired from practice a while ago," Lucas said, scrolling through a website on her laptop. "But it looks like he has a private consultation clinic near Mt. Victoria Hospital."

"We need to find out exactly what happened the night Owens' family was brought in," she offered. "Did the cops investigate that fire? Why is this alleged break-in still unsolved?"

"You're not suggesting Owens burned his own house down with his family inside!" Ethan reeled.

"She's right," Lucas agreed. "If we're going so far as to assume Owens is the one who started the fire at Levenson, it would strengthen our case if he was even suspected of starting the first one as well. Otherwise the Levenson murders and that fire were out of the blue. And as much as you want to think he doesn't need a motive, the cops might not arrest him without one."

"What if my mom found out he killed his family, and that's what led to her breakdown?" Reagan said. "He goes off for cosmetic surgery, changes his name, and discovers she's a patient at Levenson. He moves here a year before the fire, sneaks his way into Levenson looking for her, gets paranoid that she's telling everybody about his crime, and decides the only way to shut her up is murder. It would certainly explain why he went after the survivors. He needed *everybody* dead because he couldn't be sure who knew the truth about him. The only problem was when she saw him she flipped out, and got immediately transferred out. He didn't realize that, and set the fire when he couldn't find her. That's why now she still thinks he's after her. Because he is."

"And the reason he's been dormant for the past fifteen years is because nobody ever goes up to Levenson," Lucas realized. "He only kills to protect his identity."

"So..." Ethan said, finally. "This has nothing to do with *me*?"

Lucas and Reagan tossed blank stares at Ethan.

"What's Dr. Ashley's address?" Reagan asked Lucas, reaching for her book bag on the seat beside her to retrieve her GPS.

*

Lucinda slowly opened her eyes, surprised to find she had fallen asleep on the couch.

Havana sat frazzled at her feet, having stayed awake the past few hours to keep watch in case her father came home. She stood up and paced over to the window that faced the street.

"I can't even believe this is happening," she said to no one in particular, then turned to Lucinda. "Would you have ever suspected something like this?"

She suddenly remembered Lucinda wasn't aware that they suspected Carter in a string of murders.

Lucinda glanced up at Havana. "I figured he might have had siblings," she said. "I just thought he wrote his family off for not being there for him after that house fire. Can you imagine how tragic that was? And he had no one."

"I know I told Ethan I'd stay here, but we're sitting around waiting for Michael Myers to show up," she said. "I think we should leave town."

"Oh, don't be dramatic," Lucinda replied. "Besides, you've got school in a couple of hours."

"I'm not going to school today, Mom."

"You want your father to walk through that door and catch you skipping school *again*?" Lucinda asked. "Really, what is it with you?" She stood up and approached Havana. She'd sat ringside to Carter's and Havana's fights, and couldn't understand why Havana pushed her father's buttons so much. "Why do you do it?" she asked. "Do you like making him angry?"

Havana thought it was a worthless argument at a time like this. She neglected to respond.

"He's just looking out for you," Lucinda said.

"He's looking out for himself!" Havana exclaimed, on the verge of shattering her mother's world with the truth. She barreled through the stop sign. "You want to know the real reason the cops are looking for him? Because they want to question him about the 25 bodies they pulled out of Levenson Asylum last night." She stormed off into the kitchen, avoiding the disappointment she could sense creep into her mother's eyes.

Lucinda felt the wind drain out of her. The cops truly believed it necessary to question Carter, which meant they had a serious reason to tie him to something. But this? She couldn't reconcile what it was Havana was indicating, so she started into the kitchen after her. "What bodies?" she was asking.

Moments later, the front door opened and Carter entered the empty living room. He could hear chatter in the kitchen, but his own mind was too muddled to make sense out of what was being said. He looked disheveled, having not slept all night himself. He brought a trembling hand up to his head and pinched the area between his eyes. Suddenly, he knew he was home. He glanced around as if to get his bearings.

As soon as he'd heard Havana mention the name Robyn Edgefield yesterday, control of his own decisions was displaced by old instincts to maintain his freedom. Robyn Edgefield was the vault that contained his darkest secret, and all it would take was that prying Ethan Foster finding out what she knew. Left with no indication as to *where* Robyn was, he tracked down her former colleague Dr. Ashley in Greenville, hoping to use the threat of a malpractice suit to squeeze her whereabouts out of him. It failed, and the consequences of the confrontation detonated a time bomb.

After their meeting, Carter could hardly remember getting behind the wheel. The drive home from Greenville had been automatic given his state of mind. His head was still swirling, a jumble of the past 24 hours. He heard Lucinda's voice tearing into his thoughts from the kitchen.

"…no reason to think we're not safe here," she was saying.

"We're *not!*" he heard Havana reply. "Any one of us could be the next victim!" They were frightened and nervous.

Carter started for the stairs located between the kitchen and the living room, and had almost completely ascended when Havana and Lucinda emerged from the kitchen, crossing into the living room and heading for the front door. Havana was carrying her purse.

"Let's just go down to the police station and they can explain it all to you because clearly you're not going to believe me," Havana said.

"Fine," Lucinda replied. "I'm sure he isn't the only person wanted this badly for questioning, and I refuse to believe he's even capable of something like that."

Havana started to open the door, then remembered she'd given Ethan her car last night. "We have to take your car."

Lucinda turned and led the way back towards the kitchen. Her car was parked in the garage. She stopped just as she got to the base of the stairs.

"My keys are up in the bedroom," she said, starting up the stairs. "I'll meet you out in the garage."

She headed upstairs as Havana trekked into the kitchen and out the back door.

As Lucinda rounded the corner into the first bedroom at the top of the stairs, she found Carter standing in the middle of the room, staring down at their bed.

She gasped as the sight startled her. "Carter!" she exclaimed, trying to regain control of her breathing. "When did you get in here?"

"I love you, Cinda," he said, his tone barely above a whisper. "That's why you need to leave town. Both of you."

"Why?" she asked, fearing a confession. "Did something happen?"

"Yeah," he admitted. "Something happened. Twenty-five years ago." His voice was a shaky, horrified whisper. "I'm not the man you think I am."

"Twenty-five years ago?" Lucinda asked, doing the mental calculation. "The fire?"

"I didn't know what else to do. It was the only way to deal with what had happened. The accident. I had to make a decision," he explained. "And Daniel knew. He knew she was dead. He knew how she died. But he didn't know she fell. She fell, and it was an accident. He would've never told them that. And every day since then has been the predator I've been fighting against to stay alive."

Lucinda was lost. "What does this have to do with anything?"

"Everything." He started past her out of the room. She grabbed her keys off a nearby dresser and followed him out, stopping him at the top of the stairs.

"Where have you been, Carter?" she asked him. "The cops have been looking for you. Is there anything else you want to tell me?"

"I already told you to leave town." He stepped down onto the first step and she grabbed his arm to stop him.

"Carter, wait!" she yelled. "Tell me where you've been!"

"Trying to prevent a mess!" he told her, anger rising. "I knew Ethan Foster was trouble, and you didn't believe me. My hunches weren't wrong, and now he's roped my daughter into this, and shit is front-page news! There's only one ending. Evidently the first one was to be continued."

"You're not making any sense!" she exclaimed, trying to pull him back to her. A feeble attempt to reach for his shoulder caught the air ahead of him instead, and she felt herself lose balance. He grabbed her arm just as she began to tumble past him, and pinned her against the wall inches before it gave way to the railing. The angry look in his eyes slowly transformed into terror as the past replayed itself for him presently.

A tense and breathless moment passed without either of them moving until Havana appeared at the bottom of the stairs.

"What are you doing?!" Havana cried. "Let her go!" She started racing up the stairs, reaching for her mother.

"It... it was an accident," he uttered, allowing Lucinda to flee towards Havana at the base of the stairs.

Without looking back, Havana and Lucinda ran into the kitchen and headed for the back door, Havana punching 911 into her cell.

"It's Havana Owens!" she screamed into the phone when the dispatch answered. "You've gotta get here now! He just almost killed my mother!"

Carter heard Havana's voice trail off as she and Lucinda ran out the back door. There *was* only one ending to this, so the cops couldn't find him here when they arrived.

T W E N T Y   S I X

The parking lot in front of Dr. Harold Ashley's office was littered with cop cars, an ambulance, and hoards of curious bystanders when Ethan pulled his jeep into a parking space across the street.

He climbed out of the jeep along with Reagan and Lucas, and they quickly made their way across the crowded lot and as close to the yellow crime scene tape as they could get. Some police officers were darting into and out of the front entrance of the one story building, others were taking statements from several of the bystanders who were on the other side of the yellow tape. A news crew had arrived on the scene, and was setting up a shot nearby.

Lucas allowed his eyes to scan from one side of the scene to the other, taking in as much detail as he could. An older gentleman standing to his left had his cell phone in the air and was taking video of the scene.

"What happened?" Lucas asked him.

"Doc was found shot to death this morning," he replied. He nodded towards an elderly woman speaking with one of the detectives near the corner of the building. She was seated on the sidewalk, her gray dress and white blouse sporting unmistakable streaks of crimson stains. The detective was on one knee at her side, scribbling in a pad as she dabbed at her puffy eyes with a Kleenex. "She's the secretary. From what I could tell, she came in and found his body. Must have happened last night sometime."

Hearing this, Reagan felt a rush of anxiety overcome her. She took Lucas's arm in her hand and tugged him away from the crowd.

"We have to go," she told him.

"Yeah, I know," he agreed. "If this has anything to do with what's going on back home, then we don't need the cops to find us here."

"If?!" she retorted. "What do you think this was? A robbery?"

"It's a possibility," Lucas replied. The detective-to-be in him was prone to giving the benefit of the doubt. "We don't know what enemies this man had."

She didn't need him to play devil's advocate right now. Here was one more person who had a connection to Owen Carter, Robyn Edgefield, and the 1986 fire who was dead all of a sudden. This wasn't a random act of violence. This was a loose end.

"Last I checked, no one knows where Owens is. He could be lurking around here right now," she told him, firmly believing that Owen Carter was still killing anyone who found out who he was. "What if he spots us? It won't take a genius to figure out we know, and we still have to make it back home."

"Nothing is gonna happen to you," he told her. He understood that this was emotionally close to home for her, and could tell she was growing more and more worried. "I won't let anything happen to you."

"This has been going on for over twenty years, Lucas. It's older than I am," she said. "I'm expendable." The realization shook her to her core.

"Not to me," he said, taking her face in his hands.

Her eyes began to water. "I just don't want to take any chances," she said. "I feel like he's after my mom, and given what's happened to Dr. Ashley, I'm starting to think he's gonna go through whoever he needs to in order to find her. That means me, and anyone I love, including my father… and you."

They both stood there like Adam and Eve in the bareness of what she'd just done. A small part of him briefly believed she might have said it just to convince him that they needed to leave, but it was quickly chased away by the fact that he'd already agreed with her. In her protective, roundabout way, she'd said she loved him, and every ounce of him knew she meant it.

"Let me and Foster take you to the airport," he said, finally. "I'll get you a ticket, and send you someplace like Chicago or New York. Anywhere but here." His intent was to get her out of harm's way. He'd just found out they were no longer toying around in their relationship. It was serious. He'd fought her endless insecurities for the title to her heart for over the past year, and now that she told him he had it, keeping it safe became his only priority.

"Hiding is not the solution," she told him. "Sure, it kept my mother alive all these years, but look at what it cost *me*. Retribution is here and now. I need to do this for her. You can't ask me to run away from it."

He hugged her tightly. "I just want you to be safe," he said. "Otherwise, you're just running around here as bait."

An idea struck her, and she pulled away from him suddenly. "Maybe that's it!"

He could see the wheels of plot spinning behind her beautiful eyes, and immediately knew what she was thinking.

"No!" he said, adamantly. "Absolutely not."

Before she could plead her case, the two of them were interrupted as Ethan approached with his phone to his ear.

"Stay put, we're on our way," he said before shutting off the phone. The urgent look in his eyes told Lucas and Reagan this wasn't good news. "Owens showed up while Havana and her mom were home."

"Are they okay?" Lucas asked.

"Yeah, they got out and went to the police station," he said. "The cops got there too late. Owens is gone again."

"Where would he be headed next?" Lucas found himself trying to anticipate Carter's next move.

"He's trying to find my mother," Reagan said, hoping the request she made for Glendale to transfer Robyn securely and discreetly had either gone through or was in progress. She glanced over at Lucas. "It might be our only choice," she said, referring to her idea. "We know what he's after."

"No," Lucas repeated. "That can be Plan F."

"Either of you want to fill me in?" Ethan asked.

"It seems like Owens is going after anybody who might know where my mother is," she explained. "I'm her daughter."

Lucas rolled his eyes, dissatisfied with this plan.

"I'm your bait," she said.

TWENTY SEVEN

Jeffrey rushed into the police station in a panic, and sprinted to the nearest desk.

"I'm Jeff Edgefield," he stammered. "I'm looking for my daughter. Did somebody bring her in?"

"Mr. Edgefield?" Havana was standing at a water fountain nearby. She'd gotten a call from Reagan asking her to be on the lookout for him. She approached Jeffrey. "I'm Havana Owens. I'm a friend of Reagan's."

"What happened?" Jeffery asked, still panicking. "She called and told me to meet her here ASAP."

"I'm sure they're fine," Havana said. "She probably just wanted to make sure you hurried."

"What's going on?"

Ushering him towards the area where she and her mother were sitting, Havana explained to Jeffrey that Reagan's involvement in this particular class assignment put her and several of her classmates in the path of a killer, and Reagan wanted Jeffrey to meet her here at the police station where she knew he'd be safe until she arrived.

He immediately figured it had something to do with Levenson. It made sense to him now why Reagan had been pulled back into that project despite his intentions to shelter her from it. He remembered the questions Reagan had asked him earlier about the guy Robyn might have recognized that night.

"Owen Carter?" he asked Havana. "Is he involved in this?"

Havana nodded. Reagan had also filled her in on their suspicions that Robyn likely knew that Owen had killed his wife and their son in the 1986 fire, and Owen was murdering anyone who may have been exposed to that knowledge, including the doctor who treated them back then, whom they'd just discovered dead.

None of them noticed Detective Ferguson approach, carrying a large cup of coffee.

"Mrs. Owens?" he said.

Lucinda sat up. For the past three hours they'd been here, she'd regressed into a defeated version of herself, having to deal with the guilt she felt for not having suspected any of this – if it were true. A small part of her still clung to the possibility that it was just a misunderstanding. Detective Ferguson's tone separated her from hope once and for all.

"I need to ask you if you knew any of your husband's relatives," Detective Ferguson said.

Lucinda shook her head, her face was a mask of dread.

"They pulled 22 bodies out of a cave in the basement of Levenson," he continued slowly, trying to make sure she could follow. "Twenty-one of them are related to Owen Carter."

"His entire family?" Havana asked, stunned.

"One of our guys recognized a photo of Lewis Carter from a missing persons report," he explained. "That's what made us look into Owens' connection to the rest of them."

"It was his brother," Lucinda said, still in a state of shock. "Lewis was his brother. But that doesn't automatically mean Carter's responsible. Does it?"

"We also got the lab results back on that DNA sample obtained from Genevieve Davis's fingernails," Ferguson continued. "Of course, we'd need to run a test with your husband's DNA to be sure, but... it looks like he's our guy. All the evidence is circumstantial at this point, but we're putting out an APB. We're gonna get him."

Lucinda collapsed into tears.

"You said there were twenty-*two* bodies...?" Jeffrey asked, wondering who was the last one.

"The other victim was named John Radley," Ferguson said. "He had been released from Glendale Institute in 2001 after being transferred from Levenson following the fire. After Terrance Todd's suicide, John Radley was the sole survivor."

As Ferguson took a sip from his cup, the doors to the police station swung open and Ethan, Lucas, and Reagan entered. Jeffrey rushed over and threw his arms around Reagan, and Havana did the same to Ethan.

"They're putting out an APB," she told him.

"That's good news," Ethan said. "But it's not good enough."

Ferguson lowered his cup and glared at Ethan. "You and your friends have done good to kick-start this investigation. You can step aside now."

"You don't understand," Lucas continued. "There's been another murder. Dr. Harold Ashley in Greenville. He was the doctor who treated Owens after a house fire back in '86."

"Yeah, we think we know who Owens is targeting, and who he's gonna go through to get to her," Ethan said. "We've got a plan."

"I said step aside," Ferguson repeated. "None of you own a badge, and this ain't *The Shield*. We've already got our hands full dealing with this and news reporters who don't know how to give up. If you get in the way, I will not hesitate to book you on obstruction. And furthermore, Greenville is not my jurisdiction. If they have questions about this investigation while they're looking into whatever happened with that doctor, I have a phone number, an email address, a Facebook account, and my Twitter handle is @NoneOf*Your*Concern. Now, are we clear?"

He waited for an answer, his eyes darting from Lucas's to Ethan's.

"We're clear," Lucas said.

They watched as Ferguson trotted away down a long hall the length of the station. Once he was gone, Havana turned to the rest of them.

"I can't go back to that house," she said, fear coloring her words.

"We can end this tonight," Reagan told her.

"You heard what the detective just said." Lucas lowered his

tone to a stern whisper. "We are *not* getting involved. We need to let them handle this."

"With what? An APB?" Reagan asked, incredulous. "They haven't been able to catch him in two days. What's an APB gonna do? We *know* what he's after."

"I don't like the sound of this," Jeffrey said. "What is it that you want to do?"

"We need to lead him to Robyn Edgefield," Ethan answered.

"Well… not really," Reagan clarified, reaching into her pocket for her cell phone. "We need him to think I know where she is so he'll come after me, and I can lead him right where we want him."

"Can't I just put you in a cage with a hungry lion?" Jeffrey asked, vehemently opposing her idea.

Reagan stepped away to converse with whomever she had phoned. Jeffrey turned to Lucas, his only other shot at talking Reagan out of whatever she had planned.

"I thought she got out of working on this project," Jeffrey said.

She had, and Lucas knew that lifting Robyn Edgefield's file out of the basement at Levenson was what pulled her back in. It was his fault she wasn't going to let it go, and the least he could do was stand by her side now when she needed him more than ever.

"It's the only way she'll be able to protect her mother," Lucas answered, truthfully. The cops would have to handle this by the books, and Ferguson was right about one thing, none of them were cops. They would just need to ensure that the ends justified their means. Reagan's plan needed to work, so he needed to help her execute it.

Stung, Jeffrey knew if all their suspicions about Owen Carter were correct, he wasn't going to stop until he'd murdered his way to Robyn.

He would have to trust his daughter.

Reagan ended her call and returned to the group.

"It's all set," she said. "Pilar is an intern down at the television station. I told her my mom was at Levenson the night of the fire, and of course the reporters are slobbering for any scoop they can get."

"You're gonna put this all over the news?!" Havana asked, worrying about the subtlety given the order they'd just gotten from

Detective Ferguson.

"Of course not," Reagan replied. "Just gonna drop a few breadcrumbs. Like Hansel and Gretel. And we all know how that ended."

"This isn't gonna work," Ethan said. "Owens isn't doing this for attention. He's not doing it out of habit or boredom, or for the thrill of killing. He's not one of those serial killers who gets off on the media coverage. It's none of that, and the man gave us this lesson in class last week."

"He's trying to stay one step ahead of the police charging his ass on a hundred and twenty-plus counts of first-degree murder," Lucas said, wrapping his arm around Reagan's shoulder in support of her plan. "That's why he'll be watching."

*

Two hours later, Jeffrey, Ethan, Havana, and Lucinda were gathered at Lucas's apartment, huddled around the television, watching as Reagan prepared for her exclusive mid-day news interview. Lucas had gone with her to the television station, knowing that the plan was for Reagan to explain how these recent discoveries at Levenson had affected Robyn Edgefield.

"And now we move on to the story that has literally gripped this town in fear," the anchor started. "Fifteen years ago, a massive fire at Levenson Asylum left more than a hundred people dead – all of the not-so-fortunate survivors were hunted and murdered in the horrific aftermath. Yesterday, police discovered more than two dozen recently deceased bodies in the charred remains of the building, inciting a resurgence of the same horror fifteen years later. Here with us now is Reagan Edgefield, the daughter of Robyn Edgefield, a patient who had fatefully gotten transferred within hours of that tragic fire. How are you today?"

Reagan gave a sorrowful nod, trying to dial down her degree of awareness in order to pull off her plan convincingly.

"It's been a struggle," she said. "My mom wasn't there during the fire, but she was there right before, and with Levenson being back in the news all of a sudden, it's sort of unlocked something in her memory."

"Like what?" the anchor asked. "I mean, one of the patients, Terrance Todd, has gone down in infamy as the one who started the fire and mercilessly murdered all the survivors. Has Robyn Edgefield indicated that she might have crossed paths with him that night?"

"She's indicating a lot," Reagan said, looking straight into the camera and imagining she was speaking directly to Owen Carter. "She's not saying much yet, but she saw things that night, and... you know we're all afraid that what they found up at Levenson yesterday is somehow connected to what happened that night. Needless to say, she's been anxious. She is, by many accounts, the *only* remaining survivor from that night."

"Well, of course there was the thirteenth survivor," the anchor corrected.

The news about John Radley being found among the victims had not yet been made public. Reagan had dropped that "only remaining survivor" breadcrumb just to entice the killer.

"The one who was taken into custody along with Terrance Todd," the anchor continued. "He has to still be out there somewhere, which feeds into a theory among locals that perhaps he was an accomplice, or possibly the actual killer given what's happening now and how your mother has been reacting."

"You can understand why I'm not eager to support that theory," Reagan said. "The last thing we need is people suspecting my poor mother under the same logic."

"Has she spoken to the police?" the anchor asked. "Do they know about her concerns?"

Jackpot. This was the question Reagan had been waiting for. She looked into the camera and warned, "Tomorrow morning," she said. "When she's up for it."

With that, whatever move Owens was going to make, he'd have to make it before then.

The time clock began.

TWENTY EIGHT

"I never thought I'd be back out here again," Lucas said, stepping out of Reagan's car and staring up at Levenson in front of them. He tucked a flashlight into the waist of his jeans and tossed another one over at Ethan, who did the same.

Their plan was to lure Owen Carter back to the hell he had created, douse it with gasoline, trap him inside, and burn Levenson down all over again. It would appear to be a twisted suicide laced with masochistic irony.

They had left Jeffrey and Lucinda at Lucas's apartment, it being the least likely place Carter might show up with murderous intentions. Havana stayed behind as well, but not without putting up a fight about letting Ethan go without her. She wanted the chance to face her father before his demise. She sensed she would have needed the closure. Ethan argued that he didn't want to risk her getting hurt. Lucinda had been on the distant end of vacant since leaving the police station. She was clearly having a hard time handling the fact that she had fallen in love, bore a child, and spent eighteen years of her life falling asleep with a killer.

For additional cautionary measures, Havana had called James at the police station and told him that until her father was found, he should expect to hear from her every hour just to check in. He seemed okay with that, and even offered to stop by Lucas's apartment once his shift ended to make sure all of them were okay. Even though he was the one police officer any of them trusted not to mishandle any information they might have shared, he'd been purposely left in the dark about their plans at Levenson.

Reagan popped her trunk, and after donning latex gloves to conceal fingerprints, the three of them each grabbed two jugs of gasoline and headed towards the asylum for the final time. They forced themselves to ignore that what they were doing was conspiring to commit a murder. This killer had gotten away with it for over two decades, and had recently made it personal. That was all the justification they needed.

They took turns entering the broken window of the building and passing the six jugs of gasoline into the lobby, careful not to disturb the yellow police tape that now decorated everything. Once they were all inside, a chill crept over them. This place had become a crypt. Buried here along with those 25 bodies, including Frank, Genevieve, and Darren, had been a host of secrets, lies, and pure evil.

"Let's get this over with," Lucas said. He'd never found the thrill in being here.

They spent twenty minutes splashing gasoline on the blackened and rotted wicker furniture piled in the back of the lobby and then continued down the two halls that extended down the left and right wings of the building. Everything was deathly still, which only served to heighten the sense of urgency. Twenty minutes on the first floor felt like an eternity, and they'd only emptied two jugs of gasoline – just enough to spread flames.

They started up the grand staircase that Lucas and Ethan recognized from recent nightmares. Having previously only seen the burned out building's exterior, Reagan was slower than the guys, and took her time expecting the boards were fragile. Her caution was at battle against her racing pulse. Owens was after her, after all, and they had driven her car out here in case he was strolling around town looking for her.

They covered the second floor in half the time, emptying two more jugs even though they decided it unnecessary to go into any of the numerous patients' rooms located along the front hall. They found that a short hall ran parallel to the stair landing and led to a back hall that also ran the length of the building. On the upper floors, the structure was like a college dormitory. They splashed gasoline on the doors of many of the back hall rooms.

When they met again at the stairs, Ethan noticed the photo of Dr. Theodore Sweeny, Asylum Administrator, lying shattered against the base of the wall. He aimed his flashlight at the cubbyhole it had been covering, and spotted a couple of the dusty pistols.

"Looks like the police weren't as thorough as they claimed," Ethan said, reaching in and grabbing one of the pistols. "This looks like the one that was laying next to Darren's body..." He realized this must have been where Havana and Genevieve had found that pistol – the one he'd heard fire the night his dad went missing. Genevieve had been armed when she encountered Owens, and he wrestled the gun away from her before he killed her.

He checked the chamber to make sure it was loaded, and then tucked it into the waist of his jeans as they continued up the stairs towards the third floor.

*

Carter rounded the side of the burned out building, staying close to the wall. He had found a back road, possibly a service entrance driveway, which offered him the cover of trees. He knew the cops were looking to question him, and he wanted to avoid them at all costs until he had a chance to finish this once and for all. Levenson Asylum had played too big a role so far not to house what he was after.

He glanced around the front yard, and spotted a white Corolla parked on Grand Street. This was it.

He slid along the front wall and slipped into the broken window, tearing at the police tape to get inside. He glanced around the smoky gray lobby; the dust and ashes on the floor had been all but mopped up by the masses of footprints. He saw the sizeable blood stain at the foot of the grand staircase, and the faint footprint traces that tracked it upstairs. He climbed the stairs silently, hoping he still had the element of surprise working for him.

He wanted this over with as soon as possible. Knowing it was inevitable had been gnawing at his ability to even function. His pulse quickened with anticipation. What would he say? What would he do?

He'd end this.

*

"You gotta check this out," Ethan said, peering into one of the last rooms on the third floor hall. The room across from the fire exit stairway was only opened because it's door had been broken off it's hinges and stood propped against the doorframe.

Lucas and Reagan approached, having emptied one of their two remaining jugs around the third floor. Ethan carried the last one.

Intrigued by what little he could see in the room, Lucas gently slid the door aside to clear the entrance so they could step into the room.

The smell was putrid and stale, and glancing around at the furniture in the room gave them every horrific reason why. In front of them stood four narrow beds, metallic legs on wheels holding each bed up three and a half feet off the ground. While soot, dust, and cobwebs covered the beds, rust had overtaken the metal legs, and several of the beds were missing at least one wheel.

"Shock therapy," Ethan muttered. "I was wondering if we'd find something like this."

The room seemed darker than any of the other patients' rooms they'd come across, but at eye level across the left wall was a large horizontal gash of dark burgundy, the unmistakable dried spatter of blood that could have been the result of a beheading.

In the far corner, beside a heap of dusty sheets, robes, and other random garments, stood a charred porcelain basin, and on the floor beneath it lay what appeared to be a hardback Bible, it's cover sporting gruesome wounds from the ax that was planted firmly in the floor nearby. Someone had taken a rage out on God. Perhaps the culprit was whatever force could not be driven out by way of exorcism or electroshock treatment – or both, side by side, an apocalyptic showdown between Religion and Science, the mother and father of life and death. Parents of good and evil.

"I think I've seen enough," Lucas said, backing out of the room. "If we're done with the tour, can we please go do the fourth floor and then get back down to the lobby to wait for him before it starts getting dark?"

They exited the room and made it half way down the hall when they saw the figure step up onto the hallway landing from the stairs. Startled, Ethan dropped their last jug of gasoline, splashing some of it into the air. He aimed the flashlight at the figure, who turned in time for them to see it was their professor.

"What are you doing here?" Carter asked them, his tone demanding and his voice just above a whisper.

"Waiting for you, Professor Owens," Reagan said, heated. "Or is it Owen Carter?"

"I really don't have time for this," Carter replied. "You need to go."

"Oh we will," Lucas said. "But you won't be going anywhere. We know who you're looking for."

"How could you possibly?" he asked them. "Why don't you take your third grade threats and get the hell out of here."

"Not until you admit what you did to Vieve up in the attic," Ethan said. "And to my father. Did you drag him up there too?"

"The attic?" Carter asked, trying to determine what all they knew.

"You smug son of a—!" Ethan's attempt to pounce onto Carter was thwarted as Lucas held him back.

"Reagan, get out of here," Lucas said, still holding onto Ethan.

"I'm not going anywhere!" she replied. "I want him to tell me what my mother saw up there. What did you do to her?"

"What *I* did?!" Carter exclaimed. "You want to know what I did? I survived."

"At what cost?" Reagan asked, angry. "Innocent people are dead!"

"Accidents happen," he said, vacantly.

Threatened, Ethan pulled the pistol from the waist of his pants and aimed it at Carter. "Back up!"

Carter fixed his eyes on the weapon.

"Reagan, get out now," Lucas said, stretching out an arm in front of her. He knew Ethan's grief for Frank was bubbling under the surface, along with months of friction created by secrets, suspicions, and spite. One wrong move could turn Vesuvian.

Carter was standing between them and the stairs, and "this is it" was etched all over his face.

"A fire exit's down the hall," Ethan told Reagan, realizing her predicament.

Lucas turned to Reagan. "Here," he said, offering his flashlight to her. He quickly motioned towards the end of the hall behind them. "Go."

She took the flashlight but hesitated a moment, not wanting to leave him here. A number of alternatives rushed through her head before she negotiated them down to one and made for the fire exit stairway.

"It doesn't matter what Robyn Edgefield told you," Carter said. "She's irrelevant."

"What about Dr. Harold Ashley," Lucas asked. "Was *he*?"

"Dr. Ashley was an irresponsible prick with a god complex." The incident with Daniel in 1986 was all Carter could think about, and his vile contempt for Dr. Ashley was slithering across his face.

"Is that why you killed him?" Lucas continued.

"He was good as dead anyway," Carter answered. "I wanted Daniel out of his misery."

Puzzled, Lucas wanted Carter to elaborate, but Ethan wasn't backing down.

"What about my dad, huh?" Ethan's arm was trembling with fury as he pointed the gun at Carter's face. "Did you want him out of his misery?"

"You *are* your father's misery," Carter told him, coldly. "A lazy, brat son who gets everything he wants without earning it. You think you're so fucking entitled. To what? *My* sacrifices? You're not the victim. You're a fucking burden!"

"You want to know what I'm entitled to?" Ethan asked, glaring at Carter. "Vengeance."

Sensing emotion was pushing Ethan to take the shot, Lucas stepped up to his friend's side.

"Foster, stop," he said. "Think about this. If they find him with a bullet in his head, they're gonna investigate it as a homicide."

"They won't know it's me," Ethan replied, holding up his free hand to remind Lucas that his hands were still covered by the latex gloves. "Besides, I'm doing this whole town a favor. I'll be a hero."

"They'll still lock you up," Lucas said. "This needs to look like a suicide."

Slapped with the realization that they really didn't intend for him to walk out of here alive, Carter picked out the moment when Ethan seemed to fall into Lucas's logic, and made a grab for the gun. In the midst of the ensuing struggle, the two men ended up chest to chest with the pistol between them.

"You've always been a coward," Carter grunted, fighting hard to get control of the weapon. "Don't expect my daughter to visit you in prison."

"Don't expect to see her in hell," Ethan responded, and in their force to clinch, the gun went off with a deafening pop. Startled, Lucas jumped back against the wall.

Silence reverberated around them, and both of them waited to breathe or blink until either one's fall revealed who had taken the bullet. An endless moment passed until both of them noticed Lucas's body sliding down to the floor, a trail of blood painting the wall behind him.

Ethan let go of the gun, and dropped to his knees beside his friend. Lucas was slouched over, his hand covering an oozing hole in his side.

"Lucas!" Ethan shouted, frantically.

Carter bent over and lifted his fingers to the side of Lucas's neck. "He's got a pulse, and he's still breathing. You need to get him out of here."

"And let you get away?" Ethan retorted.

Carter held up the pistol. "I said get him up and go!"

Struggling, Ethan hoisted him to his feet, and draped Lucas's arm around his shoulder for support.

"Whatever trick you've got up your sleeve, it's not gonna work." Ethan said, just in case Owens was thinking of setting them up. "The cops are all over you for all of these murders, and they only close this case on the heels of a suicide." He hoped the defamatory demise of Terrance Todd was fluttering through Owens' mind. Perhaps the Hunter really would end up taking his own life. He wasn't going to stick around to find out. He wouldn't trust the justice system, either. The building was still doused in gasoline. Once he got Lucas out, he could still ignite the lobby in the event Owens wouldn't end it himself.

Carter's angry glare continued to burn. It wasn't until Ethan and Lucas were halfway down the first flight towards the lobby that Carter finally moved, his anger suddenly infiltrated by confusion. *All of these murders.*

He lifted his eyes towards the ceiling, remembering what they'd said about the attic. He started for the flight of stairs that would lead him to the fourth floor and slowly began his ascent.

Once he reached the fourth floor landing, he listened for any noise other than the fading croak of the stairs beneath the weight of Ethan and Lucas, but heard nothing. He approached the narrow stairs that led to the attic and started up. Reaching the top step, his attempt to push open the door was futile. He gave it a nudge, but to no avail. Finally, he slammed his shoulder against it, and the door flew open into the short, dark hallway. He immediately noticed a beam of light emanating from beneath the door across from him. He reached for the knob and slowly opened the door into the room.

Reagan was lying on the floor on her side facing him. The flashlight was just a few inches out of her reach. She looked lifeless. Carter stooped down to check her pulse, and discovered she was unconscious, but still breathing.

Then he heard the very near creak of a wooden door slowly being pushed shut behind him.

His heart stopped. He knew who it was, and swallowed the lump in his throat before he spoke:

"Hello Daniel."

Then everything went black.

†WE₦†Y ₦i₦E
LEVENSON ASYLUM – SEPTEMBER 1996

Ten years ago, I watched my father murder my mother and set her body on fire. It was the scene that replayed over and over in my mind, often pulling me out of my sleep soaking wet. The images were so vivid and suffocating that waking up to them in this small hospital room only exacerbated the plague they inflicted on my psyche. The doctors might have thought they were doing their best to extract this nightmare out of me, but truthfully, the scars that covered my body were far worse beneath the surface. Underneath was a hell they could never imagine.

Tonight they would.

My room was located on the fourth floor of Levenson Asylum. It was the ward rarely visited by guests or orderlies. They considered us the hopeless cases, and kept us locked in our solitary rooms simply figuring since we didn't cooperate whenever we were called in for a session with one of the staff psychologists, we didn't deserve consideration. I had nothing to say. The people I saw regularly looked at me like I had broken out of hell. They could see it. My skin was still charred in places. Most of my hair had been singed to the follicle and would never grow back again. I was their monster, ostracized for being my father's victim.

They didn't know me, nor did they want to know me. The professionals kept wanting to know why I was so closed-off, and considered me angry. I told them nothing because they felt nothing for me, and I could sense it. I knew that feeling well. All I'd ever be was another story they could talk about after dinner with their families, and forgotten about until the following session.

I'd learned early on that there was nothing to love about me, and I sought refuge within the walls of this room until even they began to turn on me. Solitude will rape a haunted man, and impregnate him with unbearable claustrophobia. My thoughts of self-preservation turned into wicked manifestations of the innocence that was stolen from me. My desperate need for affection turned into weeds and withered under the magnified heat of scrutiny. At certain times throughout the day, I could see orderlies peek in through the little glass window on the door, and quickly back away when my eyes met theirs. They wanted to be afraid of me, because it gave them a reason to pretend I wasn't their responsibility. The story of my life.

I began to memorize their faces, and they became substitutes for a father I never expected I'd see again. They preferred I wasn't a part of their world. Acknowledging so meant facing the truth that the world had some very dark and very ugly secrets. They didn't know who I was, or where I came from. I'd been dropped off by a doctor, and asked to be dealt with along with the dozens of mentally disturbed killers taking up residence here. Because to someone, I wasn't any better than these. I was the most helpless one here, and they looked at me as if the killers were normal.

Thoughts of suicide were frequent – not as a way out, but as a way to somehow give the dust what it wanted. They'd find my body, finish the cremation, and send the remains into the wind. No prayers necessary. Whatever soul resided here I'm sure had all but vacated these condemned premises.

I shut down systematically, and sadness was the first to go. Tears were painful. Their salt left blisters on my skin. I turned the memories of my mother into relics that I only allowed myself to observe on special occasions, until the moments were so spread out that the sound of her voice and the smell of her skin evaporated. I had no photos of her and hardly looked like her son since the fire. Soon, the only evidence of her was the purpose in my blood. I was still alive for a reason.

Over time, as my mother's image faded, those vivid scenes in my nightmares turned into bold feelings. My parents were played by good and evil. Good was burning up in the bathtub, and my reluctant confrontation with Evil was always interrupted by the explosion of fire.

I thought my father's substitutes here at Levenson would become the best chance I had at completing that confrontation and putting the nightmares behind me. When I was sixteen, I awoke from a dream in the middle of the night only to find my father peering at me through the window on my door. He'd made it home in time, and was going to come in and tell me goodnight. I wanted to cry, but there was nothing left inside. I curled into the fetal position and pretended to sob. The last thing I wanted was for Daddy to leave.

Fate was the key that unlocked the door that night, and Daddy came into my room. I could feel him silently staring down at me, judging me as a monster he wouldn't take responsibility for creating. When he'd stood there long enough, he made the mistake of turning his back to exit the room, and I pounced, wanting to stop him from starting that final argument with Mom. It threw him off balance and he stumbled.

I had snapped his neck before he hit the floor.

For an hour I sat beside his body, and watched his face become a stranger's. This wasn't Daddy.

To hide the orderly's body, I stole his keys, dragged him out into the regularly empty hallway and up a narrow flight of stairs to an attic. This attic became my secret garden where I harvested varieties of Evil. Over several months, I'd found my father a handful of times, and reacted vengefully whenever he dared to peek into my room with ignorant, disgusted, and condemnatory eyes. Each encounter was a tease. On some level, I knew these substitutes weren't Daddy, but seeing them gripped with fear and grasping in vain for life brought me just to the brink of closure, and then it was too late for them, and I was still his unwanted son. It was frustrating not being able to get Evil to disappear from me. Instead, it wanted grand scale, and this garden was Eden, packed with poisoned apples.

Tonight I planned a bumper crop. With the keys I'd gathered from all of the dead orderlies, I snuck out of my room and headed up to my attic where their bodies were all stashed. I dressed myself in the uniform one of them was wearing so that I could pass as an orderly, and donned a black fedora hat I'd found in a trunk up here a few nights earlier. Then, I fashioned blindfolds and nooses for each of my victims out of their clothing. Twenty minutes later, the bodies were hanging from the rafters. I'd blindfolded them because I'd had enough of the disapproving glares from Daddy. This way he couldn't see what I had done. No one could.

It was a harrowing sight, them hanging there, but it was phase one. My confrontation with Evil was going to climax tonight, and I was overcome with a sudden sensation of Good. I could feel my mother with me, but I read her presence as vindication. I could hear a faint lullaby, one I hadn't heard since before she died, and it pained me that I couldn't hear her voice singing it. I had to pull her back. This was my chance to remember her voice, so the seven year-old Daniel Carter inside started to sing it. "Daddy loves me, Daddy loves you. Yes he does, yes he does. He'll be home tomorrow, he'll be home tomorrow. You will see, you will see."

The singing stopped, and the dry, lonely echo of my own voice resonated in my ears. Just as I was about to leave the attic for phase two, I heard a scream from the hallway. The door was ajar, and someone had seen this. There was no turning back now.

I ran down the stairs after my unexpected visitor, and chased the woman as she ran frenetically down the main stairs, screaming incoherently and pointing upstairs behind her. She must have slipped out of sight after dinner and roamed her way up here where she probably figured no one would find her. She was wrong.

She glanced back, saw me coming after her, and stopped on the landing of the third floor. Our eyes locked for a moment, and I could vaguely sense recognition between us – perhaps in a past life, in a time before Levenson. She had a warm yet fragile vulnerability about her. I thought she was going to faint so I stopped as well, deciding to bring her up to the attic once she was unconscious. She silently turned to face the wall, slowly brought her head back, and then slammed it forward into the concrete. She repeated it several more times until blood caked on her face.

She had definitely seen the attic, and was trying to pound the image of those bodies hanging up there out of her head. Was she going to continue until she had knocked herself out?

Careful not to be seen, I backed up the stairs when I noticed two nurses approaching her. They wrestled to stop her from injuring herself, but she fought them to continue pounding her head against the wall and let loose a piercing monotonous scream that initiated an aftershock of unsettling grunts, groans, and screams from patients in nearby rooms.

This was perfect timing.

Another male orderly rushed over to help them get her to the ground where they flipped her onto her stomach and proceeded to tie her hands and feet together behind her back. The woman continued to scream, repeating a refrain no one else could understand but me: "You will see, you will see."

As they carried her off, I continued down the stairs until I reached the lobby. Visiting hours were over, but several staffers were in the office at the back of the lobby updating charts and checking out schedules for tomorrow. The night shift hadn't quite started yet, and many of them were hustling to finish so they could clock out on time. Other orderlies and nurses were making their final rounds. No one was paying any attention to the lobby. This place was slack in its efforts as an asylum for the criminally insane.

The kitchen was located down a hall to the right of the office. As I passed by the office, I heard one of the staffers curse before picking up the telephone and requesting a vehicle for an urgent transport for a Code 14.

I entered the deserted kitchen, aware that dinner had ended shortly over an hour ago, and started for the stoves. I turned them all on, and taking a page out of my own nightmares, searched for whatever flammable agents I could find. I wanted them all to burn. For thinking they knew me. For never caring. For being and not being Owen Carter.

In ten minutes, the kitchen was in flames, and it was spreading fast. I grabbed a vat of cooking oil and poured a trail as I backed out of the kitchen towards the hall. I dropped the container and walked back towards the office, tipping my head a bit so that the fedora obscured my face.

"Final rounds," I shouted towards the office to no one in

particular. Who knew if any of them even heard me over the commotion to secure a transfer for a patient named Robyn Edgefield. I wasn't concerned. She'd never get out in time.

I walked to the front entrance and casually locked the doors. Panic would ensue, and any additional confusion would only make things worse. Then, I crossed to the base of the grand staircase and started down the hall that extended to the left of it. I made a show of peeking into every windowed door I passed, staring into the lives of the maniacal killers I'd arrived less than, but would leave far superior to. I stepped inside the last room on the hall, and found myself standing in front of a large table surrounded by four wooden chairs. There was a large mirror on one wall.

Vanity, I thought. Do they think making these criminals face themselves was anything less than an ego boost? It was unfair that their skin wasn't a map of their sins, while I bore the scars of my father's crime. Here I was in a room of cruel and unusual punishment. I looked into the mirror, and saw my face for the first time. The vision paralyzed me. I was painted the hideous color of hate, and with every second I stood there it was seeping into my pores, being picked up by blood cells, and migrating through every nucleus of my being. Fueled by this anger, I grabbed one of the chairs and dragged it out of the room towards the door at the end of the hall. I propped the chair underneath the doorknob so that it wouldn't open from the other side. These criminals would burn for sure. I hurried back into the room with the mirror, and knowing from my previous late-night excursions of the halls that there was a fire exit stairway on this side of the building, I passed into an adjoining room that housed a large wooden electric chair. The room smelled rancid, so I quickly made for the door on the opposite wall where I found the fire stairway. I stepped into the tight space and secured the door behind me. Below, stairs led down into darkness. Since fire rises, I started to descend the stairs seeking refuge in the shelter of the dark and desolate basement, and waited for the confrontation to finish.

*

The flames were ravenous. Waves of orange were screaming

heavenward out of every window. Billowing black smoke swallowed the stars. Screams and sirens intertwined in a melody of horror.

Levenson Asylum was four floors of fire. Inside, nurses and orderlies tried fruitlessly to get as many people out as possible. An explosion in the kitchen had alerted the staffers in the office that something had happened, and a ball of fire seemed to engulf the entire right wing of the first floor at once. They simply didn't have enough staffers to even attempt order in this chaos. Over the past few months, several orderlies had gone missing, and now, it was taking everyone on call to run around to make sure all the patients' rooms were opened.

The county had dispatched several fire engines to the scene, but their arrival was too late. The lobby was teaming with violent, unrestrained patients streaking hazardously about, making it impossible to herd anyone. The flames engulfed the exits, and doors that shouldn't have been stuck shut were not budging. People became indistinguishable, and soon, those who weren't on fire were trying desperately to find each other and avoid bumping into those who were.

Once the firefighters had entered the premises, several of them stood in the lobby not knowing where or how to even start to fight this inferno. Victims were screaming in pain, sirens were wailing in the distance, and for forty-five eternal minutes, hell was happening.

T H I R T Y

Irate, Carter had barged into Dr. Harold Ashley's private office unannounced. His own daughter had just fed him a name he hadn't heard since 1986: Robyn Edgefield. If the nurse had anything at all to suddenly talk about, Carter needed to know if Dr. Ashley was involved and what any of this had to do with the alleged murders taking place at Levenson that made Havana feel threatened.

"Can I help you?" Dr. Ashley asked him, less than intimidated considering the anger in Carter's eyes.

"It hasn't been that long, has it?" Carter asked. "Twenty-five years?" He leaned across the desk to peer down at Dr. Ashley. "Or was my child not the only one you turned into a lab rat over the years?"

Dr. Ashley stared up at him, peering into the black hole of his past.

"Have a seat, Mr. Carter," Dr. Ashley said, forcing himself to remain calm.

"Just tell me what the hell is going on."

"With…?!"

"Robyn Edgefield!" Carter stressed. "Does she know about how I told you to treat Daniel that night?"

"You mean how you told me to kill him?" Dr. Ashley asked, boldly.

"You're playing a very dangerous game right now," Carter spat through gritted teeth.

"You made the rules," Dr. Ashley replied. "Unless you don't remember trying to blackmail me."

"Well this is not the way you want to counteract," Carter threatened.

"Just because I might not have anything over her, doesn't mean she won't go to jail for the rest of her life for the role she played in that. If she opens her mouth, I'm bringing both of you down. I am the grieving father. I can still go to the medical board and let them know that you pumped my dying son full of whatever that was you cooked up while she watched. So if I were you, I'd figure out where my best interests lie, and take care of this."

"First of all," Dr. Ashley started. "Nurse Edgefield quit that night. I haven't heard from her since I asked her to leave us alone in your room. If you're worried about something she has to say, good! You should be. And secondly, save the threats. It's a waste of my time. Nobody is going to believe a 'grieving father' suddenly wants to bring a malpractice suit over something that happened two decades ago. You don't have proof. You don't have witnesses. All you've got is a guilty conscience, a disturbing psychological problem, and an 18-year-old expiration on the statute of limitations. Is there anything else?"

"I guess there was nothing psychologically disturbing about you turning a child into a science project." Carter barked back.

"But see, I was trying to save his life," Dr. Ashley said. "You wanted to end it."

"You forced me to make that call!" Carter exclaimed. "You made him worse, and then only told me about it to cover your ass. If he had died from the first injection, you would have told me he died from his burns, and we both know it."

"Rehashing this is not going to change anything. You ordered me to kill him," Dr. Ashley said. "And if blaming me is the only way you're going to clear your conscience, why don't I just fill you in on all the details? You want to know what it's like to cause death? You want me to tell you how unbearable the guilt has been all this time?"

"I already know," Carter said, breaking. He had killed Catherine, but until now could only admit as much as her accidental slip on those stairs. The fall was an accident. The bathtub was murder. "It... it was an accident," he stammered, trapped between the memories of her fall and setting her body on fire. "I stood to lose too much. I had to do something."

Dr. Ashley stared at Carter for a long moment before responding. "So did I," he said. "And killing that little boy... was not gonna happen."

The brick wall that hit Carter sent shockwaves through his legs, and they almost gave way from beneath him.

"What?" he asked.

"You've got nothing on me, Mr. Carter, because there is nothing," Dr. Ashley said. "Daniel survived. I gave you cremated remains of a John Doe, and sent Daniel someplace where he could get some help. For ten years, I sent money for him to stay there and prayed to God that he would never cross paths with you."

"Daniel's alive…" Carter's world was dizzying. He could hardly verbalize the only question he had. "Where did you send him?" he managed.

Dr. Ashley continued to stare at the pitiable man before him. What harm could this information do now? The facility had burned down fifteen years ago.

"Levenson," he answered. "Levenson Asylum."

*

A palm landed hard across Carter's face, bringing him back to consciousness. He was in the attic at Levenson, seated in an old wooden chair. His hands were tied together in his lap. At his feet, Reagan Edgefield was still lying unconscious on the floor, her hands also tied together in front of her. The very next thing he noticed was the dark figure dressed in a long black overcoat and fedora hat. He was slowly pacing back and forth at Carter's side, but suddenly stopped and bent over, bringing his gruesome face within inches of Carter's.

Carter turned his head slowly to look at the son he hadn't seen in 25 years. The fire had left such a mark that skin could not grow back to cover large portions of his face. Pink and black scabs had formed on top of scabs, and blood had left a trail in the deep grooves where Genevieve Davis's fingernails had clawed into him.

"Daniel…" muttered Carter.

"Welcome home," Daniel whispered, his resentment filling the dimly lit room.

"What is this?" Carter asked.

"Let's call it a father-son moment. The one and only." Daniel disappeared behind Carter to retrieve a small oil lamp. Turning it on, the orange light gave the room a haunting glow, eerily appropriate. He sat the lamp next to the door, and picked up the pistol he had taken from Carter after he'd knocked his father unconscious.

"Get up!" Daniel pointed the gun at Carter, forcing him to stand to his feet.

"Why did you do all of this?" Carter asked, horrified.

"Stand up on the chair," Daniel ordered.

Carter took a quick assessment of the situation, and realized he was at his son's mercy. He carefully climbed up onto the chair, and immediately noticed the makeshift noose now hanging neck-level from a beam in the rafters.

"Son—"

"Don't!"

"You didn't have to do this," Carter continued, drilling for an untapped well of emotion.

"*You* didn't have to do it," Daniel snapped. "I'm not the one the cops are looking for," he reminded him. Had he known it was Havana's DNA that loosely linked the Carter bloodline to Genevieve's murder, he would have thrown in the Sophoclean element that both of Carter's own children contributed to his demise. "This might actually be the easier way out for you."

"And what happens to you?" Carter asked.

"What do you think?" he retorted, bitterly. "I've spent the past 25 years building up to this."

"So you kill me, and then walk out of here? Where are you gonna go?"

"1282 Turner Lane," Daniel answered, rattling off Carter's home address without pause.

Horrified, tears started to form in Carter's eyes.

"That's it…" Daniel goaded. "At least now we know you're human. You can cry."

Carter pleaded, "Don't hurt them."

"That's only making it worse," Daniel said. "Because you didn't give a fraction of a damn about me or my mother when you killed her! Now you're telling me you care about them? They don't even know what you did to her."

"That was an accident!" he shouted. "Catherine slipped on the stairs, and she fell."

"For all I know you pushed her."

"That's not what happened!" Carter screamed.

"I should believe you?" Daniel's contempt seethed. "I should trust you? Where did that ever get me? Other than a front row seat to you tossing a match into that bathtub. By mistake, right?"

Carter couldn't find the explanation because he'd never forced himself to remember if there was one.

"I heard the whole thing," Daniel said, antipathy radiating from him like heat. "You arguing. Her falling. You dragging her body to the bathroom. I watched you light the match."

For the first time in all these years, he felt tears in his own eyes. Knowing his dad was eliciting emotion out of him and drawing tears that would burn his blistered face awoke a rage inside hot enough to vaporize them before they fell.

"And the funny thing is," he continued. "I might have slept through all of it if you had given me any reason to think you cared at all about me. That's what hurt the most. None of this would have happened. Maybe it's just who you are as a father. Fucking incapable."

"So you become a murderer?" Carter asked.

The question was laced with condemnation. Daniel peered up at him with a scowl. "Genetics," he snipped. "Or maybe it was something I picked up when I was seven. Nature, nurture, take your pick – I could give a shit because I ended up here, not even knowing if you were still alive. Though I can't really say I was any better off thinking you were dead. I was stuck here chasing a ghost until... things got out of hand. And when this didn't cut it, I figured I'd just go after whoever knew you. Until I stumbled across this *new* you. Imagine my surprise."

Daniel slowly reached up and removed the fedora from his head. He tossed it aside, giving Carter a good look at his scars. His scalp was mostly bald with small patches of hair growing wherever it could. His face and forehead were canvases of dark red, brown, and burgundy, with speckles of yellow and green where pus had dried into the skin.

"Why do you get to move on?" Daniel asked him. "Why do you get to be happy when nobody else can? Not me. Not my little sister. Not even her boyfriend. What, do you hate him just for the hell of it?"

Carter stared at the wall to his right. "He reminds me of you." The disgust finally broke the surface, and he pitied himself for it.

To Daniel, the admission had been a flash fire, singeing the scars caused by his father 25 years ago.

"You didn't even want to remember me?" Daniel struggled to keep the hurt out of his voice, but the revelation had slapped the little kid who only wanted to spend time with his father. He paused, allowing the anger to harden him. "Is that why you told Dr. Ashley to kill me that night?"

Unnerved, Carter brought his gaze back to Daniel. "How would you know that?"

"What don't I know?" Daniel began to slowly pace back and forth in front of his father. "I've been that uneasy feeling you've had walking to your car in the parking lot at Westmore every night these past few weeks." He traced the scratch marks left by Genevieve on his face -- in return he'd taken her life and her car. "I followed you to Dr. Ashley's office. Got an earful. So did you. I knew it'd only be a matter of time. And here we are." He stopped pacing, and stood directly in front of Carter, who was still standing on the chair, the noose dangling in front of him. "I just wish I coulda gotten the doctor here. The trifecta: father, son, and you yourself said he had a god complex. He did save my life," Daniel added. "But he put up a fight. He would have known I did this. I had to put him down."

"I told him you would have been better off not having to live like this," Carter said, trying to appeal. "I was thinking about what was best for you, Daniel. You were going to be in constant pain. That wouldn't have been fair to you."

"*That's* funny," Daniel said, noting the irony. Still clutching the pistol in one hand, Daniel reached up with his other to hold the noose still, and motioned for Carter to stick his head into it.

"Stop and think about what you're doing!" Carter begged. His booming pleas to Daniel were reaching Reagan. She slowly began to stir on the floor. "You don't think I've had to live with what happened to you and your mom all these years? Every breath I take is full of guilt."

"Well this'll put a stop to that," Daniel smirked.

"You undisciplined little shit, you never did anything I asked you to do!" Carter shouted angrily, hoping it would continue to rouse Reagan. "This is what you want your life to be? Full of hatred and vengeance over a mistake that happened when you were seven?"

"No! You wanted me dead! So your mistake was my eighth birthday," Daniel spat. "If you knew how to take responsibility—"

"It would've ruined my life!" Carter yelled.

"Look what you did to mine!" Daniel's rage was rising to match his father's.

Reagan opened her eyes, confused. The back of her head ached, and she searched her memory until she recalled being struck on the fire exit stairway. She glanced around the room, hearing the argument ensue between this cloaked figure and Professor Owens standing on a chair over her.

"I didn't make you go out and kill all these people, Daniel!" Carter said, hoping Reagan was coherent enough to put the pieces together. "You want to talk to somebody about taking responsibility, you are a mass murderer!"

"And you're a coward!" Daniel's venom was acidic within him. "I did what I did because of you! This fire, 'The Hunter,' your students, your entire family... I did it all because you got away with murder. You are this evil I can't control, and if you think I won't go after your new family, you have fatally underestimated me."

"What..." Reagan stammered. "What's happening?" She looked up at Daniel, horrified by the scars that made up his gruesome face.

"He's my son," Carter told her. "He's the one who did all this."

Daniel looked down at her, his face twitching in rage. He pointed the gun at her chest. "I need to know where Robyn Edgefield is," he demanded.

Horrified, she summoned the strength to fight back.

"Fuck you!" she shouted.

He squeezed the trigger, planting a bullet into Reagan's chest.

He lifted his red, angry eyes to his terrified father and tossed the gun to the floor. "Moving on."

T H I R T Y O N E

Ethan had reached the bottom of the grand staircase in the lobby when he heard the gunshot. He'd been struggling with carrying Lucas, trying to be careful not to cause any more blood to seep from his wound. Enough of it had already trailed their path down three flights of stairs, and he could see Lucas's color was draining.

Out of breath and sweating from hefting Lucas's weight, he stopped beside a column just in front of the entrance foyer, and rested Lucas on the floor against it.

"Lucas," he said, searching his friend's face for any sign of life. "Come on, man."

He reached two of his fingers to the side of Lucas's neck to search for a pulse, but he didn't know where he was supposed to be feeling, and his own heart was racing so fast he could swear it was causing his own extremities to throb.

"What was..." Lucas was fighting to stay conscious. "What was the noise?" His voice was tiny and his breathing was shallow.

"Gunshot, I think," he answered. "Sounds like Owens shot himself. Saved us some trouble." He hoped that was the case. "I still think we should torch this place. Think you can walk out of here with me?"

"Rea..." Lucas stammered. "Reagan?"

"She's outside, remember?" Ethan said, trying to encourage Lucas to gather up some strength to climb out of the broken window. He crossed over to the busted window and glanced out towards the car. It was starting to get dark, and from what he could see of the yard, the car was parked just out of sight.

He stepped back from the window and stared down at Lucas. Pulling him through the window wasn't going to happen. How had the cops gotten the bodies out of the tunnel? There had to be a back entrance somewhere.

"Don't try to move, okay?" he told Lucas. "I'm gonna check around back to see if there's a service entrance or something."

With the flashlight beam guiding his path, he sprinted towards the back of the lobby to find any hall that would lead somewhere, giving himself ten minutes to make it back to Lucas.

*

"I thought I was the one you were after," Carter said, staring down at Reagan's lifeless body. "What do you need with Robyn Edgefield?"

"She saw me," Daniel replied. "She's the only person left who knew what I did up here that night."

"What makes you think she'd say anything if she hasn't already?" The noose lay around his neck like a boa constrictor just waiting for the first sense of danger to coil.

"I won't risk it," Daniel said. "You're stalling. Now step off the chair."

"Not until you tell me that this ends here," Carter declared. If Reagan and Robyn were still in Daniel's way, there was no telling what his intentions were with Lucinda and Havana.

"What do you want me to do?" Daniel asked, stepping in front of him. "Because I believe you were the one who taught me about promises."

"Look," Carter started, defeated. "Nothing is going to change what happened all those years ago, and you can't even imagine how sorry I am."

"I can't even care," Daniel corrected, frigidly.

Carter realized he was up against pure evil, and nothing he said would reach his seven-year-old son.

"How do I stop you?" he asked.

Daniel took one step back to give his father room, but still remain close enough to be the last face Carter would see. "Drop."

Down to his only option, Carter stared into his son's cold, chilling eyes for a long moment. Even if he had the chance, it wasn't like he could turn him in to the police without incriminating himself. This was going to be the final act. Daniel wanted him dead, and given those 25-year-old circumstances, maybe he deserved it. He took a deep breath as Lucinda and Havana raced through his mind. Neither of them would be prepared for either outcome.

Bracing himself, he swiftly reached up to grab the rope above his head, and jumped, kicking his feet out in front of him with all the force he could muster while hanging onto the rope so that the noose wouldn't tighten around his neck. His feet slammed into Daniel's torso, sending his winded son backwards and tumbling over Reagan's body. As his own body swung back after the force of the kick, Carter struggled in the precious seconds to plant his feet back onto the chair before Daniel recovered. Though his hands were still tied in front of him, he quickly removed the noose and stepped down from the chair.

Daniel stood up and ran over to tackle Carter. The two of them fell to the floor, and Carter immediately scanned the room for the pistol. The light from the oil lamp by the door afforded no help, and soon Carter could feel Daniel's hands around his throat, squeezing.

"Daniel..." Carter choked out.

He tried desperately to loosen Daniel's hands, but his strength was fading fast. Just before he blacked out, he felt Daniel's grip slip away, and his weight climb from on top of him. Seconds later, pain tore through his body as Daniel planted his foot into Carter's side over and over again, and at last, slammed it across Carter's face as if his head was a football headed towards a field goal. Blood splattered the floor.

When he opened his eyes, he could sense tightening in his chest, and wasn't sure if it was soreness from Daniel's attack, or a biological response to the situation. Choking on the blood in the back of his throat, he twisted onto his side and coughed up what he could. His vision was blurry, but he didn't see Daniel anywhere.

He sat up, hissing over the pain in his sides, and struggled to his feet. Reagan was dead beside him.   He knew Daniel was around here somewhere, but Carter had nowhere to run even if he wanted to. Thousands of dollars he'd spent on surgeries to reconstruct a face he'd now never be able to show again if he wanted to stay out of prison.

And again, Daniel was to blame.

He picked up the oil lamp from beside the door and glanced around one last time for the missing black pistol. No luck spotting it, he left the room.

He carefully climbed down the narrow stairs that led to the fourth floor, waiting for the sound of the gunshot that would precede the stinging pain of its bullet – if he'd feel it at all. He'd almost prefer Daniel to just blow his head off so it'd be over sooner. But Daniel had years of anger bottled up inside, and a quick finish was not going to satisfy him. If Carter had gone through with the hanging, at least Daniel could have had the satisfaction of watching him struggle for his life, which seemed to be how he was deriving his pleasure.

He reached the fourth floor, and slowly headed down the main stairs, giving silence the opportunity to betray Daniel. Once he reached the landing on the third floor, he heard a faint noise in the hall behind him. He turned around, holding the light out in front of him. The glow was a dim orange orb. Beyond it's boundaries was a darkness as vast and violent as the universe. He kept backing towards the top landing of the stairs to go down, his tied hands extended with the light in front of him.

"Daniel…" he said, figuring it better to assume Daniel was there. "Let's just end this."

"Only one of us is leaving here alive," came the husky reply.

It startled Carter, and he tripped over a jug on the floor behind him. It was the sixth jug of gasoline Ethan had left behind earlier. He fell to the ground, feeling the cold liquid emptying the jug. He scampered back to his feet, keeping the oil lamp high and away from himself, having smelled the unmistakable aroma of gasoline. This wasn't good.

"I don't want to kill you—" Carter said, still not knowing how far away Daniel was.

"What changed?" Daniel asked.

"But I'm not gonna let you go after my family," Carter continued. The time to consider Daniel his family was past. He didn't – or couldn't – care how that made Daniel feel. There was simply no saving him anymore. He had to protect Lucinda and Havana.

Daniel slowly stepped into the faint orb of light. "Stop me." His threat was guttural, and sent chills up Carter's spine.

Carter saw the jug he had tripped over was now on its side between himself and Daniel. The remaining gasoline inside was level with the mouth of the jar. The rest of the gasoline was all over the floor between them. He had one shot to do this, and wasn't entirely sure his aching body would get him away from the explosion quick enough to avoid going up in flames himself before he was certain Daniel was dead.

"I have nowhere to go," Carter said, near tears and prepared to die. "My students are convinced I did this. They've got the police looking for me. If I walk out of here, whether you're dead or not, they're gonna put me in prison for everything you've done. I have no way to prove I'm innocent. If this is it for me... then this is it for *us*. Because I *will* stop you from going after them." With that, he heaved the oil lamp at the jug, and it crashed onto the floor with a wave of flames that raced off in every direction like a tsunami.

Carter turned around and started for the end of the hallway, his gut reaction to survive kicking in – an endearing human instinct that was now working against him. He might have been better off with the noose.

Before the fire caught up to him, he glanced around and saw Daniel's form leaping through the flames toward him. Carter spun around and caught Daniel as he crashed into him. The two fell to the floor, fighting each other within the sea of fire. Rolling around in the hall, the flames quickly attacked Carter's gasoline-splattered clothing. He managed to pull Daniel to his feet, and stood him against the wall beside the stairs. He leaned back and brought his head hard against Daniel's. Daniel fell backwards, tugging Carter with him. Both of them lost their balance and toppled down the stairs. The two of them. Father and son. Fire trailing them all the way down.

*

Ethan returned to Lucas after ten minutes, having found the service entrance. Lucas was conscious, but fighting to remain so as they struggled towards their exit. The service entrance was down the hall past the kitchen, which seemed the most damaged by the fire.

They emerged from the building expecting to be greeted by the fresh air of springtime dusk. Dusk was present, but the fresh air had been infiltrated by a fog of black smoke hovering out of the floors above.

"I'm gonna run around front and get Reagan," Ethan said to Lucas. "We'll drive the car around here and get you to the hospital." He was glad to be able to make that his priority now that the building was on fire. He figured Owens must have ignited the place before shooting himself. There was a touch of poetry in Owens finishing what he started this way. Maybe he was hoping to get rid of everything once and for all.

He ran around the side of the building, leaving Lucas alone again with the bleeding hole in his side. He'd been covering it with his hand, which was now completely stained and coated. He could still feel himself drifting in and out of consciousness, and wondered if this was going to be what killed him. He fought against the thought, only to replace it with the horrific look on Reagan's face when she saw him like this. He needed to pull himself together before she got here. He needed to look better than this when he finally told her he loved her.

Hoping this would just be a brush with death, being shot had certainly taught him not to take those words for granted, or think that he had all the time in the world to express himself to Reagan. She had rearranged those exact words in a sentence to him this morning, and he wasn't going to let this day end without letting her know he loved her, too.

The wait for Ethan to return stretched on, and it was getting harder for Lucas not to pass out again. He wondered what could be keeping them. This building probably wouldn't be structurally capable of withstanding another fire, and it seemed the one it was currently engulfed in was spreading fast. The top three floors were screaming smoke and flames.

Moments later, Reagan's Corolla rounded the corner of the other side of the building. It was approaching fast, and screeched to a stop on the gravel of the rear driveway. Ethan jumped out of the driver's side and ran over to Lucas.

"Did Reagan come back here?" Ethan was shouting, frantic. He had his phone to his ear, waiting for Reagan to answer on the other end.

Lucas could hardly understand the question.

"Where's Reagan?!" Ethan asked him again. "She wasn't at the car! Her phone's going straight to voicemail again." He ended the call without leaving a message, remembering that Reagan was always having trouble getting a signal. Part of him wasn't buying that explanation, and feared the worst.

Lucas finally noticed the passenger seat and the back seat were both empty. Something wasn't right. Someone was missing.

"Reagan...?" he uttered, concerned. "Why isn't she...?" He was fading. "I told her to leave, remember?"

Ethan punched 911 into his cell, and glanced around for any sign of Reagan. The flames were growing and the building was under siege. There was just no way.

"We gotta go back in..." Lucas managed. His voice was still weak. "Foster..."

A thunderous crash on one of the upper floors signaled a beam had crumbled, and the top floor suddenly caved inward, sending a plume of thick black smoke into the air.

"Oh my God!" Lucas cried. "Rea!" His loudest shout was but a hoarse whisper. He desperately needed to save her, and could only attempt to crawl towards the service entrance, still calling her name in tears.

He could feel Ethan's one-armed effort to pull him back while he spoke urgently to the 911 dispatch on the phone.

"I told you to leave..." Lucas was saying, trying terribly to disregard the pain that was going to stop him. *"Reagan!"*

And the pain won. Lucas collapsed on the grass behind a burning Levenson Asylum as Ethan ended the call with 911.

E P I L O G U E
ONE MONTH LATER

Ethan pulled up next to Lucas's truck on Grand Street and turned off his jeep. He and Havana got out, not surprised that they had found him here.

"I couldn't spend this day without her," Lucas said, not turning his eyes away from the blackened, erect first and second floor remains – all that was left of Levenson. "She should've been there. Sitting two seats down from me. Her name should be on a degree, not some memorial."

There were no words that would comfort Lucas right now. Ever since the fire, he had blamed himself for not escorting Reagan out of the building himself. Instead, here he was on their graduation day, staring at her final resting place.

They could only assume Reagan had waited for them to finish their confrontation with Owens before she had one with him of her own. Her only objective had been to stop him from going after her mother. They would never know if she'd shot Owens or if he'd shot her after she set the fire. Either way, they were sure she had sacrificed her life to burn Levenson to the ground.

They told the police they'd followed Owens up to Levenson that night, and hoped to catch him as he left – only he never did. When they realized he'd set the place on fire again, they ran in to try to get him, and he confronted them all with a gun – which explained how Lucas got shot and why Reagan was his final victim. The cops readily accepted that he'd felt backed against the wall, which led him to suicide, and the case was closed.

Unfortunately, firefighters found no identifiable human remains anywhere on the first two floors that still stood, and decided both Reagan Edgefield and Owen Carter must have perished on one of the upper floors.

The three of them had each lost someone to the dark and skeletal catacomb in front of them. Lucas would never be able to hear Reagan say "I love you, too." Havana still needed answers from her father, and Ethan needed acceptance from his. Perhaps these were embers always destined to remain in the wake of burning emotions like ashes that never go away.

"Want to come with us to Mr. Edgefield's house?" Ethan asked Lucas, reminding him that Jeffrey was having a graduation dinner for them in honor of Reagan, Genevieve, and Darren.

"That reminds me," Lucas said. "I'm supposed to call and invite James."

"I already did," Havana said, starting back towards the jeep.

Lucas hopped off the back of his truck and slid into the driver's seat.

"Race you back?" Ethan suggested before starting up his jeep.

"We are *done* with your bright ideas for the rest of this decade, Foster," Lucas shouted back, jokingly.

Conversation drew their attention away from the smoky remains of Levenson, and no one saw the dull flashlight beam seeming to float slowly forward out of the darkness beyond the still broken first floor window. The light approached the window's edge, it's carrier stalling as the two vehicles drove away, leaving the charred asylum almost totally dark.

And then the light went out.

ABOUT THE AUTHOR

A native of South Carolina, Raynard Gadson graduated from Winthrop University in 2005 and moved to New York City to pursue his passion for bringing stories to life. With comedy, drama, and suspense being his favorite genres to write, his style is largely influenced by a range of legendary storytelling icons from Sophocles, to Alfred Hitchcock, to Bill Cosby, to Wes Craven. He is the 2012 recipient of Winthrop University's Outstanding Young Alumni Award, and was recognized by Academy of Television Arts and Sciences in 2011 and 2012 as a staff member of the Daytime Emmy Award-winning *The Dr. Oz Show*. Raynard currently works as a television associate producer in New York City, and loves feedback and/or Levenson-related conspiracy theories. Email him at gadsontr@gmail.com.

ACKNOWLEDGMENTS

I am extremely grateful to have been blessed with this immense passion for writing. Not only has God endowed me with a restless imagination, He's put a number of people in my life to help me nurture it. I have to thank both of my families, the Gadsons and the Oldens, for always letting me do my own thing, my teachers at DeLaine Elementary and Lakewood High and professors at Winthrop University for giving me the platform to create, recreate, and share my stories. When it comes to "Ashes" specifically, my sincerest appreciation and gratitude to Erik Salmi, Jason Lee, and Steven Van Patten for inspiring and motivating me at various stages of this project, LaTria Garnigan for helping me edit, and Brandon Stevens for burning up the alphabet.

www.ingramcontent.com/pod-product-compliance
Lightning Source LLC
Chambersburg PA
CBHW030131180626
46812CB00002B/649